# Snowbirds

# Snowbirds

CRISSA-JEAN CHAPPELL

Published by
Merit Press
an imprint of F+W Media, Inc.
10151 Carver Road, Suite 200
Blue Ash, OH 45242. U.S.A.
www.meritpressbooks.com

ISBN 10: 1-5072-0069-2
ISBN 13: 978-1-5072-0069-8
eISBN 10: 1-5072-0070-6
eISBN 13: 978-1-5072-0070-4

Printed in the United States of America.

10   9   8   7   6   5   4   3   2   1

Cover design by Sylvia McArdle.
Cover images © Getty Images/Diane Labombarbe.

*This book is available at quantity discounts for bulk purchases.
For information, please call 1-800-289-0963.*

# dedication

for the *Rumspringa* girls

# acknowledgments

Thank you to my agent, Wendy Schmalz, for believing in this book. I'm grateful to my editors, Jacquelyn Mitchard and Stephanie Kasheta, and everyone at Merit Press. Big hugs to Mom and Dad, the Chappell and Erskine families, Jonathan, who spotted the lantern in the sky, Team 305, and Harlan, my rock. Shout-out to Suzanne Reeves, May-Lin Svantesen, Kelli Hicks, Jackie Dolamore, and Joyce Sweeney. You were there from the start. Thanks so much for your encouragement along the way. I'm especially grateful for the Anabaptist communities in Pinecraft, Florida, and Lancaster, Pennsylvania, who patiently answered my questions, and most of all, the snowbirds on Bahia Vista. I will never forget your generosity and kindness.

# chapter one
# pinecraft

All the trees have been chopped down. Me and my best friend, Alice, used to play hide-and-seek in this empty lot. Now it's just a field of stumps. I listen for night birds—whippoorwills and owls—but hear none. Only the rumble of traffic, growing closer, then farther away, keeping time like a pulse.

Alice is waiting for me by the chainlink fence on Friday night. The first thing I notice is her hair.

"What do you think, Lucy?" She strokes the loose curls below her neck.

I touch my own hair, which is pinned under a prayer cap and damp with sweat. I've never even trimmed the ends.

"It's going to take forever to grow long again," I tell her.

"Good," she says, kneeling in the dirt and unzipping her backpack. She dumps out a pile of skinny jeans and a tank top studded with rhinestones. We're not supposed to wear store-bought clothes. The faded blue denim is softer than anything I've ever worn.

"But now you can't get baptized."

"I don't care," she says, lifting up her skirt and tugging herself into the jeans. "I'd rather be shunned than join the church."

I shiver. "Don't say that."

If Alice were shunned, we'd never see each other again. And that's not the worst part. She wouldn't go to heaven when she died.

There's only one place left to go.

"So what are you going to do?" I ask.

She takes a deep breath. "Me and Tobias are driving to the bus station tonight after the party."

"You're running away?"

7

When Alice told me to meet in our hiding spot, I knew she was in trouble. I figured she got in another fight with her mom. I had no idea it was this bad. Ever since I can remember, Alice has been talking about running away from the Old Order.

I didn't think she'd actually try.

Headlights trickle across the empty lot. A truck pulls up and two boys get out. They start walking toward us through the tall grass. One of them waves his flashlight at Alice. He's wearing a T-shirt crisscrossed with bones, as if he's turned himself inside out.

"Took you long enough," she says, running up to him. So this is Tobias, the boy Alice mentioned in her letters. She kisses him so hard, I have to look away.

"Who's that?" he snaps, and I know he's talking about me. "Thought I told you not to bring anybody."

Alice grabs my hand. "This is my best friend, Lucy."

"Whatever," Tobias says. "You got the money?"

Alice digs inside her backpack. She takes out a roll of crumpled bills in a plastic bag. More money than I've ever seen.

"Been saving up all summer," she says, waving it in his face.

The other boy whistles.

"I wouldn't go showing that off."

He's taller than Alice's boyfriend. Stronger in a lean muscle kind of way. When I hear him talking real slow, I figured he's Old Order Amish too. But he's zipped into a hoodie with flames curling down the sleeves.

"This is Faron. He's driving," says Tobias. "So where is this party anyway?"

"On the beach," says Faron, jingling his keys.

I can't leave Alice alone with these *Rumspringa* boys. They're already walking to the truck.

Alice slings her backpack over her shoulder. "You're coming with me, right?"

I open my mouth, ready to say no.

Instead, I follow behind.

## chapter two

# rumspringa

When I was little, me and Alice used to look for shells on Lido Key before dawn. We'd grab our buckets and flashlights and comb the Sarasota beaches in our long dresses and bonnets. Sometimes a man jogged past and stared. Catching a glimpse of us was like digging up a secret. I'd cover my face, just like Dad taught me.

After our buckets were full, we dumped out the sand dollars. I showed Alice how to crack the shells. Inside were five tiny "doves." We soaked them in a bowl of bleach until they turned pure white.

I keep the doves in a mason jar on my dresser. It's the first thing I see when I wake up. Same as it's always been. Nothing ever changes in Pinecraft. Every morning, it's the same routine. Chores and more chores.

Today I better work fast.

That's because the snowbirds are coming.

On Friday, I rise with the sun. The quicker I get my chores done, the sooner I'll be with Alice. This afternoon, the buses will pull up near Big Olaf's ice cream shack like they do every year. The Old Order Amish will flood Bahia Vista Street in a tide of bonnets and straw hats. I'll search for Alice's smiling face in the crowd.

*"Lucy, I've got so much to tell you!"*

That's for sure.

Alice could talk a pelican out of a fish. At least, that's how Dad puts it. He says we couldn't be more different. Me, with my long fingers that darken to the color of pinewood floors in the sun. Alice, tiny and fair-skinned, her pale eyes always hunting for shade.

"Different as summertime and winter, you two," Dad likes to say, though it's never winter in Florida.

In the corner of my bedroom, a row of plain cotton dresses—sky blue and seashell pink—droop inside the mahogany wardrobe Dad built for me. Alice says I'm lucky. In my church, I'm allowed to wear pastels, while she's stuck with muddy brown. Maybe she's right, but lately, I'm tired of putting on the same clothes day after day.

If I don't head for the kitchen, Dad will yell at me. Fried eggs and toast is the most I can do. Mama used to bake all kinds of sweets. Pecan twists studded with chocolate chips. Cinnamon rolls curled tight as sailors' knots. Best you ever tasted, Dad says.

I never got a chance to find out.

Mama got sick after I was born. Sometimes I wonder if it was my fault. I try to picture her in Heaven with the Lord, but it feels so unfair, the fact that she's gone. I know it's selfish, but that doesn't stop me from thinking it.

My dad built all the furniture in the house. The ladder-back rocking chair. The "bench table" (flip it upside down and you've got a place to sit). The wooden star nailed to the wall. It's supposed to hang on a barn door, but there aren't any barns in Pinecraft.

After breakfast, he leaves his coffee mug in the sink like I'm his maid. Would it hurt if he washed his own dishes once in a while?

"You heading over to meet Alice?" he asks, scratching his beard.

I nod. "The buses are coming this afternoon."

"Well, you need to finish up here first," he says, waving at the laundry basket near the sink. The damp pile of rumpled jeans is stacked so high, it's overflowing. Guess I should've taken care of that earlier.

We're Mennonite, not Old Order. Still, my dad refuses to buy a clothes dryer to go with the washer. He calls it a "worldly indulgence." In other words, something we don't need. I'll have to string his wrinkled pants in the broiling sun, a clothespin wedged between my teeth. Dad's got a big list of "worldly" things, like TVs and electric toothbrushes. Still, he keeps a radio in his workshop. It plays gospel music all day long.

I grab the sponge and start scrubbing.

"Lucy," he adds, turning to leave. "Don't forget."

I glance up from the sink. "What's that?"

"Our little visitor," he says, staring at the floor.

At first, I think he's talking about Alice. Then I notice the stain by the door, swirled like the folds inside a conch shell.

*Our little visitor.*

Yesterday I forgot to lock the back door. No big deal in Pinecraft. Everybody leaves their porch screens wide open. Windows, too. But when I wasn't looking, a raccoon snuck inside the house and "let loose." Must've been real hungry, if he was prowling around in the daylight, poor thing.

"I won't forget," I tell Dad, reaching for the dish towel. I move so fast, the cup slips through my fingers and smashes on the floor.

Dad pushes back his straw hat and sighs. "Lucy, your head's always in the clouds."

"Sorry," I mumble.

No matter how I try, I'll never be perfect enough for him.

He traces the raccoon stain with the edge of his boot, as if he could erase it, just by wishing. "Might take a little more elbow grease than Murphy's Oil," he tells me. "Our visitor schmutzed it up."

No kidding, Dad.

He picks up the broken cup and throws it in the trash. "Get a move on before the day's gone. Then you can go meet Alice. Not till then, you hear?"

"Yeah, I heard," I mutter under my breath.

Maybe I can't cook worth a fig. But give me a bucket of nails and a hammer. My hands are bumpy with calluses, the fingernails worn down to nubs. Last summer I built a plank-style table all by myself. Too bad we had to sell it in Dad's shop. That table sure beats any pie I ever tried to bake.

I grab the coffeepot and scatter a handful of damp grounds over the raccoon stain. That way, the pinewood can soak up the color. All it takes is a dishtowel and a good scrub. Soon the floor's almost new.

As I scrub, my gaze drifts around the kitchen. Nothing's changed, as long as I've been breathing. Our place is like most in Pinecraft—a plain, ranch-style house with a screened-in porch. The orange grove shading the backyard has been there forever. Dad planted the littlest tree when I was born. The branches are twisty and snarled like an old man's knuckles, the fruit bruised with canker.

"That tree's not much to look at," Dad will say, shaking his head.

That's why it's my favorite.

When I'm finally done with raccoons and coffee stains, I carry the laundry basket outside into the sun. The backyard is thick with heat and the breeze smells like thunderstorms. I'm already sweating in my long dress. Better get moving fast. I kick the screen door open and step onto the porch, where Mama's needlework hangs on a nail:

LOVE MEANS EVERYTHING

The corners are stitched with tiny pink roses. I stare at the delicate cursive, so tight and perfect. Sewing's just another talent I don't have.

"One more thing," Dad calls across the yard.

I drop the basket on the porch.

It's always one more thing with Dad.

"Need help with the McCullers' gazebo," he says, heading for the workshop. "The frame could use a little sanding."

My heart sinks. "Can I go meet Alice first?"

"You know the rules, Smidge," he says.

Dad could totally finish by himself, but "many hands make light work." At the end of summer, he's always trying to keep up with new orders, building gazebos for rich people in Sarasota.

"Okay," I tell him. Hopefully, it won't take too long. I watch him disappear under the mossy oaks, humming a gospel tune I know by heart.

Guess I should be thankful. Sometimes we go months without a paycheck. Then it's macaroni for supper every night. Yeah, I love Dad's mac and cheese, but it starts tasting like glue after a couple nights in a row.

I walk over to the clothesline. My bike's leaning against the porch. The crate tied above the back wheel is crammed with hibiscus blossoms. For a second, I think about sneaking off to pick more flowers. All I want to do is escape.

As I pin Dad's wrinkled shirts to the line, a flock of jade-green birds swoops across the sky, cackling like I'm the joke. Quaker parrots. They're from somewhere far away. Nobody knows how they got here. Still, I often catch a glimpse of them flicking through the branches, with their sharp eyes and bright beaks.

I wave at the parrots, half expecting them to wave back. I'm so busy looking up, I knock over the laundry basket, spilling Dad's clean shirts in the mud-soaked grass. Of course, he's hanging outside the workshop, keeping an eye on me the whole time.

"Head in the clouds," he says.

• • •

I'm racing through Pinecraft Park on my rusty old ten-speed. Hope I'm not too late. I don't want to miss the buses when they pull up to Bahia Vista Street. Alice will be there, waiting for me at Big Olaf's ice cream shack. That's where everybody goes to meet their Old Order friends from up north—friends they haven't seen since last year.

On Sundays, the picnic tables near the canal are crowded with Amish-Mennonites in pastel dresses. We spend the whole day eating after church. Dad says I need to learn how to bake something to share with everybody. But I'm much better at eating shoofly pie than baking it.

"You can smell scorched soup from a mile away," Dad always says. And I know he means us. Dad, who loved Mama so much, he didn't get married again. And me, the girl who builds gazebos like a man. Never bakes any sweets for the summer bazaar. Rides her bike a little too fast. Falls asleep in church while everybody else is singing.

Last weekend, I didn't have anything to sell at the bazaar. So I whittled a bird from a piece of driftwood with Dad's pocketknife. Later, I heard Mallory Keller say it was "ungodly" for a girl to carve animals out of wood. Who cares? A knife's good for more than scoring pie crust.

Mallory and her friends are playing volleyball in a patch of sand near the picnic tables. When I zip past, they turn their heads away. I'm no good at volleyball, either. Dad really wants me to learn to play, but I'd rather be on the beach catching hermit crabs and digging up sand dollars.

Dad says I need more friends. In other words, girls who aren't Old Order. But nobody's half as much fun as Alice.

I stand on the bike pedals, my skirt flapping in the breeze, and zip toward Bahia Vista Street. Big Olaf's ice cream is packed. Girls with their pale dresses circling the parking lot on skates. Boys in suspenders, clattering back and forth on Razor scooters. Entire families on three-wheeled bicycles. All waiting, just like me.

A little girl races ahead in her bare feet. I sort of admire her determination. She's dragging one of those Amish rag dolls, the kind without a face. I used to have a doll like that, but it scared me so bad, I never wanted to play with it. What are you supposed to do with a faceless doll anyway?

"Always hold Mommy and Daddy's hand," a man shouts, running after her.

I laugh. The girl doesn't even look back. No stopping her now.

"Waiting for the snowbirds?" asks the woman on a bench. Her long-sleeved dress is the same color as the orchids in the oak trees, and her hair is tucked under a stiff white prayer cap exactly like mine.

*The snowbirds.*

That's what everybody calls the Old Order Amish. Every September, the snowbirds take a bus down to Pinecraft, Florida. They stay all winter long, then head back north to their farms when the ice melts.

"My best friend's coming down from Maine," I tell her.

"Sometimes I wish they'd take me with them," she says, watching the buses roll down Bahia Vista Street. "Been years since I've seen snow."

I've never seen snow in my whole life.

The parking lot is full of bearded old men in straw hats, all dragging suitcases. Old Order women in dark dresses follow quietly behind, their faces hidden under their bonnets. Just by looking at them, I can tell where they're from. The Midwest girls wear brown dresses and stiff, pleated prayer caps. In places up north, like Lancaster, they might have heart-shaped bonnets. It all depends on the *Ordnung*, your church's rules.

Sometimes I wonder why we're so different. Every church does its own thing. Who makes up the rules? And why does it matter?

When Alice finally steps off the bus, I gasp.

"Lucy!" she says, pulling me into a hug. "I've got so much to tell you."

We used to look like sisters. Now we don't look alike at all. Her hair is unpinned and loose, spilling down her back. She's still covered up in her apron and cotton dress, but there's something different about her. Something I can feel more than see.

Mrs. Yoder is already marching ahead. Her long black skirt almost drags on the ground. Ever since I can remember, Alice's mom has always worn black. Her husband died in some accident a long time ago. That's all I know about him.

"Enough chitchat. There's time for that later, don't you know," says Mrs. Yoder in her singsongy voice. "Hot isn't the word for this day. Soon as we're inside, I'm making sweet tea." She glares at Alice. "And you're going to do something about your hair. What happened to your pins?"

"They got lost."

"Well, they better get found."

A couple of Old Order boys speed past us on Rollerblades. They turn their heads to get a second look at Alice.

"If my mom doesn't stop talking about my hair," she whispers, "I'm going to chop it all off."

Yeah, right. The Bible says God wants us to have long hair. At least, that's what I read. It's our "crown of splendor" and we're not allowed to cut it. Girls can't wear boys' clothes because it's an "abomination." It also says we aren't supposed to eat pork, but Dad's always first in line for ribs at the church barbecue.

Together we walk down Kruppa Avenue. All the backyards in Pinecraft have clotheslines flapping in the breeze. The grass is smooth as mint candy. No cars parked in the driveways. Only bicycles tipped against the coconut palms.

Mrs. Yoder always rents the place with the blue shutters. It's just down the block from me, but it feels like another world. I leave my bike on the lawn and follow Alice inside the house. Her mom goes straight to the kitchen. Not that I'm complaining. Mrs. Yoder makes me a little nervous, like I'm going to say or do the wrong thing.

"*Sis hees dohin,*" Alice mutters, fanning her face as we head for her room.

I don't speak Deitsch, but we've been friends so long, I've picked up a little.

"Yesterday was ten times hotter," I tell her. "I'm glad summer's almost over."

"Yeah?" she says. "Feels like it just got started. At least, where I'm from."

While Alice unpacks her suitcase, I fold the quilt on her bed. The Yoders sell lots of quilts at the Amish craft fair, but Alice's mom never lets her keep any. The blue and yellow squares are "too busy," she says.

Alice's mom only brings one thing from Maine—her old-fashioned recipe book. On the cover are drawings of places I've never seen. Horses pulling buggies up a hill. A maple tree dropping its leaves. Ice skaters swirling across a pond.

I sit on Alice's bed, turning pages. In the margins of the recipes are old-fashioned rhymes and jokes.

"This one's my favorite," I tell her.

Girls with fat cheeks have hearts like flint.

Alice rolls her eyes. "What's that supposed to mean?"

"I don't know. But I like it."

On the opposite page, the same thing is written in Deitsch.

*De mad mit dika boka. Hen Hartsa we do woka.*

The words float over me like seashell music.

"It's Old German," Alice says. "Nobody talks like that anymore."

"You do."

"How come you don't?" she asks.

I shrug. "My church has different rules."

Me and my dad belong to the Beachy Amish-Mennonite church in Florida. We're different from the Old Order up north.

I'm allowed to have things that Alice can't have, like electricity in the house. But my dad won't let me listen to the radio or watch TV. Dad says it's a road to wickedness. He says I should be thinking about the next world. Not the one we're living in.

"You're so lucky," Alice says. "If I lived in Pinecraft, I wouldn't have to get up before sunrise and feed the chickens. Or wash my clothes in a stupid bucket. Or spend my whole life doing chores."

"I've got chores too," I remind her. "Lots of them."

"Like what?" she asks.

"I hang the laundry out to dry. Same as you."

"But your dad's got a car, right?"

"He borrows Mr. Showalter's truck on the weekend. It's not really ours. My dad only uses it for hauling lumber."

"Well, at least you've got that."

I stare at her curls, the way they shine.

The bedroom door swings open and Mrs. Yoder marches into the room. She drops something on Alice's dresser. The metal hairpins.

"Fix your hair," she says.

Then she turns and leaves the room, just as quickly as she appeared.

Alice gets up and sweeps her hand across the metal pins. They clatter on the floor like nails.

"My mom hates it when I dress English," she says, meaning clothes that aren't plain. "But I'm not baptized yet. She keeps talking about me joining the church. It's like I don't even get a choice."

"Are you going to do it?" I ask.

"She can't make me do anything," Alice says, looking at the floor. "What about you, Lucy? Isn't your turn coming soon?"

My turn.

It's already been planned. A week from tomorrow, I will kneel in front of the whole church and say my baptismal vows. Then

I'll be Amish forever. Dad's been talking about it ever since I was little.

Can't I wait a little longer?

I reach down and scoop up her hairpins.

"You don't have to get baptized," Alice tells me. "You know that, right?"

Dad would be so disappointed if I didn't join the church.

"It would look bad if I wasn't baptized. Everybody would think I messed up."

Alice grabs my hand. "Do you want to be stuck in Pinecraft for the rest of your life?"

"Pinecraft isn't so bad," I say, a little defensive.

"But there's a lot more to see," Alice says. "If you don't go looking for it, you'll never know what you're missing."

Maybe it's true. The world's a lot bigger than Pinecraft. Too big, it feels like sometimes.

"Promise you won't do it unless you're sure," she says.

I squeeze my fist around the metal hairpins. They're made of stainless steel and stronger than anything you can buy at the drugstore.

"Promise?" she says.

I put her hairpins on the dresser.

"Keep those stupid pins," Alice tells me. "I don't need them anymore."

• • •

Later that day, we walk to Pinecraft Park. The clouds streaking above the canal are wispy and thin, as if they've been combed. "Mare's tails." That's what they're called. A sign it's going to rain. I keep my ears pricked for thunder, but it's way too quiet.

"Was the bus ride okay?" I ask.

19

Alice is walking so fast, I can barely keep up. "What?" she says without looking at me. It's pretty obvious she's not listening.

"Never mind."

We used to talk until our throats hurt, once she got here. Now we're not talking much at all. I get the feeling she's holding back something. Whatever it is, I'll find out soon enough.

When we reach the canal, Alice finally slows down. Behind the fence where the bearded old men play shuffleboard, the boys jump and shout on the basketball court, their sneakers skidding across the concrete.

"They're *Rumspringa* boys," Alice whispers.

*Rumspringa.*

The word means "running around." If you're Old Order, you can act English once you turn sixteen. You're allowed to try out worldly things, in case you're not sure about getting baptized. It's your last chance to decide if you're going to stay Amish forever. As far as I can tell, nobody ever walks away from the church. Of course, that doesn't stop them from having as much fun as possible, if only for a couple of years.

My dad says it's wrong to step over the line of temptation. The Old Order can even wear English clothes—baggy jeans and tees. At least, the boys always do. If you asked me, the rules aren't the same for girls. Still, I never hear anyone talk about it. They'd probably love to swap their long dresses for jeans.

I know I would.

Everybody says the *Rumspringa* girls have the same choices as boys, but I don't believe it. Not when you see them sweating in their long dresses, while the boys run around in T-shirts. You see boys drinking more, too. When they toss their beer cans in the park, Dad says it's just "boys being boys." He says girls wouldn't do something stupid like that.

Girls aren't supposed to mess up.

Yeah, that's what he really means.

"So why did you ignore my letters?" she asks, staring at the ground.

Now I get it. Is that what's bothering her?

"I'm really sorry."

"Yeah?" Alice still won't look at me.

"I feel bad for not writing back."

That's the truth.

"So why didn't you?" she wants to know.

When I try to come up with an excuse, it doesn't sound right.

"I've been so busy helping Dad at the shop . . ."

She nods. "That's what I figured."

I'm not sure she understands. Alice's world up north is so different from mine. Living on a farm without electricity, it's work, work, and more work. That's how she describes it in her letters. To be honest, I was fascinated by it. The "chicken chores" and early morning cow-milking. The tangy scent of wood smoke lacing the paper.

There's another reason I haven't answered Alice's letters. We used to talk about all kinds of things. When I told her my secret—I don't want to spend the rest of my life in Pinecraft. I want to go to college and study the ocean—she didn't make fun of me. She listened.

Lately, all she talks about is boys.

A plane slices across the sky, leaving a trail like a zipper.

Alice squints. "How does it stay in the air without falling?"

"The wings push it up," I try to explain.

"But the wings aren't moving."

"Yeah, but the plane's going really fast. So that makes it lift."

"Whatever." She crouches down and digs inside her sock. I have no clue what she's doing. Then she pulls out a silver tube of lip gloss. Where did she get that? I bet she's had it a long time because there's hardly any left. Just a stubby lump of pink.

"Here," she says, slipping it into my hand. "It's almost gone anyway."

I'm embarrassed, just holding it. On the bottom, it says, *Summer Passion.* I glance around the park, hoping nobody sees me.

"Go on. Try it," she says.

Okay. Here goes.

I dab on the lip gloss. "Feels weird."

Alice laughs. "Don't you wish you had *Rumspringa?*"

Actually, I'm dying to know what it's like. A small taste of freedom. But there's no *Rumspringa* for Mennonites. That's one of the reasons my church broke off from the Old Order, a long time ago.

The Old Order girls keep their secrets hidden. They whisper to each other in Deitsch, hunched at picnic tables under the oaks. They move a little quieter, as if they're trying to take up less space.

The *Rumspringa* boys are different from the guys in Pinecraft. They hang out in packs like dogs and make a lot of noise, drinking beer in the park. That's why there's so much broken glass sparkling in the dirt. To be honest, it's really annoying. Sometimes I wish they'd get back on the bus and go home.

I wipe off the lip gloss on the back of my hand, but my mouth feels sticky. If Dad caught me wearing makeup, I'd be grounded for life.

Alice leans against the chainlink fence. "Have you kissed anybody yet?"

I look away. "What about you?"

She smiles.

"Tobias."

I can't believe it. Alice is a year older than me, but sometimes I feel like she's my little sister. She's always asking questions. What's this thing? How does it work? I used to think she'd never catch up. Now I'm the one falling behind.

"Don't be jealous, okay?" she says, grabbing my hand. "I can't wait for you to meet him."

Maybe I am a little jealous.

"There's a party on the beach tonight," she says, never taking her eyes off the boys. "It's going to be so amazing. You should come."

Yeah, right. There's no way Dad will let me go. If I can have things like cars and washing machines, why can't I have *Rumspringa* too?

I watch the boys lunge at the basketball net. "How are we supposed to get there?"

"Easy. Tobias knows somebody with a car."

A car is the first thing the *Rumspringa* boys want. And if they want something, they'll find a way to get it.

"What if my dad finds out?"

"Just tell him you're going to the Friday Night Youth Fellowship."

My stomach burns. "I can't lie to Dad."

"You don't have to lie. When it gets dark, walk over to church," she says. "Then call my cell."

"Your what?"

Alice reaches into her bag. She takes out a sparkly pink cell phone. "Pretty sweet, huh? My boyfriend gave it to me."

Dad has a cell phone for work, but he never lets me borrow it. Alice's cell looks brand-new. On the back, her name is spelled in tiny plastic diamonds.

"So I'll see you tonight?" she says.

"Maybe."

"Come on, Lucy. Remember when we used to sneak out?"

Me and Alice used to climb the mango trees in the empty lot near my house. Hours would pass without our feet touching the ground. I never felt so free.

"Let me give you the number," she says, taking a pen out of her bag. She pushes back my sleeve and scribbles on my wrist like she's drawing a tattoo. "There. Now you can't lose it."

I almost want to rub it off.

"I have to go," I tell her. "My dad needs help at the shop."

She makes a face. "You're always working."

"Tell me about it."

"At least we're finally done with school," she says. "If I had to do that again, I'd go crazy."

When you're Old Order, you have to drop out of school in eighth grade. The boys go straight to work with their dads. They usually end up in a factory, building furniture or painting RVs. That's what Alice told me.

She never said what girls are supposed to do.

In Florida, the rules are different. I finished all my classes last year. Tenth grade. That's as far as it goes. A lot of my friends were homeschooled. Nobody goes to college, unless you're studying something like nursing.

"Don't you miss school?" I ask.

"Yeah, right," Alice says. "I couldn't wait to get out of there."

"It's better than sanding lumber all day."

Although I love whacking nails with a hammer, love the smell of sawdust and cedar, sometimes I wonder if my fingers will ever feel soft.

"If you don't get out of Pinecraft now, you're going to be stuck here forever," Alice says. "Soon as I save up, I'm moving to California."

I can't listen to Alice anymore. Her head is full of dreams. I've got big dreams too. I want to go to college and learn about the ocean. Swim with dolphins and sharks. Watch loggerhead turtles lay eggs under the full moon. The world is a living thing that changes and grows.

Try explaining that to Dad.

When I talk to Dad about college, he says it's too much money. But I've been looking up schools at the library. A nice lady who works there helped me apply for scholarships. I've got my hopes on a school for marine biology in St. Petersburg. I sent the applications last summer. I still haven't heard back.

"I really have to go," I tell Alice, handing her the lip gloss. "Here. Keep this. My dad's going to kill me."

As I turn to leave, she reaches inside her bag.

"Got a present for you," she says, handing me something wrapped in brown paper.

"You didn't have to do that."

"Yeah, I know," she says, smiling.

I tear off the paper. "Is it a book?" I ask hopefully.

It is.

*The Blue Planet: A Natural History of the Oceans.*

"Because you love the water so much," she says.

As I turn the pages, I look at pictures of animals from far away. Seals bobbing in the frozen seas of the Arctic. Tiny fish with enormous eyes, glowing in water so deep, we could never find them. Birds that migrate for thousands of miles without ever stopping to rest.

I stare at those pictures a long time.

"Don't you like it?" she asks.

"It's beautiful. But I can't keep this."

"Why not?"

"You know why," I say, wiping my face.

If Dad catches me with a book about the e-word—*evolution*—I'll be in big trouble.

For a minute, Alice doesn't say anything. Then she gives me a big hug.

"You're supposed to say thank you."

• • •

When I get home that afternoon, Dad's on the front porch. He's been working in the yard all day and his face is slick with sweat.

"Been waiting for you," he says, marching across the lawn.

I hide the book behind my back. "Me and Alice were just—"

"I don't want to hear about Alice," he snaps. "Understand? I need you working here at the shop. Not running all over Pinecraft."

"I'm sorry."

"You left my good shirts on the line. And you forgot to pull out the pockets. The jeans are still wet."

He's disappointed in me again. Why can't I do anything right?

"I'll take care of it," I say, moving toward the clothesline.

Dad grabs my wrist. "What's this?"

The book tumbles into the grass.

I lunge for it, but Dad's quicker. "If you keep reading so much, it's bad for your eyes. You hear?"

Yeah, I've heard that before.

He flips through *The Blue Planet*, not saying a word. The more Dad reads, the deeper he frowns.

"Where did you get this?" he asks.

"It's a present. Alice gave it to me. Please. Can I have it back?"

"You have enough books," he says. "You don't need more."

He's wrong.

I can never have enough books.

Dad goes over to the workshop. The garbage bins are heaped with plywood boards. Rusty nails. Whatever he can't use. He shoves my book into the pile.

"Don't be filling your head with lies," he says, walking away.

*The Blue Planet* isn't a lie.

It's the world we live in.

When he's finally gone, I plunge my hand into the garbage. I feel around for my book, but I can't move those heavy boards out of the way.

That's when I make up my mind.

I'll go to that party with Alice tonight.

I don't care if I have to lie.

## chapter three

# floating

Faron's truck is parked behind the empty lot. It doesn't look like it can go very far. A piece of rope dangles from the bumper. The faded red paint is scabbed with rust. I stand there, looking at it.

He slides behind the wheel. "You girls coming or what?"

Guess I don't have a choice.

"Can't you talk?" he says.

"Yeah," I tell him. "When it's someone worth talking to."

He blinks, as if he doesn't know what to do. Old Order boys are weird. That's for sure.

Alice tugs herself up into the truck bed. There's a lot of junk tossed in the back—fast-food wrappers and crumpled beer cans. I crouch next to her on the rubber mat. Already this feels like a big mistake.

We swerve onto Fruitville Road, speeding past motels with names like Seabreeze and Sundial and a mini golf course shaped like a pirate ship. All the parking lots are lit up, but their spaces are empty. A car swerves in front of us, blaring its horn. I scoot down lower and hope nobody sees me.

"Isn't this fun?" says Alice, waving like a princess on a float.

Fun isn't exactly what I'd call it.

When we pass the drugstore near the highway, Alice thumps the glass between us and the boys.

"Can we stop for a minute?" she shouts at Faron.

"What for?" he says.

"I need something."

"You think this is a taxi?" he says, but we make a U-turn and pull into the parking lot.

The boys sit in the truck while me and Alice climb out. The drugstore is surrounded by a wall of scorched-looking palm trees. My dad never buys anything here. He says it's wasteful, the money people spend on things they don't need.

Tobias leans out the window. "Don't take too frickin' long. You hear?"

"Yeah, I hear," Alice mutters.

"What the hell are you getting anyway?"

"None of your business," she says, blowing a kiss.

We march up to the store's gleaming front entrance. The door swishes open, all by itself. There's a line of people waiting at the cash register. Little kids shoving potato chips in their mouths. A lady with plastic curlers in her hair.

"They're so strange, those Amish girls," she says under her breath.

It's me, not Alice, she's staring at. My long-sleeved dress. The prayer cap on my head. The things on the outside that make me different.

Go ahead. Keep whispering like I can't hear you.

"Look at all this stuff." Alice whistles as she drifts through the store. I still don't know how to whistle. She's walking so fast, I can't help feeling like she wants to get rid of me. If she's trying to pass as English, she probably doesn't want me hanging around in my plain clothes.

Alice disappears around a corner. I'm trying to keep up, but a couple of girls are blocking the aisle. They're so busy squeezing lotion on their hands, they won't get out of the way.

"Excuse me," I mumble.

"Oh. Sorry," says the dark-haired girl. But she's not sorry. She grins at her friend, who's even smaller than Alice. They're both in denim shorts and flimsy tank tops, their bare shoulders pink with sun.

Her friend giggles. She's got a million rubber bracelets stacked up her arms and rainbow streaks in her hair. Maybe I'd dress like that, if I lived in their world. They're like me and Alice. The same, but different.

"Where's your horse and buggy?" she asks.

"It's my day off," I tell her, pushing ahead.

They're laughing at me. I can tell by the way they're glancing back, then looking away, like I'm too dumb to notice. This is why I hate shopping outside Pinecraft. Sometimes I just want to hide in my room with my books and never go anywhere.

Alice is in the next aisle, reaching for something on the shelf. I'm still thinking about the girls, their fun clothes and perfect teeth. All of a sudden, I feel dizzy. I need to get away from all these people. I head straight for the door and step outside.

Faron's pickup truck is a bright red smear across the parking lot. The boys are sitting behind the windshield, their faces lit by the streetlight. They've got the windows rolled down and I can hear them talking. I crouch down behind a car and pray they don't see me.

"I thought this place would be different," says Tobias, reaching under his seat and pulling out a can of beer.

"Different how?" Faron asks.

Tobias cracks open the beer and takes a long gulp. "I don't know," he says. "Florida's not so great. I mean, yeah. The girls are real pretty. But they're kind of stuck-up." He wipes his mouth on his sleeve. "Everybody's got money down here. You see the cars in this parking lot? All brand-new."

"Not the one you're sitting in."

"Yeah, that's the problem. Up north, it's all beaters. That's because it snows every frickin' day," he says, glancing up, like it might snow inside the car. "Girls won't even look at you unless you've got money."

"If you think money's going to solve all your problems, you're in for a big surprise," says Faron.

"Well, it got me away from home."

"Freedom, huh? That's what you want?"

"Doesn't everybody?"

"The whole world's looking for it," says Faron. "Most of the time, they don't go farther than their own backyard."

"Whatever. Soon as I'm up north, I'm getting my own ride," says Tobias. "Maybe an old-school muscle car."

"Let me guess," says Faron, lighting a cigarette. "You want a big old spoiler on the back?"

"Yeah." Tobias grins. "That would be awesome."

"Don't waste your money on a spoiler."

"Why not?"

"It won't make you go fast."

"But it looks cool."

"Looks don't mean nothing," says Faron. "If you can't go fast, it ain't worth driving."

"Speaking of looks, who do you think is prettier? My girl or yours?"

"The quiet one? She ain't mine."

Tobias laughs. "Only fair to share. What do you say?"

"I say you need to shut your mouth." Faron tugs up his hood and climbs out of the truck, like he can't stand to listen to Tobias anymore. He leans against the bumper, looking up at the night sky, as if he's counting stars. He's got his back to me, so I quickly turn and head inside the store.

It doesn't take long to find Alice. She's in the exact same spot where I left her.

"Where did you go?" she asks.

"Just needed some fresh air," I mumble. My head is pounding. The dizzy feeling won't go away. "So what are you going to buy?"

She grabs a tube of lip gloss off the shelf. "Nothing," she says, cramming it inside her sock.

"You better put that back," I whisper.

"Why?"

"You're going to be in so much trouble."

Alice smirks. "Only if I get caught."

A man in a white jacket is at the cash register, watching us. He catches my stare and I look away.

"Now it's your turn," Alice says.

I glance at the shelves. Lip gloss that's guaranteed to last through every kiss. Foolproof mascara that lengthens and shines. I don't want any of it, but Alice has a way of talking me into things.

"Come on, Lucy. Hurry up."

I reach for a bottle of nail polish. It thunks on the floor, gushing pink ooze. I'm so embarrassed, I want to run out of the store.

Somebody puts a hand on my shoulder. The man in the white jacket. He glares at the stain on the carpet, then at me.

"Start explaining," he says.

My fingers begin to tingle. A buzzing drills my ears, like the sound of all the thoughts zinging through the world. The man's voice fades away. Now I'm on the floor, looking up at the ceiling.

I open my mouth to scream.

Nothing comes out.

Alice is next to me, stroking my forehead. "Lucy," she keeps saying. "Please get up."

The man in the white jacket is standing behind us, talking on a cell phone. When I open my eyes, he gets this strange look on his face.

"I think you two should leave," he says.

Alice grabs my hand. We run out of the store into the parking lot. By the time we reach the truck, I'm out of breath.

"Are you okay?" Alice says, gasping. "I mean, was that for real? You weren't faking?"

*Why would I fake something like that?*

"Yeah, it was for real."

"Were you sick?" she asks.

I try to describe it. I'm stuck in my body and I can't breathe. Can't even move a finger. I want her to believe me, but I'm not sure she understands.

"I've had those kinds of dreams," she says. "Scares me so bad, I wake up screaming."

"It wasn't a dream," I tell her.

"How do you know?"

"I'm not dreaming now, am I?"

Alice is quiet.

The shame burns through me. "Please don't tell anyone."

"I won't," she says. "As long as you don't tell Mom about me and Tobias."

I promise. But the way Tobias was talking about girls, you'd think he wasn't even her boyfriend. I don't trust him. Not one bit.

We climb back into the truck. I'm still thinking about dreams, how they slip away like the tide in the morning light.

"About time you got back," says Tobias, cranking the window.

Alice leans back against the truck bed. She slides a finger in her sock and pulls out the tube of lip gloss. "So when you passed out. . ." she whispers to me. "Did you see anything special? You know. Angels or something?"

I shake my head. "No."

She smears the lip gloss across her mouth. "I never believed in them anyway."

chapter four

# water tower park

The truck slows onto a dimly lit street. Dozens of cars are lined up at Water Tower Park. I've played Frisbee golf here with Dad lots of times. The rusty baskets are scattered around the woods, each target flagged with a number. In the distance, the tower rises above the oaks.

"This doesn't look like the beach," says Alice.

We get out and start walking. Tobias wastes no time, cracking open another beer. He passes it to Alice and she tilts her head, gulping it down.

"Here." Faron shoves a damp can at me. "There's only one left, but we can share."

I tip back the can and swallow a warm, sudsy mouthful. I don't like the taste of beer, but I like how it loosens something inside me.

"You're from Pinecraft, right?" he says.

My face burns as I take another sip. "How did you know?"

He points at my dress. "The girls back home, they only wear gray or brown. Nothing fancy like yours."

"It's not that fancy," I say.

Alice comes up behind me and grabs my arm. "Let's go. I want to dance."

The Old Order girls are dancing behind the oak trees. They remind me of ghosts swaying in their long dresses.

"I don't know how."

"It's easy," she says. "I'll show you."

Everything's easy for her.

"We're supposed to be having fun," Alice says, pulling me closer. "So what do you think of Tobias?"

I shrug. "He's okay, I guess."

"Well, I think he's amazing. I mean, he's not like other boys." She looks back at him and smiles.

"Go on," I tell her. "I'll wait."

The loud music is making me nervous. Same for the beer going sour in my mouth. I just want to get out of here. I turn around so fast, I bump into Faron.

"Whoa," he says, laughing as I take a step backward. "You in a hurry or something?"

I glance up at him, all the planes and angles in his face. I'm probably staring. Faron turns around and his eyes meet mine.

"Want to go someplace quiet?"

"Sure." That sounds good to me.

As we walk through the woods to the canal, he doesn't say much, but that's okay. The *Rumspringa* boys are always running around, making noise, but Faron is quiet and still. I feel pulled to his stillness. It's exactly what I need right now.

When we reach the footbridge, I lean over the railing and peer down. "This canal used to look a lot bigger when I was a kid," I say, breaking the silence.

"That's because the world got smaller."

His sneaker bumps mine and I don't move.

"Are you from up north?" I ask.

He nods. "Drove down from Maine last summer."

I figured he was on *Rumspringa*. Now I'm confused. If Faron drove to Pinecraft last summer, he's not a snowbird.

Then what is he?

"Alice is from up north, too," I say.

"Old Order."

"Yes. Her mom's trying to push her into getting baptized."

"Don't blame her for running."

"What if Alice doesn't join the church? I mean, will she . . ." I struggle with the words. "Is she going to be shunned?"

"If she ain't baptized, they can't shun her."

"But she can't go home."

We're both quiet for a moment.

"You never felt like running away?" he says.

I scrape a piece of flaking paint off the railing. "Not really," I say, which isn't even the truth. "What about you?"

"Sure," he says, tugging up his hood. "But the world's too small a place to hide in."

Is Faron hiding from something?

"Well, running away isn't going to fix anything," I tell him.

He reaches into his pocket and takes out a pack of Reds. "You got it real easy, growing up in Pinecraft."

"What makes you say that?"

"It's different here," he says, flicking his lighter. "You've got a lot of nice things."

"Like what?"

"Well, you can go to the beach anytime you want."

"There's beaches up north, too."

"Not like this," he says. "The Florida Amish have it real good. You can drive a car. Watch TV."

"My dad won't let me watch TV."

"Yeah?" says Faron, blowing out smoke. "That's probably the one thing you don't got."

"What about *Rumspringa*?"

"You don't need it," he says.

"Why not?"

"Because it's always *Rumspringa* in Florida."

He's laughing at me. Does he think this is a joke? I dig my fingernails into the railing, scraping away more paint.

"So where did you get that truck?" I ask, trying to put him on the spot.

"Built it myself."

I'm surprised. "You built it?"

"Most of it's scrap," he says. "Saved up, working in my dad's lumber yard. He really hated that old Ford. Used to make me park it behind the barn."

"So you're working for your dad?"

Faron tosses his cigarette. "We don't talk no more."

Now I get it.

He's been shunned.

What would it feel like if your family pushed you away? It scares me, just thinking about it. No Sunday picnics. No Christmas, either. No afternoons on the front porch, watching my dad carve driftwood into windmills and birds. I'd probably miss that the most.

"Is that why you're in Pinecraft?" I ask.

"Yeah," he says. "After my dad kicked me out, I jumped in my truck and headed south. Then I just kept going."

I don't know what to say. For some reason, I can't stop shivering. I hold onto the bridge railing with both hands, but my fingers won't stay still.

"You cold?" he says, unzipping his sweatshirt. "You're shaking something fierce." Before I can answer, he drapes it over my shoulders.

Now we're both quiet.

"Never heard crickets like that," he finally says. "Must be a million of them, chirping up a storm."

"They're not crickets," I tell him. "Those are *coqui* frogs. They're invasive."

"What?"

"The *coquis* don't belong here. They're eating all the native tree frogs. Pretty soon, we won't have any left."

Why am I talking about frogs? He must think I'm really weird.

Faron grins. "Maybe they can be friends."

Too bad it doesn't work like that. I've read enough to know. If you don't fit in, the world's going to swallow you up.

"What about gators? Ever seen one in this canal?" he asks.

"There aren't any gators in Water Tower Park."

"Okay. I dare you to walk to that tree over there." He points at a straggly palm. "Bring back a leaf."

What does he think I am? A dog that plays fetch?

I stand there, not moving.

"Thought you weren't scared," he says.

"Fine."

This is so stupid. I start making my way down the canal, lifting the hem of my dress. When I reach the palm, I tear off a frond. Sure, there aren't any gators. But as I head back through the dark, I can't help looking over my shoulder once or twice.

"Here's your prize," I say, handing the leaf to Faron. He nods like I've done a real good job and tucks it behind his ear.

"Thanks, *fehlerfrei*," he says.

*Fehlerfrei*. An Old Order word that means "perfect."

I look away.

Maybe he thinks I'm "high-minded," as Dad would say. Trust me. I'm anything but perfect.

Something tickles the back of my neck. It scares me so bad, I jump. Then I turn around and see Faron holding that stupid palm leaf. I'm so mad at him, I tug his sweatshirt off my shoulders and toss it in the dirt.

"Hey," he says, scooping it up.

"Probably time you washed that thing," I tell him.

He brushes it off. No big deal. As he tugs himself into the sleeves, he says, "Don't get so fired up."

I've really had it with him.

"We should probably go back now," I say.

Faron's hooded face looks down at mine. "You got someplace to be?"

When he smiles, a jolt burns through me. I bet he's used to girls following him around. *The quiet one.* Well, if he thinks I'm going to laugh at his jokes all night, he better guess again.

I turn and start heading across the bridge. I shouldn't have walked so far alone. I just wanted to get away from that party. The loud music. All those people. Now I'm shaking again, but it's not like music can hurt you.

"Lucy," he calls out.

I keep walking toward the lights behind the trees. I need to find Alice and talk her out of running away. If she's looking for a place to hide, where could she go?

The world isn't big enough.

## chapter five

# sunrise

All around me, the music pounds. In church, we never sing like that. We're not even allowed to clap. That would be like showing off.

I push through the crowd, searching for Alice. She's not with the Old Order girls dancing behind the oak trees. They're all dressed plain. I can tell where they belong, just by looking at the length of their skirts. The color of their bonnets. Alice is the only one who belongs nowhere.

"Alice?" I shout over the music.

Nobody pays attention to me. They're snowbirds. And they know I shouldn't be at this party.

I keep moving toward the park entrance. There's a bunch of people drinking in the woods. They could almost pass for English in their hoodies and jeans, but there's something weird about those *Rumspringa* boys. I don't want to talk to them, but I've got no choice.

As I walk closer, the boys start talking in Deitsch, big words that sound strange and familiar at the same time. I'm so nervous, I take a step backward.

"I'm looking for my friend," I tell them.

The boys laugh, like this is real funny.

"Me and you can be friends," says the guy in the baseball cap. He shoves a plastic cup in my face.

"No thanks." I push it away.

"You got a problem?" he says, grabbing my arm.

I can't believe he's touching me. I try to pull myself free, but he doesn't let go. I reach for the plastic cup and throw it at him. Beer soaks through his T-shirt and darkens his jeans.

I take off, running. But you can't run very fast in a dress. Or very far. I don't stop until I reach this big open field near the parking lot. It's so empty. No one's around. Then I notice a girl in skinny jeans and a tank top, face-down in the grass, as if she fell asleep.

Alice.

I run over to her, stumbling in my long skirt. "Alice, it's me."

She doesn't move.

"Please wake up."

I shake her. Hard.

Alice slowly raises her head. She gives me a long stare. "I'm so wasted."

"What happened? Are you sick?"

"Tobias got me another beer. I probably drank it too fast," she mutters. "Thanks for leaving me."

"I didn't leave you."

"Yeah, you did. I saw you walking by the canal with Faron."

A rush of heat floods my neck. "We were just talking."

"That's all?" She gets up, swaying a little like she's going to fall.

"Are you okay?" I ask.

"I'm more than okay."

"Well, you don't look it."

"Me and Tobias got in a fight," she says, brushing herself off. "Whatever. He's being really stupid."

"Where is he?" I ask.

She doesn't answer.

I glance at the cars streaming out of the parking lot. "We should probably head back."

"You're not coming with us?"

"Where?"

"Everybody's going to Lido Key to watch the sunrise."

"The beach?"

"Yeah. Don't you want to go?"

Of course I want to go to the beach. Watch the colors paint the sand. Dig for coquina shells that wash up at dawn. But I've got work in the morning, and Dad's going to be looking for me.

"I can't go."

Alice rolls her eyes. "Can't you have fun for once in your life?"

"This isn't fun anymore."

"Then leave," she says.

I wince, as if I've been slapped. "Fine."

If she's going to be mean, I'd rather leave this stupid party.

I start walking toward the parking lot. When I glance back, Alice is gone. I'm scared for her, but I'm still angry because of the way she's acting tonight. It's like she turned into somebody else.

How am I supposed to get home now? I can't figure out what to do. It's too far to walk to Pinecraft. The buses don't start running for a couple more hours. Then I spot Tobias in the swarm of people leaving the park. He's got some kind of camera in his hands. He's so busy messing with it, he doesn't notice me.

"Tobias," I call out and he spins around.

"Oh, it's you," he says, like I don't even have a name.

"Alice was looking for you."

"Yeah?" he says. "Where is she?"

"You just took off without her?"

"Hey, I'm not in charge of her life."

I want to scream at him.

He brushes past me and drifts into the crowd. I stare at the ground where his sneakers have stamped patterns in the dirt—three pointy leaves and a pair of stripes. Let him deal with Alice. I'm tired of following her around. She's supposed to be my best friend, but all she talks about is Tobias. I can't believe she'd ditch me for a boy.

All this time, I've stood in the background while Alice races ahead. Now I want to take a step forward. Where? It doesn't matter, as long as it's away from here.

The parking lot is filled with cars all leaving at once. I'm blinded with noise and light. When I try to cross over, I stumble in my long dress and fall on my hands and knees. A truck slows in front of me, blocking my path.

The window rolls down and Faron leans out.

"Been looking all over for you," he says, swinging the door open. "What are you doing out here?"

I stand up and brush myself off. "Walking home."

"Looks more like you were falling. You want to get killed?"

What a stupid question. I don't want to go for a ride with him. Still, it's better than standing out here in the middle of traffic, waiting to get run over.

I pull myself inside the truck and scoot next to him. "Can you drive me back to Pinecraft? I need to go home."

"You're going to miss the sunrise," he says.

I stare at the rabbit's foot swinging from the rearview mirror. "I've seen it before."

"Is that right?"

"Yeah, I've seen it a million times."

He grins. "You ain't never seen it with me."

# chapter six

# low tide

L ido Key is quiet at dawn. The breeze smells like low tide and
magnolia blossoms. All across the beach, the Old Order girls
stand near the shore, laughing as the water swirls around their
ankles. They came to watch the sunrise, but they're looking in the
wrong direction.

"When I was little, I'd get up early and dig for sand dollars," I
tell Faron. "You couldn't walk across the beach without stepping
on them. Now they're all gone."

"What happened?" he asks.

"Some people were drilling for oil and it leaked into the Gulf.
Now the water's messed up. See?" I point at a dead shark that's
flopped in the sand. A lemon shark. They look a little scary, but
hardly ever bite.

"We should have a funeral," I say.

"A funeral for a shark?" he says, looking at me.

"At least bring it back in the water." I kind of feel sorry for that
shark lying there in the sand all alone. I start walking over to it.

"Most girls would be scared, getting close to a shark."

"It can't hurt me." Why would I be scared?

"True," he says. "It ain't right, leaving it out in the open."

I crouch down and grab hold of the shark's tail. It's too heavy
for me to pull by myself. Faron comes up next to me. Together we
carry it into the tide. All the muscles in his arms are straining as
he drags it toward the water. But Faron is strong. You have to be
strong, if you're Old Order.

I help him pull the shark back into the Gulf. Together we wade
knee-deep in the surf until we're almost swimming. Then we let
go.

43

"Your shark's back where it belongs," says Faron as we walk to shore. "Now it can go to sleep."

What does he mean, "go to sleep"? Is that how Faron imagines death? If my dad heard me talking like that, he'd say I'd been reading too much.

Sometimes at night I try to imagine it. I wake up, shaking from a dream I can't remember. Maybe that's the closest thing to death. I know it sounds strange, but I feel a little better, knowing the shark has a quiet place to rest.

"That shark must've been sick," I tell him. "You don't find them washed up on the beach like that. They can see real good."

"Yeah?"

"Even better than us."

I'm talking a lot, but Faron's listening. "How do you know all this stuff?"

I shrug. "Books mostly. I like to read."

"You like to read about the ocean, huh? Wouldn't you rather feel it?"

My face heats up. "I just like reading. That's all."

"You don't want to be out there?" he says, pointing at the tide. I do.

"There's a school for marine biology up in St. Pete. It's only an hour away, but my dad thinks it's a waste of time. He says it costs too much money, but he just wants me to stay in Pinecraft forever. He doesn't know I've been applying for scholarships online."

"That's your dad," says Faron. "What about you, Lucy? Is that what you really want?"

Nobody's ever asked.

"I want to study the ocean." It feels good, saying it out loud.

"You want to swim with the fish, huh?"

"And the sharks."

Faron laughs. "Man, you're something else. What's so great about sharks anyway?"

"Sharks have been here a long time. They're like living fossils."

"Fossils?"

"You know. Like the dinosaurs."

The teachers at my school didn't believe in dinosaurs. They said the plesiosaur bones at the science museum are made of plastic.

"How can a shark see anything in that dark water?" he asks.

"Sharks can sense electricity. That's why they're really good hunters. Everything that's alive has electricity inside it."

"Including us?" he says.

"As long as your heart's still beating."

When Faron smiles, I can't help smiling back.

"Maybe that's why people believe in souls," he says.

I'm stunned. All my life, I've been asking questions. How does a soul get inside your body? Does it switch on like a light bulb? Or is it simply part of the secret places inside us, like the ocean in a seashell?

"Do you think animals have souls?" I ask Faron.

"If we do," he says.

I look away. "You shouldn't say things like that."

"Why not?" he asks.

"Because it's wrong."

"What's wrong? Thinking it? Or saying it?"

I really don't know.

We keep walking on the beach. The sky is lighter now. Soon the sun will be up. I've never been alone with a boy all night. But it's easy, talking to Faron. I feel like I could ask him anything. When we stood together on the bridge, I thought he was making fun of me, joking about how it's always *Rumspringa* in Florida. But I was the one judging him.

I've got another question for Faron. A big one.

"Why did you get shunned?"

He stares out at the Gulf. "My dad was pushing me to join the church. So I caved in. Then I left and never looked back."

"You changed your mind about baptism."

"After I joined the church, I thought I'd have all the answers. Instead, I got more questions. Here's the deal. They want us all thinking the same, you know? Why is it so bad if I don't follow the church's rules? Why do they get to choose what's right and wrong?"

We should think for ourselves. Is that what Faron's saying?

"At first, I just went along with everything," he says. "Sure, the Lord made the world in six days. Maybe I can't wrap my head around it. Or maybe it's just . . . you know. A way of explaining something so big, we'll never understand it. But when I asked my dad if it's true, he got real angry." Faron shakes his head and sighs. "I was asking too many questions. Guess I should've kept my mouth shut. That would've made everybody happy."

"If you weren't sure about being Amish, why did you go through with it?"

"Felt like I had to."

"But it's supposed to be your choice."

"That's what they say. As long as you make the right one."

*Rumspringa* doesn't sound so good anymore. By the time you're old enough to drive, you're supposed to have your whole life figured out. If you're Old Order, you've got two choices: join the church, or walk away forever.

"It's not fair."

"Of course it ain't fair. But that's the way it goes."

"Why can't you start over again? Everyone deserves a second chance."

Faron doesn't say anything.

"Don't you think?"

"Want to know what I think?" he says, leaning in close. "I think I want to kiss you."

*What did he say?*

I'm so stunned, I don't know what to do. I lower my head. Faron hooks a finger under my chin, tilting my face upward. When he brushes his lips against mine, I'm right there, feeling his closeness. I never imagined my first kiss would happen like this. Not on the beach, where headlights cut between the chainlink fence, dim, and grow brighter.

This can't be happening. I mean, this isn't supposed to happen. I could be in big trouble, kissing an Old Order boy who's been shunned. What if somebody sees us?

Faron pulls back. I'm so embarrassed, I can't even look at him. Then he tries to kiss me again, but I turn away.

"What's the matter?" he whispers.

"Nothing. I'm fine."

He grins. "Thought you weren't scared of anything."

I am scared.

It's all so strange and new. As long as I can remember, I've been told to stay away from *Rumspringa* boys. Now I'm caught in the warmth of his arms and it feels so good, I don't want him to let go.

I look down at his hand.

Then I notice the scars.

"How did it happen?" I ask gently.

"Got pulled into a saw at my dad's lumberyard." He stares at the faint lines slashing his knuckles. "Took a month just to learn how to tie my shoes again."

"I'm sorry."

"Don't be sorry. I'm okay now. It's in the past," he says. "That's where the past belongs."

I know he's not okay.

Not even close.

Faron isn't like Tobias. He's different from the *Rumspringa* boys. Older inside. And stronger too. He doesn't run around, making a big noise. When we're alone together, he leans in with his whole body, listening to me. Most boys don't listen at all. They're too busy talking.

I'm used to being alone. All I need are my books for company. Now Faron's got me thinking. Maybe it's okay to speak up and ask questions. When he kissed me, I didn't want it to end. And when we were talking on the beach, I wished I could stop time.

He's like a book I want to keep reading.

"Come on," he says. "Let's take a walk. The sun's coming up."

It's almost morning. Low tide. The shore is crusted with shells. When I was little I'd swim until my toes wrinkled. Now there are signs everywhere. DANGER. BEACH CLOSED. It makes me sick, just thinking about it. A hole bleeding poison into the sea.

"This is the best time to look for sand dollars," I tell Faron. But when I glance at the sand, I don't see any. "Did you know they've got a secret?"

"What's that?" He smiles at me.

"If you crack open the shell, you'll find the doves."

"Doves?"

"Yeah, they're tiny bits hidden inside."

"But you'd have to break it," he says.

It's true. I didn't believe until I cracked my first sand dollar. I wanted to see what was inside. Hold it in my hand. Then I knew it was real.

A siren cuts through the early morning quiet. Red and blue lights sway across the sand. There's a police cruiser near the seawall. Sarasota Beach Patrol.

"Let's go. The cops are kicking everybody off the beach," says Faron.

The crowd is already moving away from the shore. Old Order girls in long, dark dresses. They all look the same. But where's Alice? I thought she'd be here. I feel bad that I waited so long to look for her. The siren pierces through me. So does the guilt.

"Come on," Faron says, looking over his shoulder. Why is he so nervous?

"I need to find Alice." I turn and start running in the other direction.

"Lucy," he shouts.

I push against the crowd. Maybe Alice never made it to the beach after all. If I had a cell phone, I'd call her. But it's just another thing I don't have. I keep moving, calling her name. Alice was carrying a lot of money. More than I've ever seen. I bet she saved up all summer.

Tobias saw it too.

I'm thinking so hard, I don't even notice the cop. He's waving a flashlight and motioning for me to leave.

"Go home," he says. "The party's over."

I glance at the seawall, but Faron is gone. I'm blinking back tears as I walk to the bus stop on Ringling Boulevard. The seagulls wheel above me, silent and watchful, and slowly, it begins to rain.

• • •

The sun is on the horizon. I get off at the bus stop in Pinecraft and walk home as fast as possible. Maybe I can sneak inside the house before Dad wakes up. Too late. He's already working outside, sanding lumber.

Dad glares at me. "Do you have any idea what time it is?"

"It won't happen again."

"I got up this morning and you weren't here."

My stomach burns. I feel horrible, knowing he was worried about me. My dress is soaked, the hem crusted with sand. I'm so embarrassed, I can't even look at him.

"I'm sorry."

"You were with Alice. Is that right?"

He probably went next door and talked to Mrs. Yoder. Did she tell him about me and Alice sneaking out? Yeah, I bet she did.

"I know you girls are close," Dad says. "But now you're running around all night, doing who knows what."

"We stayed up late, talking. That's all." The words come out fast. I hardly recognize the way I sound.

"Don't raise your voice at me, Lucy. You've been running a bit too much with that Old Order girl. And it's going to stop."

"But—"

"Get inside," he says. "Your face is dirty. Better wash up before the neighbors see you."

I go in the house and head straight for the bathroom.

All this time, Alice kept her secrets to herself. Now I've got one of my own. I hold it close, buried someplace deep, like the doves inside a sand dollar. Slowly, I take off my prayer cap and let my hair spill down my back. I peel off my dress. Then I sit in the tub until the water turns gray.

## chapter seven
# keeping secrets

I'm on the porch, snapping green beans for supper, when I spot the Old Order woman in her long dress, making her way through the moss-draped trees. Mrs. Yoder never comes to my house. I'm so surprised, I barely hear what she says.

"Alice is gone."

A shiver runs across my skin. "Gone where?"

"I was hoping you'd tell me."

All day long, I've been carrying Alice in my mind. I can't talk about what happened at Water Tower Park. Or ask if anybody's seen her after the party. I don't want her to get in trouble.

We're both in trouble now.

"Don't just stand there, catching flies," says Mrs. Yoder. "I know you girls were together last night."

I stare at the orange trees in the front yard. Their branches shift and bend as a breeze picks up. It smells like something's burning far away.

"Am I correct?" she asks.

"Yes," I say, a little too quickly.

"I'm thinking Alice has run off again."

So it's not the first time. Then why do I feel so worried? And why didn't Alice tell me about it before? I thought we could tell each other everything. It hurts, the fact that she never shared this secret with me. In my head, I keep going back to the party. All those Old Order girls on the beach. But Alice wasn't there. What happened to her after I left the park?

I shouldn't have left her alone.

"Well?" says Mrs. Yoder.

"I don't know where she is."

Mrs. Yoder frowns. "You're telling half the truth, Lucy Zimmer. And that makes a whole lie."

The front door swings open.

"What's this about?" Dad wants to know.

Mrs. Yoder steps onto the porch. She marches up to Dad like I'm not even there. "My daughter, Alice, is missing."

Dad glances at Mrs. Yoder, then at me.

"Come inside," he says, motioning for us to follow him.

In the kitchen, we sit around the table. Mrs. Yoder and Dad on one side. Me in the chair with the wobbly leg. The chair keeps rocking as I tell them about last night.

Not everything.

Enough.

"What's the matter with you, Lucy?" Dad says. "That was a foolish thing to do, going to Water Tower Park at night."

If he finds out I was with a boy, I'll really be in for it.

Mrs. Yoder stays quiet the whole time. She's not crying or anything. That's what's strange about it.

Her sharp little face turns to me. "Where did you go after the party?"

"I didn't go anywhere."

"You went straight home?"

I shift my weight in the chair. "That's right. I took the bus."

"And you went by yourself?"

I nod.

"What about Alice?"

"She wanted to stay longer, I guess."

"You guess?"

I don't know what else to say.

"You're protecting my daughter, aren't you, Lucy? Just like when you girls were small."

I look down at my hands folded in my lap.

"You and Alice have always been good friends. I can't believe she'd run off without telling you. Didn't she say something?"

Yeah, she did.

And it still hurts.

"I never should've come down to Pinecraft this year," says Mrs. Yoder. "Not with Alice on her *Rumspringa*."

"What's Pinecraft got to do with it?" Dad's losing his patience now. He turns to me. "So you're running around with these Old Order kids last night. They're down in Florida on *Rumspringa*. The Lord knows what they're doing in Water Tower Park," he says. "Probably drinking. Am I right?"

I can't even look at him.

"Answer me, Lucy."

"It was just one beer."

He shakes his head. "Does that make it okay?"

"No."

"Alice didn't leave the park by herself. That much, I can guess. Did she go off somewhere with a boy?"

It's not easy, hiding the truth from Dad.

"I don't know what happened after the party."

That's all I can say.

Alice wanted to go to Lido Key and watch the sunrise. But I never saw her leave Water Tower Park. I drove to the beach with Faron, a secret I can't tell anybody.

Mrs. Yoder leans across the table. "Lucy Zimmer," she says in a voice so cold, I flinch. "Don't lie to me."

Dad slams down his fist. "My daughter's no liar."

The house is quiet.

I listen to the clock ticking above the stove.

Finally, Dad pushes back his chair. "We were just about to have supper," he tells Mrs. Yoder. "You're welcome to stay and eat a little."

That's how Dad handles everything, as if a slice of Key lime pie could solve all your problems.

"All right," says Mrs. Yoder, still looking at me.

Dad pats my hand. "Come outside for a minute. I need some help."

I know he doesn't need help, but I follow him anyway.

When we reach the koi pond in the backyard, he says, "I'm really disappointed in you, Smidge."

The way he's talking, I feel like the ground has split between us.

He opens a can of orange pellets and flings a handful at the koi. They flail against the surface of the water like knives. "Why did you keep quiet about your friend? You could've talked to me."

"I'm talking now."

"Okay." He yanks a hanky out of his pocket and mops his neck. "I'm listening."

I glance across the road. Some Old Order boys are rattling down Kruppa Avenue on metal scooters, while a couple of girls shuffle quietly behind.

"Alice doesn't want to get baptized."

"And why is that?" he asks.

I lower my gaze. There's a calico scallop at the bottom of the pond, leaning against a rock.

"Lucy," he says. "Your turn's coming soon."

Next week, I will stand in front of everybody at church and say my baptismal vows. That's the main thing we have in common with the Old Order. We both believe that baptism is a grown-up decision.

Ever since I was little, I've been getting ready for this day. Now I'm having second thoughts. If I go through with it, I'll have to stay Amish forever. I'll probably never leave Pinecraft. And I'd never go to school and learn about the ocean.

Dad sighs. "It's time you started acting more grown-up. Think about what I'm saying here."

I think too much. That's what Dad says.

He dips his thumb in the water. All the fish swarm around it, waiting for food. That's how much they trust him.

"What's going to happen if Alice doesn't get baptized?" I ask.

"If your friend isn't baptized, I'm afraid she's lost."

"But what if she did it just to make everyone happy? Wouldn't that be like lying?"

Dad doesn't say anything. He closes the screen over the pond, keeping the fish safe for the night. Then he walks back to the house.

• • •

That night, I toss and turn under my quilt, the one Mama sewed for me. No use trying to sleep. I get up and go to my dresser. Everything reminds me of Alice. The mason jar filled with seashells and tiny doves. The shoebox I keep under my bed, stuffed with my best friend's letters.

I open the box and take out the envelopes, so delicate and scented like wood smoke. As I trace Alice's old-fashioned cursive, my eyes sting, but I can't look away.

*January 17*
*Smyrna, Maine*

*Dear Lucy,*

*The ice storm hit something fierce last night. Mom told me to bring the horses in the barn. I couldn't find the red mare so me and Shepherd (that's what we decided to name the dog) went out looking for her. Mom says horses don't have enough sense to find their way home. But she's wrong.*

*They've got more brains than most people I've met. Maybe they can smell the storm coming, just like I always know when it's going to rain. Or the way green things can smell sunshine before they twist out of the dirt. What makes plants and animals so different from us?*

*Sometimes I walk out on the frozen lake at twilight. The sky is so big I could fall into it. Everything turns this purply color, like the jellyfish on Lido Key (I can't wait to see you at the end of September. Then we can swim at the beach every day). Don't you wish we could make time move faster?*

*Lucy, I miss your letters. You used to write all the time (I'm not judging you, I swear. I really wish our "paper conversations" could go on forever). You'd tell me all about Pinecraft. The sand dollars on Lido Key. The doves hidden inside the broken pieces. I didn't believe you until I saw it. Sometimes you have to see to believe.*

*You're so lucky down in Florida. No farm chores. No horse and buggies. Everybody riding around on bicycles. Palm trees and beaches. And you wear nice dresses in the prettiest colors (I love pink and purple best of all). Also: your dad lets you watch TV (I know you're not allowed to have a TV in your house. Still, I'm so jealous).*

*One day, I'm moving to California. I know it sounds crazy, but I can't stop thinking about it. I'm going to be in the movies. Then I'll be famous. Mom says if you've only got money, then you've got nothing. But I think things would be better if we had a little more.*

*It's still dark here every morning. Before sunrise, I get up and milk the cows in pitch-blackness. You can see the steam rising off their backs like gauze. Did I tell you? We lost a calf last winter. I don't know what happened. I held her in my arms all night. When I woke up, she was gone.*

*PS: The red mare finally turned up. She was waiting for me outside the barn. Wish she could tell me where she's been hiding. Mom says it's all my fault. But I think that mare would've run off sooner or later. I could tell, just by looking into her eyes, so soft and full of secrets. There's no holding her back. All the rope in the world can't keep her still. Next time, she'll be gone. Just you wait and see.*
*238 days until Florida.*

*Alice*

I watch the headlights dive across my bedroom wall. I remember how free Alice looked, waving like a princess in the back of that truck. I try to picture her chasing after that mare. The frozen lake. The calf that died in her arms.

All she wanted was a little freedom.

What's so wrong about that?

I think of Faron, our kiss on the beach. I hold the secret tight, curled like my fist in my lap. There's no letting go of it. I used to tell Dad everything. But I can't tell him what really happened after the party. Or the things Faron told me before we kissed in the sand.

I listen to the water splashing in the bathroom sink. Dad's finally getting ready for bed. Footsteps creak in the hall. After what seems like forever, the light under my door goes out. I wait a couple minutes. Then I sneak out of my room.

The house is so quiet, I can hear the whippoorwills calling back and forth, like they do every night. It seems so wrong, the fact that they're still singing, and yet everything has changed.

Dad keeps his cell phone in a kitchen drawer. I'm not allowed to use it. He won't even let me borrow that phone. Not unless it's an emergency. Well, if this isn't an emergency, I don't know what is.

Alice wrote her number on my wrist, hidden inside my sleeve. The ink has smeared like a bruise. I can barely read it. My fingers won't stay still as I type the number into Dad's phone.

I lift the phone to my ear. There's a click and a staticky noise, as if I'm drifting through space. It rings once, twice.

"Hey, what's up?"

"Are you okay?" I whisper. "Why didn't you go to the beach? I was looking everywhere for—"

"You know what to do. Leave a message."

*Beep.*

I snap the phone closed. Lean back against the kitchen counter. My heart's pounding so fast, I feel like I'm going to pass out. Why didn't Alice pick up her cell? I'm getting really nervous now. But I'm still angry at her, too.

I try calling again. Same thing. No answer. Did the battery go dead? Or did something else happen?

Something I don't want to think about.

A light clicks on in the kitchen. Dad's standing in the doorway, looking at me.

"Smidge? What are you doing up?"

"Couldn't sleep," I tell him, sliding the phone back in the drawer. Too late. Dad's already seen it.

"Why are you on the phone?" he says, frowning. "I don't want you using that cell without my permission. You know better."

"Sorry," I mumble.

"Who are you calling at this hour?"

I stare at the floor.

"Answer me," he says.

"I was trying to call Alice."

He looks confused. "Your Old Order friend has a cell phone?"

"Someone gave it to her," I explain.

"And did you get through to Alice?"

"No," I say, my voice shaking. "I'm really scared, Dad. I think she's in trouble."

He throws his arms around me. For a moment, he holds me close, like when I was small and I'd wake up screaming from a nightmare.

"Come on," he finally says. "It's late. We can talk about this in the morning."

I have to find Alice. But how? I'm always stuck here, working for Dad. I can't just leave. He won't let me take off by myself. I don't even have a car. And besides, even if I could drive away from Pinecraft, I don't know where to go.

Maybe she's just run off, like her mom said. But I've got a shivery feeling deep inside. It doesn't make sense, Alice disappearing without telling me where she's headed. She's always been my best friend. Growing up, we were both alone. No brothers or sisters. Alice lost her dad a long time ago. My mama got sick after I was born. I don't even remember what her voice sounded like.

When we were little, Alice used to tell everybody that I'm her sister, but it isn't true.

We were just pretending.

## chapter eight
# head in the clouds

The next morning I'm late for church. It's so quiet in the house, I figure Dad's left without me.

Now I'm really in for it.

I kick the covers off my bed. No time to get ready. I grab a pale blue dress from my wardrobe and quickly pin up my hair. It's always freezing in church. I'll have to bring my cardigan, even though it feels like a hundred degrees today. I don't know why they crank up the AC. Maybe it's supposed to keep us from falling asleep.

When I go into the kitchen, Dad's drinking coffee with our neighbors, the Showalters. They usually give us a ride on Sundays. Everyone turns and stares at me. I'm so embarrassed, I want to close my eyes and disappear.

"I thought you weren't going to make it." Dad frowns.

Why didn't he wake me up? Yeah, I know it's my responsibility to get out of bed on time. Still, it's kind of strange that he didn't knock on my door. I feel like everybody's been talking in the kitchen for a while.

Talking about me and Alice.

"Let's get going," says Dad, grabbing his jacket off a chair.

Our church is on Honore Avenue, just a couple miles away, but it seems like the drive takes forever. Dad sits up front with Mr. Showalter and his son, Jacob, who's the same age as me. I'm squashed in the back with Mrs. Showalter. She doesn't even say good morning. She keeps staring at the window like there's something real interesting out there. All I see are houses lined up in a row.

As we get closer to the highway, there's a lot more traffic. Big cars going fast. Nobody walking anywhere. The homes get bigger, too. Most are tucked behind fancy metal gates or peach-colored walls. I can't tell if they're trying to hide from the world. Or keep their own world in.

The parking lot is full outside the church. Mr. Showalter's going to have to park across the street at my old school. Sometimes I really miss it. Then I remember how weird it got toward the end. A lot of girls dropped out last year and started waiting tables. Some went off and got married. Guess you don't need more school for that.

I rush out of the car and head across the road. The Beachy Amish-Mennonite Fellowship isn't much to look at. It's not like the glittery churches on holiday cards. No stained glass windows. Just a plain white building shaded by mossy oaks. If I were Old Order, I wouldn't have a church. That's because everybody meets up in their homes.

As I push open the door, everyone's singing the first hymn, "I'll Fly Away." It's my "heart song." In other words, my favorite.

Some people might think it's strange—the fact that we don't sing along to a church organ or a piano. Nothing fancy like that. I still love it. There's only our voices, lifting up the words together in harmony.

I move over to the row of pews on the left, blending into the swarm of pastel dresses and prayer caps. Maybe it's wrong, but I really wish I could sing like Kara Horst. I scoot next to her, moving my lips and making no sound. Kara frowns as I squeeze into her row. She's kind of showing off, dragging out the last *ahh-lay-loo-yaaaaah.*

Dad's across the aisle from me, standing with a group of bearded men in dark vests and white shirts. In our church, women aren't allowed to sit with men. Everybody looks straight ahead at Pastor Troyer. I wonder if he mouths the words, too.

After the hymn, Pastor Troyer goes over the list of prayer requests. He leans over the podium, droning on about Hilda

Schwartz's gallbladder operation. Sounds like she's been having that operation for years.

"Let's not forget our Old Order brothers and sisters," he says, pushing back his glasses. "Alice Yoder, as you may already know, has been missing since Friday night."

When I hear him say Alice's name, everything goes hazy. I grab the pew in front of me, trying to keep my balance.

Mallory Keller turns around and stares at me. She was in my class last year. Now she works at the fruit stand on Bahia Vista Street. I know why she's staring. Everybody thinks I saw what happened to Alice after the party.

I'm keeping secrets.

That's what they think.

When it's time for the sermon, I sink back into the pew. I was rushing around so much this morning, I forgot my Bible. It doesn't matter anyway. I can't concentrate. The pastor's voice drones on. I'm not really listening. He's saying something about the Holy Spirit, how it changes shape, but stays the same. It might look like a dove. Or a river of flowing water. Maybe it's like the Gulf, the currents that circle so far from the coast, yet always come home again.

Did Alice ever make it to the beach? I can't stop going over everything that happened before she disappeared. What if I'd talked her out of going to Water Tower Park? And what if I'd never left the house that night? Would she have gone to that party without me?

Is there anything I could've done to keep her safe?

Finally, the sermon's over. Not that I heard much of it. When Pastor Troyer says, "Let us pray," everybody turns around. We kneel on the floor and lower our heads on the pews like we're saying bedtime prayers. My knees ache, but that's nothing compared to the hurt I'm holding inside.

All of a sudden, the Garver's new baby lets out a long, hiccupy wail. I know exactly how he feels. I squeeze my eyes open and stare at the floor. There's a plastic Ziploc bag under the pew. It's filled with tiny sea creatures. Starfish. A dolphin curved like a question mark.

"Hi," whispers the little girl in the next row. She wiggles her fingers at me.

"Hi yourself," I whisper back, and she smiles real big.

I bet she loves the ocean as much as I do. Too bad those plastic toys are the closest she'll ever get to their secrets. She won't find out that dolphins have their own language. They even give each other names.

After the prayer, we turn around and sit in the pews again. Now it's time for Pastor Troyer to pass around the microphone.

"If anything's weighing on your heart this morning," he says, "stand up."

It's always the men who get a chance to talk. The girls stay quiet, like they're scared or something. Scared of what? I really don't know.

Mr. Holtzer stands up. He runs the little post office near Big Olaf's, and, believe me, he's always got something to say.

"The Old Order girl who's missing," he says, frowning, and my blood turns to ice. He's supposed to talk about the sermon. Not Alice. "I don't think this *Rumspringa* nonsense has any place in Pinecraft. It's only going to get worse."

"Thank you, Brother John," says Pastor Troyer. It's always *Brother this* and *Sister that*, as if we're all one big family. Of course, that's all for show.

I'm so jittery, I can hardly breathe. Then Jacob Showalter stands up. I've never seen him talk in church before. His round face turns pink as he reaches for the microphone.

"Can I say something?" His voice cracks. When he stands up, the entire church turns and gawks at him.

"The Old Order aren't that different from us," he says.

Now I'm really surprised. I didn't expect him to defend the Old Order.

"But I agree with Brother John," he adds. "They don't belong here."

Everybody starts talking at the same time. I'm trying to catch my breath. Just holding on to one small thing. The pew's smooth pinewood ridges. Sweat prickling between my shoulder blades.

"The Old Order have been visiting Pinecraft since I was a boy," says Mr. Showalter, putting a hand on Jacob's shoulder. "It didn't used to be this bad. Now we've got these *Rumspringa* boys stirring up trouble in our neighborhood, throwing wild parties on the beach. Do we want our girls to be next?"

Dad gets up and says, "Hold on a minute. There's no reason to judge the Yoders so harshly."

"And why is this your business?" says Mr. Holtzer. "Because your daughter is friends with the missing girl?"

I can't stand to listen to him attacking Dad. This is so unfair. I won't sit still and stay quiet. Not anymore.

"Alice didn't do anything wrong."

My voice comes out shaky, but no doubt, everybody hears it.

Mallory Keller twists around in her seat again.

Another head turns.

More faces stare.

The buzzing swells inside my fingertips, rising like the tide. I can't hear the men talking anymore. *Please God. Don't let it happen.* I squeeze the pew so tight, my knuckles burn.

Then I sink to the floor.

Voices shout across the church as I float away.

*What's wrong with Lucy?*

*Is she sick?*

I'm looking up at the pews. All those women in pastel dresses, leaning over me. The stern-faced, bearded men, afraid to get too close.

When I open my eyes, Dad pushes his way through the crowd and throws his arms around me.

"She's only doing it for attention," Mallory whispers.

Slowly, Dad helps me sit up.

"There's nothing wrong with my daughter," he says, glaring back at them.

I have to get out of here. It's too much. The faces watching me. The too-close smell of their sweat.

"Can you stand?" Dad asks.

"Yeah, I'm fine," I tell him, but it isn't true.

I get up and start walking toward the door. I can feel everybody's eyes on me, but I don't dare turn around. I grab the handle and push it open, letting in fresh air and sunlight. I keep walking across the church lawn, never looking back.

Why is this happening? Maybe I'm sick, after all. Or the Lord is punishing me. He can see inside our hearts. And if He looked inside mine, He'd know I'm sorry for not telling the truth.

Traffic races down Honore Avenue. I stand under the palm trees, watching the cars go by. Everybody in a hurry to get somewhere.

The world didn't stop turning because Alice is missing.

I almost wish it would.

• • •

After church, we usually eat a big lunch. If the sun's not too hot, we sit on the picnic benches in Pinecraft Park. I don't mind so much. At least I get to be outside. Unfortunately, most of the time, I'm dragged someplace I don't want to be. Maybe it's because my dad's alone. Everybody feels sorry for us. It's all smiles and pass the apple crumble. Soon as we're gone, they're talking up a storm behind our backs.

When we go to somebody's house, the girls stay in the kitchen, heating up casseroles and quiche, while the men sit in the living room, drinking coffee. It's like there's some invisible rule about what we're supposed to do. (I can't even cook toast, so if people come to our house, we usually cheat and buy a family pack of fried chicken from Winn-Dixie.) After stuffing ourselves into a food coma, everybody goes home and takes a nap.

Pretty exciting, right?

At least, that's how it's always been.

Nobody invites us to lunch after church. First time ever. Dad says it's no big deal. We could eat at the Amish diner on Beneva Road. Or Der Dutchman on Bahia Vista. That's the restaurant where a lot of girls from school ended up waitressing. Out front, there's a glowing sign that says, "Eat in our Amish buggy!" The so-called buggy is just a covered booth with wheels.

"It's okay," I tell Dad. "I'm not really hungry."

"You sure?" he says, frowning.

Usually I'm first in line. Eating is one thing I'm good at. After what happened today in church, I can't even think about food.

"Yeah, I'm sure."

He nods. "Okay, Smidge. I've got some warmed-ups we can heat on the stove." That's Dad's word for leftovers.

It's a long walk home, but the Showalters don't offer us a ride. They're already heading down the street to Pastor Troyer's house. Mrs. Showalter's talking real loud so everybody knows that's where she's headed.

Walking home, I remember the first time Alice and her mom showed up in Pinecraft. It was Sunday after church, just like today. Me and Dad were eating lunch in the park. Sure, I'd seen the Old Order before. The men weren't so different from my dad with their beards and straw hats. But when I saw the little girl in her long dark dress, her face hidden by her bonnet, I got a shivery feeling deep inside.

"Don't stare," my dad told me.

She was sitting all alone at the picnic table with her mom. When the Old Order woman turned her head, the girl snatched a strawberry off her plate. I started laughing so hard. Then the girl looked at me like we were sharing a secret. She popped the strawberry in her mouth and smiled.

"Why don't you invite her over?" Dad asked.

I glanced up at him. "Is that okay?"

"Of course it's okay."

"But they're Old Order."

"Doesn't matter," he said. "We do things a little different, but we're all family."

I walked over to their table. The girl's eyes got real big. She seemed kind of surprised. Her mom was watching me the whole time, not saying a word.

"My dad says you can eat with us," I told them.

The Old Order woman didn't move. At first, I thought she was angry at me. She murmured something to the girl. I couldn't understand the words. After a minute, the girl stood up. She didn't look me in the eyes. Her voice sounded so strange, twisting up and down. I had to listen real careful to understand.

"What's your name?" she said, clutching her skirt. "I'm Alice."

Later I heard my dad and Mr. Showalter talking about the Yoders. Something about Alice's dad. He'd been in an accident. Alice was heartbroken and needed a rest. She and her mom were visiting family down in Florida. But nobody had ever seen the Yoders before.

I liked Alice right from the start. Her easygoing laugh. The way her blue eyes sparkled when she talked. After that day, we were inseparable.

"See you tomorrow, Lucy," she said, waving goodbye.

I looked at her fingernails, the bright red stains.

## chapter nine
# words and pictures

On Monday, I'm in the workshop with Dad, sanding wood for a gazebo. The planks are already drilled with holes. Then somebody can screw it together later and pretend they built it themselves.

"Quite the little helper," says Mr. Showalter, opening the door. He and Jacob are always hanging around the shop, getting in the way.

"Lucy does good work," says Dad and a rush of pride surges through me.

"Is that right?" says Mr. Showalter. "Wouldn't she rather be in the kitchen?"

If I wasn't so angry, I'd probably laugh. The only thing I know how to cook is "bumps on a log," celery smeared with peanut butter and raisins.

Mr. Showalter eases his weight against a sawhorse. "A shame about her friend. The widow's girl hasn't turned up yet?"

That's what everybody calls Alice's mom.

*The widow.*

I glance up at Dad.

"No word about Alice," he says.

"Her mother says she snuck out to a party," says Mr. Showalter, looking at me. "I heard you were there too, Lucy."

I can't make up a lie. Dad already knows I was at the party.

"A lot of people were there," I say.

"This was in Water Tower Park?"

I nod.

"That park's quite a few miles from here. How did you get back?"

"I took the bus." Why won't he leave me alone?

"The buses don't start running until six. Did you go anywhere else that night? Say, maybe the beach?"

How does Mr. Showalter know I was at the beach? Maybe his son, Jacob, heard about it. Not that Jacob would ever go to a *Rumspringa* party. He won't even swim in the canal at Pinecraft Park because "it's filled with leeches."

Mr. Showalter keeps talking. "My son found Alice's cell phone near the seawall this morning."

"On Lido Key?" I'm shaking so hard, I let go of the sandpaper.

"That's right," he says. "But how did it get there?"

Now I'm stuck.

There's nothing I can say.

Except the truth.

"Alice wanted to see the sunrise on the beach."

Dad frowns. "You and Alice went where?"

"Alice wasn't with me. I went by myself."

"How did you get to Lido Key?"

I stare at the sawdust piled on the floor. "I got a ride."

"A ride from who?"

He waits for my answer. I want to run away, but I'm trapped in the workshop and there's no going around it. If Alice is in trouble, I need to be honest about what happened that night at the party.

I swallow hard. "A boy drove me to Lido Key."

"I can't believe I'm hearing this. Do I know this boy?" Dad's voice is getting louder. Now I'm really in for it.

"His name's Faron."

"Is that Andy Mast's Faron?" he asks.

In Pinecraft, you're always somebody's somebody. But Faron isn't from here. He belongs to no one.

"Not one of those boys from the park, I hope," Dad says.

A *Rumspringa* boy.

"That's the Old Order boy who's been shunned," says Mr. Showalter, like he's the expert on everything. "Got himself a red truck. Drives all over Pinecraft in it."

"Shunned?" Dad's so upset, he can barely talk.

"He just gave me a ride to the beach. That's all."

"You will not be running around with Old Order boys, Lucy. You hear me?" he says.

"Just because somebody's been shunned, doesn't mean they're a bad person." Me and Dad have talked about the *bann*, how we both think it's old-fashioned and hurtful. He doesn't seem to remember that now.

"And what were you doing at Lido Key? The beach isn't safe at night. You should know better."

"I'm sorry."

Dad shakes his head. "Why didn't you tell me?"

I used to tell my dad everything. Lately, we don't talk much at all.

"Don't mean to scare you, Lucy," says Mr. Showalter. "But do you know if Alice has her own cell phone?"

"Yes, she does," I say, a little confused.

"Her name was on the back," says Mr. Showalter.

In my mind, I see Alice's phone, the fake diamonds spelling her name. Did she make it to the beach after all?

"The cell phone was in a Ziploc bag. Thought it was kind of strange, carrying it around in something like that. Nice phone, too. Probably cost a lot."

Alice's money was in that plastic bag. I remember her showing it off. All those bills wrapped in rubber bands.

"Do you still have the cell phone?" I ask.

"Been planning on giving it to her mother. Can't bring myself to do it."

Dad shakes his head. "You should give it to the police."

"Well, it's none of my business," says Mr. Showalter. "What a shame. Always knew Alice Yoder was headed for trouble."

"I'll tell you what's a real shame," says Dad. "This *Rumspringa* business. Who lets their girls go running around, doing whatever they please?"

"It's not like that," I say, but he isn't listening.

He puts a hand on my shoulder. "If you truly cared about Alice, you'd tell the truth. Speak up. It's the right thing to do."

I remember my promise to Alice. I'm not supposed to tell anyone about Tobias. But if she's in trouble, he's not a secret worth keeping.

"Both of you girls were at Water Tower Park on Friday night."

"Yeah, but then—"

"Then what?"

I've already said too much. I'm so embarrassed, talking about what I did that night. Drinking beer at the party. Lying to my dad. Kissing a boy on Lido Key, the morning Alice disappeared.

No matter what I do, I'll never be perfect enough for him.

I can't talk to Dad about boys. If he found out about me and Faron on the beach, I'd be in so much trouble. But I need to have my own life. That's something Dad won't understand. Maybe it's selfish, but I'm not going to tell him everything that happened at Water Tower Park that night.

"Alice has a boyfriend. His name's Tobias. They were talking about running away."

"What happened then?"

"They got in a fight. I didn't see them leave the party together."

"So Alice left by herself?"

"Yes." It feels like I'm lying. I wasn't there, so I don't know if this is true.

"Is this boy from Pinecraft?"

"I don't know."

"Do you think he might've hurt your friend?" Mr. Showalter asks.

When I don't say anything, he narrows his eyes at me. "I will keep Alice Yoder in my prayers. It's in the hands of the Lord now. As you know, He sees everything."

My heart is thudding fast. Does it make me a bad person if I keep a secret that only the Lord can see?

"We're all praying for Alice to come home," says Dad.

I rub my eyes, but the sting won't go away. "Can I take a break for a minute?"

He nods. "We'll talk more later."

I need to find Jacob. How does he know about the party? He never hangs around the Old Order. You won't find him playing basketball with the *Rumspringa* boys. Or drinking beer in Water Tower Park.

Jacob's on the back porch, sitting in Dad's rocker with a plate of snickerdoodle cookies. Everybody says he's going to marry me someday. I'd rather be alone than get stuck with Jacob Showalter.

"Hey Lucy," he says, holding out a cookie. "Want the last one?"

"No thanks." He always licks his fingers.

I sit in the chair next to Jacob and peel off my work gloves. Dad got them real cheap at Goodwill. No wonder they're too big. Sometimes I try to imagine who wore them before me.

"Alice has been missing since Friday. I heard she was at an Old Order party or something. At least, that's what everybody's saying. I wasn't there."

"I was."

He blinks, like this is hard to believe. "So where was it?"

"On the beach. That's where you found her cell phone, right?"

"Yeah. Near the seawall. Me and Dad were out fishing for snapper. I found the cell phone in the sand. Couldn't get it to work. It was smashed up pretty good."

I stare at the shadows bleeding across the porch. "Is that all you found? Nothing else with it?"

He shakes his head. "Nothing."

A cell phone wouldn't break if it fell in the sand. Did something happen to Alice before Jacob found it on the beach?

"Must've been some party," Jacob says, licking his thumb.

"How did you find out about it?" I ask.

"I saw the pictures online."

"What pictures?"

"All over Facebook," he says.

Jacob Showalter has a Facebook page? I'd be in big trouble if Dad caught me online. He thinks it's too worldly, even though we have computers in the fellowship hall at church.

"I didn't know you were on Facebook."

"If you're not online, you might as well be dead," he tells me.

"I must be dead then. My dad won't let me have a computer."

"Why not?"

"He says it changes the way you think."

"A computer's just a machine. It can't make you do nothing."

Words and pictures can make you do wrong. That's what Dad says. They can trick you into believing things that aren't true.

"Who put those pictures online?" I ask.

Jacob shrugs. "Everybody."

The *Rumspringa* boys wouldn't have a computer at home. But they could borrow one from somewhere else. If I want to go online, I use the computers at the library. I have to take the bus to Sarasota, but Dad's got me working all afternoon. Can I get there before it closes?

As I turn to leave, Jacob hands me the last snickerdoodle.

"Sorry about your friend," he says.

I guess Jacob Showalter isn't so bad. Still, I can't imagine us getting married. I can't even imagine kissing him. In my mind, I drift back to that night on the beach. The soft warmth of Faron's mouth. His hands circling my back. The closeness of him as we talked until sunrise. It felt like we'd met a long time ago and just found our way home.

Where is he now?

"Lucy?" Jacob's staring at me as if I'd sprouted two heads. "Are you okay?"

I break the cookie in half and give him the other piece.

"Thanks." He crams it in his mouth and smiles.

Dad's on the front lawn, talking to Mr. Showalter. I can't let them see me. Then I'll have to deal with more questions.

I start walking the other way, toward the orange grove. Dad says the trees are sick with canker, but he won't cut them down. All their fruit is speckled with bumps, not smooth like the oranges at the supermarket. That's okay with me. They don't have to look perfect to taste good.

"Lucy," Dad calls out. "I want you back at the shop. Got an order for a wedding gazebo up in St. Pete. We need those planks sanded, you hear?"

Yeah, I heard.

It's always about what Dad wants.

"I'm almost done," I tell him.

"Well, hustle up. I want to get those panels drilled. That cedar needs a good coat of primer. Then we can start painting. Let it dry overnight."

"You mean we have to put the gazebo together?" Usually, we just stain the planks and ship the whole thing off in a box.

"Promised I'd have it ready by Saturday," Dad explains.

Mr. Showalter takes out his keys. "Figure we'll hitch a trailer to the Dodge and carry the gazebo to the beach. Won't that be a sight?" He grins like he's doing us a real big favor.

If I don't leave now, I won't make it to the library in time. This stupid wedding gazebo is so much work. There's no way out of it.

I'll be stuck in the backyard, sanding and painting, for the rest of the week.

Jacob comes up to us, wiping his hands on his pants. "Can I help?"

"Don't you have a paper to write?" his dad asks.

Unlike me, Jacob's still in school. He's a year behind. Too bad we can't trade places.

"Let me guess," says Mr. Showalter. "You haven't even started."

I almost feel sorry for Jacob. He looks so pathetic, wiping the sweat off his face. His wide-brimmed hat keeps sliding over his forehead, as if he'll never grow into it.

"What's the paper about?" I ask.

"Tides," he says.

A giggle sneaks out of me. Once I get going, it's hard to stop.

"Lucy." Dad glares.

For some reason, this makes me laugh even harder.

"Sorry, Jacob," I mumble.

"Go ahead and laugh," he says, kicking the dirt. "It's not like I'm failing or anything."

Mr. Showalter raises an eyebrow. "Is that so?"

"At least you picked a good topic," I say, trying to help.

"I didn't pick it," Jacob says. "How am I supposed to do a paper on tides? It's the most boring topic ever."

"We wouldn't be here if it wasn't for tides," I say.

Dad gives me a look. I know what he's thinking. Here I go again, talking about the sea.

"Is that true?" Jacob asks.

"A long time ago, the fish washed up into tide pools. They had to learn how to adapt."

"You're saying fish walked on land?" Now Jacob's the one who's laughing.

"That's enough," Dad says, startling me. "Nobody wants to hear your make-believe stories."

It's not a made-up story. It's the truth. And no matter what I say, I can't make him believe.

Mr. Showalter smiles. "Well, I think Lucy knows more about the ocean than my son's teacher. That's for sure."

I quickly look at Jacob. "You want help with that paper?"

"For real?" he says.

Dad shakes his head. "I need you here, Smidge. Or that gazebo won't get done in time."

"Let me take over for Lucy," says Mr. Showalter. "Bet you could use a little muscle, lifting those rafters."

Yeah, right. Mr. Showalter's only good at lifting a fork to his mouth. He thinks I'm not strong enough to carry those planks, just because I'm a girl. Anyway, it's not worth fighting about. If he takes over for me, I'm free to escape.

"Can you drive to the big library in Sarasota?" I ask Jacob.

He nods. "Been there lots of times."

Dad still doesn't look convinced. "That's a long way."

"Not really," says Jacob. "It's about five miles from Pinecraft."

"Can't you walk someplace closer?" Dad says, glancing at the road.

Driving is probably safer than walking. Not to mention a whole lot faster. But Dad's always freaking out about cars. He says everybody in Sarasota drives too fast. "Life's not a race," he always tells me. "Might as well enjoy today because it's never coming back."

"Okay," Dad says. "But I want you home at sundown."

Mr. Showalter can't stop grinning as me and Jacob walk to the truck. No doubt, he's hearing wedding bells.

"Thanks for helping me out." Jacob fumbles with the key, shoving it in the passenger door. He yanks it open. "Ladies first," he says, making a big deal out of this. I seriously want to smack him.

"You're helping me too," I mutter, leaning back against the seat. The Showalters always help us out. Dad borrows their truck every weekend. Sure, they've been friends a long time. Still, I can't help feeling like something's tipped in their favor, just because we're a little "less off," as Dad says.

Jacob revs the engine as we gun it down Bahia Vista. He's probably trying to impress me. But I'm thinking about Faron, his hand cupped over mine, shifting the gear stick as we drove to the beach at sunrise.

"I can't believe I have to write this stupid paper," Jacob says, messing with his seatbelt. "Who cares about tides? It's just water moving around."

He wants me to explain the tides in words. Cram it all into a couple pages, just to make his teacher happy. But he'll never understand the ocean's pulse, the way it breathes like a living thing.

Most people just want to get by. That's all they care about. They don't want to think about the threads that tie us together. The ocean, how it gives and takes from us. The tides, moving close, then sinking into cold, dark water, the way I imagine death.

Did Alice make it to the beach that night? Or did something happen to her in Water Tower Park? In my mind, I go back and forth, trying to figure it out. I see Alice kissing that boy, Tobias. The girls in their dark dresses, standing at the edge of the tide, laughing as the surf curled around their ankles.

"Can I really get this paper done by tonight?" Jacob asks.

I stare out the window. "You're going to be okay."

That's all I can promise.

# chapter ten
# ghosts

Jacob parks in the shade near the library. As soon as I'm out of the car, I want to climb back inside. There's a bake sale on the sidewalk. And the girls at the table are in long-sleeved, pastel dresses exactly like mine.

Those girls are from my church. Mallory's right up front, rearranging cookies on the plates. There's no other way inside the library. I take a deep breath and start walking toward the front entrance.

"There she is," Mallory whispers.

I know Mallory's been talking behind my back. She thinks I'm lying about what happened at the party on Friday night. I shouldn't be hanging around the Old Order. Especially the *Rumspringa* boys. That's only asking for trouble. And now trouble's what I've got.

"Come on," I tell Jacob.

He's too busy sniffing the plates. "Want anything?" he asks, taking a huge bite of a cinnamon roll.

Yeah. I want to get out of here.

Mallory smiles at me, all fake. "Sure you don't want to buy something? It's for the Youth Fellowship."

I skipped going to Youth Fellowship last weekend. Instead, I was with Alice, drinking beer in Water Tower Park. I'm embarrassed, just thinking about it. All I want is to go back in time and make things right. Yeah, like that's going to happen.

"Come on," Mallory says, motioning me over to the table.

"Meet you inside," says Jacob. He marches toward the library's front entrance. Great. Now I'm stuck here alone.

"So you're going out with Jacob Showalter now?" Mallory says.

I glance up. "What's that supposed to mean?"

"I just thought . . . since he drove you here."

"Well, you thought wrong."

"Must be nice having all these boys. You know. Drive you around in their cars."

The girls laugh.

How much does Mallory know?

I reach inside my tote bag, dig out a handful of change and drop the coins into the half-empty jar on their table. As I turn to leave, Mallory smirks.

"Guess you don't need any sweets today," she says, launching another round of giggles.

My cheeks are stinging as I turn away from their table. Did Mallory go to that party on Friday night? I didn't see her there. All the girls drifting through the woods were Old Order.

Except me.

I push open the library's door, thankful for the smell of books, the cool, air-conditioned rooms, and the quiet. The computers are lined up against a wall in the back. As I move past the rows of desks, I get a lot of stares.

"Check her out," says a boy at one of the tables, laughing with his friends. They all look alike in their baggy jeans and baseball caps.

I stare right back at him. If he's got something to say, he might as well say it to my face.

"Hey, freak," he says, louder this time. "Are you in a cult?"

I bet he's wondering if I'm allowed to use a computer. He probably thinks I'm not allowed to read.

"No, I'm not in a cult," I snap. "Are you?"

He looks confused. My homemade clothes aren't the kind you can buy in a store. It's not what a magazine tells me to wear. Or famous people on TV. The outside world has its own rules, too. It just doesn't know it.

When people look at me, they only see the outside. I'm like the statues on St. Armands Circle. Just because I'm covered up, doesn't mean I can't feel anything. Dad's always saying I've got to try harder. But I'll never be perfect enough for him.

I don't want to be a statue.

Jacob's in the next row, hunched at a computer. He's watching a music video on YouTube, sitting real close to the screen.

"This doesn't look like marine biology," I say.

He scoots back his chair. "Sorry," he mumbles, turning red. "Got a little distracted."

On the computer screen, a woman in a skintight dress is crawling out of a coffin. She wiggles her hips to the music, teetering on high heels. It doesn't seem like she's having any fun. In fact, she looks kind of sad.

"Okay," I tell him. "There's a really cool video about tides on *Discovery*. Give me a second and I'll find it."

The *Discovery* video seems to drag on forever. Jacob's yawning the whole time, not even paying attention. When it's finally over, I turn to him and say, "Maybe you should check out a couple books."

"Good idea," he says, like he never thought of it.

"And before we leave, you should probably watch that video again. Only this time, you might want to take notes."

"It's all in here," he says, tapping his head.

I doubt it.

"One more thing," I say, lowering my voice. "Can you show me that Facebook page? The one with the pictures from last weekend?"

Jacob drums his fingers on the desk. I can tell he's nervous. For a second, I think he's going to say no.

"All right," he says. "But you can't tell anybody I showed it to you."

"I won't."

"And next time there's a party, let me know, okay?"

I smile. "Okay."

Jacob reaches across the keyboard and logs on to Facebook. He clicks down a list of names and faces, scrolling through pictures. "I don't know this girl," he says, clicking away. "My friend's really into her. But he's wasting his time."

"Why?" I ask.

"She's Old Order. Even if they hook up, she'll be gone in a couple months. Seems kind of pointless."

"Was your friend at that party?"

"Nah, he just heard about it." Jacob shakes his head. "I think she blocked her profile. I can't get onto it."

After last weekend, I bet a lot of girls blocked their profiles. I'm so frustrated, I want to scream. There's got to be somebody else on Facebook who can see those pictures. Still, I can't go around asking questions about the party. That would be stupid. And I'm in enough trouble right now.

"I'll be back in a minute," says Jacob, closing his Facebook page. "Can you help me get started on that paper?"

Across from us there's another girl in a pastel dress, sitting at a computer.

Mallory.

"I'm supposed to begin with an introduction," Jacob says.

"That's a good place to start," I say, watching Mallory giggle at something on the computer—her Facebook page.

"Actually, we need to get back to Pinecraft real soon. Or my dad's going to kill me. He won't let me drive the truck after dark."

"Grab some books," I say, keeping my gaze on Mallory. "I'll help you write the intro."

"Awesome." Jacob marches off to the bookshelves. I get the feeling he'll be there a while, and that's fine with me.

I wait until Mallory gets up and heads for the restroom. When she's finally gone, I move to her computer. She's got her Facebook page open, but I'm not sure how it works. Who wants to share their diary with the whole world?

At the top of the page is a search box. I type *Alice Yoder*. Seconds later, a dozen names fill the screen. I didn't expect to find so many. Alice could be any of those girls. Or she could be gone and the names would still be there.

I scroll down the list. There's an Alice Yoder in Lancaster, Pennsylvania. And Holmes County, Ohio. In the space next to their names is a picture. I stare at their faces. They're dressed plain. All of them.

Amish girls.

Why wouldn't they be on Facebook? I remember what Jacob told me. If you're not online, you might as well be dead.

The girls are probably on *Rumspringa*. They're taking pictures with their cell phones, smiling into bathroom mirrors. They want people to see them. That's what's so strange about it.

Mallory's coming back any minute now. I have to move fast. I switch back to her Facebook page. She's friends with a lot of people from my old school. It feels kind of awkward, looking at their birthday parties and trips to the beach. Especially because they never invited me.

I keep clicking through the pictures. Ice cream melting in a cup. A bird swooping over a telephone wire. Bare toes dusted with sand. The Youth Ministry playing volleyball on Lido Key. Oak trees draped with Spanish moss.

This picture was taken in Water Tower Park. I'm sure of it. Under the oak trees, a group of Old Order girls are dancing in their long dresses. Alice has to be there. At first, I don't see anyone that looks like her. Then I spot a girl swaying in the shadows. Short hair and skinny jeans.

She looks so small. Almost like a little kid. And someone's in the background, watching her behind the trees. A boy in a skeleton T-shirt.

I drag the blinking cursor over his face.

TOBY GRANGER

Is this Alice's boyfriend?

When I click on his name, a message pops up: *Do you know Toby? See what he shares with friends . . .*

His profile is locked.

I slide the cursor back to Alice.

Nothing.

I switch over to Google and do a search for "Toby Granger." There's a snowboarder from Vermont. A boy who won a hot dog eating contest. Lots of names. This is so much harder than I thought.

Google has this thing called "images." When I click on it, the screen fills with pictures. So many faces. A guy with a pierced lip. A kid with a puppy slung over his shoulder. None of them are Tobias.

I glance back at the computer desks. Everybody's playing games or watching YouTube videos. I always look for National Geographic online. That's how I learned that sharks can see electricity. You could probably find anything on YouTube.

Can I find Tobias?

My hands are shaking as I type his name. At the top of the list is a video called *Agora*. It's just a group of boys running through a field. They're all wearing costumes—long capes and pointy hats. Their strange clothes remind me of another time, like the drawings in *Martyrs Mirror*, a book about Amish who died hundreds of years ago.

"Can you turn that down, please?"

A librarian drops a pair of headphones on my desk.

"Sorry," I whisper. When I glance up, I'm surprised. It's the nice librarian, the one who helped me look for scholarships online.

"Any word yet?" she asks, tucking a strand of purple-streaked hair behind her ear. She's probably not much older than me.

"Nothing," I tell her.

"Well, hang in there," she says, patting my shoulder. She walks back to the front desk, where another girl is waiting in line.

How much longer can I wait? And what if I actually get a scholarship? I'll have to tell Dad I don't plan on staying in Pinecraft forever. I'd feel horrible, leaving him all by himself. But he doesn't understand why I need to study the ocean. When I told him about the hole in the Gulf, he shrugged.

"Not my business," he said.

He's wrong.

It's everybody's business.

I slide the headphones on. Voices pound my ears, screaming words I don't understand. It scares me, just listening to those boys. They're running back and forth with big, wooden sticks. I can't tell if they're playing some kind of game or trying to hurt each other.

A girl steps into the frame. The glittery wings strapped to her back remind me of angels. They fell like lightning when the Lord kicked them out of heaven.

When she turns and looks back at the camera, all my blood turns cold.

"You're not supposed to be here," Alice says.

"So what?" says the voice behind the camera. "Are we playing this frickin' game at Blackwoods or not?"

That's when I know.

The boy holding the camera is Tobias.

"But you're not following the rules," she says.

"I'll make up my own rules."

The video goes black.

I tug off my headphones.

When did Alice's boyfriend make this video? I study the woods in the background. I've never been up north, but Alice told me about the leaves, how they change in the fall. All the trees are speckled gold, like sunlight crackling on the ocean.

Agora.

What does that word mean? I do a quick search. The first link that comes up is something called The Agora Games. There's a date. Friday. And a location. South Lido Park. What kind of game is this? I need to talk to the other players. Maybe they know Tobias. But Dad's got me working next weekend. How can I get out of it?

"I saw you."

Mallory is standing behind my chair.

"You were at that party," she says.

I quickly get up and move to the other desk. "You were there too?"

"Everybody was there."

Mallory waits for me to say something. When I don't, she says, "You're friends with that Old Order girl. The one who's missing."

"Do you know Alice?"

"Not really. I don't have a lot of Old Order friends."

I'm not surprised. In Pinecraft, you're either a snowbird. Or you're everybody else.

"Those Old Order girls are really weird," she says, leaning back in her chair. "I can't imagine living like that. I mean, they're so stuck in the past. They're like ghosts or something."

*Ghosts.*

"They're just different," I say.

"So what happened to Alice?"

"I don't know."

"But she's your friend, right?"

"Alice is my best friend."

"Then why don't you know?"

I glance at the stairs near the computer desks. A little girl is sitting on the bottom step. She tries to lift herself up, going backward a level at a time. Then her mom grabs her arm, saying, "That's not how we do things."

Mallory leans back in her chair. "No wonder Alice is in trouble," she says. "I feel sorry for those Old Order girls. They're so brainwashed."

"You're the one who's brainwashed."

I shove past Mallory. I can't listen to her anymore. She doesn't know anything about the Old Order. In her mind, they're outsiders. They don't go to our church. Or sit with us for Sunday picnics in the park. They dress as if they're from another time. Almost like ghosts.

"You're so lucky," Alice used to tell me.

She thought everything was perfect in Florida. I've got electricity in my house instead of candlelight. But I hang my clothes on the line, just like she does. I wash dishes by hand. Dad thinks it's better that way. "Keeps you grounded," he says.

When Alice stepped off the bus this time, it was pretty obvious things had changed. She gets to have *Rumspringa*. I don't. All of a sudden, Alice was the one with all the freedom. Yeah, I was jealous of her clothes. Her fancy cell phone. The fact that she had a boyfriend. She left me behind. That's what I thought.

"Lucy?" Jacob calls out. He's got a stack of books in his arms and a confused look on his face. But I can't deal with him. Not now.

I slam my weight against the library door and head outside. I can't stop thinking about what I saw online. The boys running through the field with their sticks. Alice. The wings strapped to her back. She never told me about this game. Maybe she didn't want her mom to find out. But why couldn't she tell me? I remember what Mrs. Yoder said the morning Alice disappeared. It wasn't the first time she ran away. Was she sneaking off to play this secret game in the woods?

The longer you hold a secret, the deeper it grows, like the poison bleeding into the Gulf.

I know exactly how that feels.

## chapter eleven

# pearls

When I get home, it's almost dark. The gazebo planks are spread out on the lawn in a circle, ready to dry. They remind me of whale bones. The ribs inside me, too. All the secret parts that hold us together, keeping our hearts safe.

Dad doesn't know I'm back yet. If I move fast, I can get to Pinecraft Park before the sun goes down. I need to talk to the *Rumspringa* boys. Maybe they know Tobias. I bet they were at the party last weekend.

*Everybody was there.*

They probably aren't going to talk to me, but I have to find out if they've seen Alice's boyfriend. There's something about him that doesn't make sense. When I saw Tobias in that video online, playing that game in the woods, it scared me, the way he shouted at Alice. It was like he thought the game was real, not make-believe. I remember the boys, their strange clothes, their fists waving those sticks, as if they wanted to hurt the whole world.

Pinecraft Park is quiet at sundown. Usually, I'll see the *Rumspringa* boys playing basketball behind the chainlink fence. Or the Amish girls in their bonnets, gathered at the picnic table, lifting their voices in a gospel song. Once in a while a girl will stand outside the fence, as if wishing she could play too. Then look away, like she's gone too far, just thinking about it.

As I walk through the tall grass, I don't see anybody at the picnic table. The basketball court is empty, the ragged net swaying in the breeze. I'm about to turn around and go home when I hear a burst of laughter. It's coming from the edge of the park, where cattails bend like heads lowered in prayer.

A couple of boys are smoking near the canal. The smell of their cigarettes drifts across the water. They're both in T-shirts and jeans, but I can tell it's new for them. They always pick the brightest colors, letting everybody know they're a big deal.

The blue in their store-bought denim hasn't faded and their shirts are too baggy, as if they belong to somebody else.

"Hello?" I call out.

The skinny one glances over his shoulder at me. He's small, but his arms are tight with muscle, like most Old Order boys who grew up on a farm.

"You looking for something?" he says.

"Maybe it's *someone* she's looking for," says his friend, blowing out a stream of smoke.

I need to get these *Rumspringa* boys to trust me. But how? I don't know what's going to make it harder—the fact that I'm not Old Order Amish. Or the fact that I'm a girl.

"I'm friends with Alice Yoder," I tell him.

"What's she got to do with us?"

Okay. Now he thinks I'm blaming him. It feels like everything I say is wrong. How can I get these boys to talk to me?

"Did you go to that party last weekend?" I ask.

"Yeah," he says. "Maybe I did. What about you, Markus?" he says, turning to his friend. "Tell me. What's a Beachy Amish girl doing in Water Tower Park?"

He smirks. "Same thing we're doing."

When I hear that stupid, high-pitched laugh, I cringe. This is the same boy I saw drinking in the woods that night. He's not wearing a baseball cap, but I remember the anger on his face when he pushed that beer at me.

"Did you see Alice Yoder at that party?"

He shrugs. "That girl was so wasted. Last I saw, she was passed out in the grass."

"And you didn't try to help her?"

"What do you think I am? Her boyfriend?"

The way he's talking so mean, it's like he doesn't care if Alice made it home. Or if she's even alive.

"Sounds like you saw a lot of things that night," I say carefully.

They're both quiet for a minute.

"Alice was walking down Bradenton Road," says Markus, tossing his cigarette in the canal. "Everybody was heading out to Lido Key, right? And she was going in the other direction."

So Alice tried to walk home after the party. What was she thinking? It's a long way to Pinecraft. Maybe six miles. Not to mention, it's all roads and highways. Why didn't she get a ride with somebody?

Maybe she did.

"What about her boyfriend?"

"Which one?"

When I see him grinning like he's better than everybody else, I want to knock the teeth out of his face.

"Alice had a lot of boyfriends back home," says Markus. "I used to see her mom walking up the hill and calling for her in the morning. Snow, rain. Didn't matter. She'd be knocking on doors, looking for that girl."

"You mean the widow?"

"She ain't no widow. That's just what Alice tells everybody. Her dad's still alive. He went missing too. Long time ago."

"Alice said her dad got hurt in some accident."

"And you believe that?"

Is he telling the truth? It doesn't make any sense. Alice lost her dad when she was little. Why would she lie about it? Or did she keep it a secret like those pictures I saw online, a secret so deep, she couldn't share it with me?

"You're asking too many questions," says Markus, moving closer. "I think we should get to know each other better."

I don't like the way he's looking at me, like he's sizing me up.

"I have to go," I say quickly.

"Yeah?" Markus grabs my sleeve. "Why so soon? You didn't even tell me your name."

"Her name's Lucy."

I spin around.

Faron is walking through the tall grass, coming up behind us. What's he doing here? I'm so startled, I barely recognize his slow, careful voice, or the way he's moving toward me, like pushing through water.

Markus lets go and I stumble forward. I look up at Faron, unable to believe that he's really here. His face is unshaven, as if he hasn't slept in a while, his hair damp with sweat, but his eyes are just as dark as I remember.

"Come on," says Faron, sliding his fingers through mine. "Let's take a walk."

We drift away from the canal. In the distance, the water is stained with the setting sun. Faron doesn't say anything as we cross Bahia Vista, where cars race back and forth under the power lines and palm trees.

"Why didn't you wait for me on the beach?" I ask.

"I waited as long as I could," he says. "I couldn't find you. I'm sorry. I was scared I'd never see you again."

"You were scared. That's right."

"I said I was sorry."

"Yeah, I heard you the first time."

I watch his face.

His expression doesn't change.

"You don't believe me," he says, tugging up his hood.

"I want to believe you."

"But you don't."

"I don't know what to believe."

"Can't we start over?" he asks. "Please. Just give me a chance, *fehlerfrei*."

"I'm not perfect, okay?"

"You're right," he says. "But I'm not perfect, either."

Now I'm the one who feels ashamed.

I want to trust Faron. But I can't let him get close to me. I have to be careful, no matter how much I wish he'd kiss me again. I know it's wrong, the way I'm aching for his kiss. But that doesn't stop me from wanting it.

Now it's getting darker. When we reach the train crossing, I sit down on the tracks. It's dangerous, but I don't care. The rails are a dull, silver stain, winding under the streetlight.

"Me and my friends used to race here," says Faron. "We'd try to make it across before the gate went down."

"That's pretty stupid."

"Yeah," he says. "But it was fun."

"Fun until you're dead."

He looks hurt. "Listen. After my dad kicked me out, I did a lot of stupid stuff. When I came down here last summer, it was even better than *Rumspringa*. For the first time in my life, I could do whatever the hell I wanted."

"You were free."

"Never had that kind of freedom before," he says, looking at the rails. "Do you even understand what I'm saying?"

"You don't have to be Old Order to understand."

"Yeah?" he says. "Because I don't think you know how it feels."

"I've got it easy in Florida. That's what you said. Well, it's not easy being different from everybody else."

Faron sits next to me. He puts his arm around my shoulder, but I pull away.

"Just leave me alone, okay?"

He reaches down and picks up a bracelet that somebody lost in the gravel. "Here's a present for you," he says. "Real pearls from the ocean." He grabs my wrist and slides it over my hand.

"It's plastic."

"Nah, these are magic pearls. I swam in the Gulf this morning and caught them myself."

"You caught them?"

"Yeah, with my bare hands." He grins.

One minute, he's making me so angry, I want to strangle him. Now we're laughing again.

I toss the bracelet into the weeds. "The Gulf's messed up. I wouldn't go swimming in it. Not even for a magic pearl."

"Where do pearls come from anyway?" he asks.

"They come from pain."

He's watching me, his face hidden inside his hood. "You think I'm stupid, right?"

I thought he was joking around. Now I feel bad. Does he really want to know?

"Oysters make pearls," I tell him.

"Yeah, I get that," he says. "But how?"

"When you put sand inside an oyster, it makes a pearl. That's why I said they come from pain."

"Glad I ain't no oyster," he says.

All of a sudden, the warning lights blink and flash. I watch the guardrail lower over the tracks.

"Are you friends with those boys?" I finally ask.

"I wouldn't call them friends."

If you're on *Rumspringa*, you get to know everybody. But Faron doesn't belong to that world. At least, not anymore.

"What about Alice's boyfriend?"

"Who?"

"Tobias. I thought you knew him."

Faron shrugs. "Ain't no friend of mine."

"You never saw him before?"

"He showed up in Pinecraft last weekend, looking for a ride to the party. Figured he was on *Rumspringa*."

"So you didn't know Tobias. But you helped him out."

"Lucy, this is Florida. We help each other."

"The ex-Amish, you mean."

"That's right."

"What if Tobias isn't Amish?"

"Never thought about that," he says. "Tobias told me to take him and Alice to the bus station. We were supposed to go after the party. But they never showed up on the beach."

"Alice wanted to go to California. She was going to be in the movies." I feel so embarrassed, saying it out loud.

"Well, she's headed in the wrong direction," says Faron. "Her boyfriend said he was going back to Maine."

Now I'm confused. "But that's where Alice is from."

"A lot of us are from up north," he says.

It's true. The buses come to Pinecraft every winter, so many, you couldn't count them all. If Tobias wanted to disappear, he chose the right place.

"Alice wouldn't go back north." I remember what she told me. Sometimes it's so cold, her eyelashes froze as she walked to the craft fair, selling the beautiful quilts that Mrs. Yoder wouldn't let her keep.

"Did you see all that money she was carrying around that night?"

"Yeah, I saw it."

"Tobias saw it too."

Faron tosses his cigarette in the gravel. "You think he stole Alice's money?"

"What do you think?"

"I don't know, Lucy. Anything's possible. Sounds like your friend got herself in a lot of trouble."

I look down at the gravel, where the dull glow of his cigarette flares and disappears. I swallow hard, but the knot in my throat won't go away. "My next-door neighbor found Alice's cell phone on the beach, all smashed up."

He looks at me. "When was this?"

"The morning after the party," I say, blinking back tears.

Faron tightens his arms around me. I sob against his chest. He's wearing the same sweatshirt from that night, the one with the flames spiraling down the sleeves, but my tears can't put them out.

The train whistle blares, then leaks away. At that moment, I can't think of a lonelier song.

"There's a freight coming," says Faron, pulling me away from the tracks.

The whistle cuts through the trees, louder this time. Now the freight's gaining speed, lighting up the branches in the pines. I cover my ears, blinking in the haze of dust and grit as dozens of cars thud past.

"Where's it going?" I ask.

"Somewhere that ain't here."

Finally the last boxcar rattles into the distance as if pulled on a string. I think about Faron racing across those tracks, looking for escape. He's never going to outrun his past, no matter how fast he goes. Or how far.

"I've been thinking about you, Lucy," he says. "Ever since that night. You and me on the beach."

I've been thinking about him, too.

"Don't lose hope, okay?" he tells me. "I'll help you find Alice. I promise."

Can I trust him?

Faron's opened up his heart to me. He didn't lie about his family shunning him. He's not afraid to ask questions, the kind that get you in trouble. He told me about his faith, how it was shaken. When I said the ocean is my dream, he listened. And he's listening now, stroking my hand, never taking his eyes off mine.

We start walking back. My head is busy, adding things up. Did Tobias steal Alice's money? Faron talks about the Old Order as if they're one big family. But I know that's not right. Just because you're Old Order, doesn't make you a good person.

As we cross Bahia Vista, I notice somebody watching us. It's Jacob. He catches my stare and turns in the other direction. Great. Now he's going to tell everybody in Pinecraft. If word gets out I'm with an Old Order boy who's been shunned, Dad will never let me leave the house. That's for sure.

"When can I see you again?" Faron asks.

"I don't know." I let go of his hand.

"Are you just saying that? Because if you don't want to—"

"I want to," I say. And it's true. I want to see Faron again. But Dad's not going to like us being together. Faron's not from Pinecraft. He's not even Amish anymore. If my dad found out about tonight, I'd be in so much trouble. But at this moment, there's no place I'd rather be.

"Tomorrow's Friday. Is there going to be another party in Water Tower Park?" I ask.

He looks away. "I wouldn't go back there."

"Why not?"

He sighs. "I can't talk about it, okay?"

"What's wrong? Don't you understand? I'm on your side."

"I know you are," he says.

"Then why can't you tell me?"

"I just . . . can't."

"But why?"

The *Rumspringa* boys near the canal are watching us. Markus and his friend. They're leaning against the fence near the basketball court. I can tell they're angry at Faron. There's something going on that he's not talking about.

"Tell your girlfriend to mind her own business. You hear?" says Markus, glaring at us.

"I'm sorry," Faron whispers.

He turns and starts walking over to the boys. Away from me. For a minute, I watch him drift behind the oak trees. Then I turn into stone.

## chapter twelve

# deep water

The next day, I'm helping Dad in the backyard, lifting the roof onto the gazebo. The cedar planks remind me of spokes on a wheel. Next come the panels, dropping into place like a puzzle.

"If you're missing one, it won't hold," Dad says.

It's the same at an Old Order barn raising. At least, that's what Alice told me. "Many hands, easy work," they say, reminding us that we're all together.

Then why do I feel so alone?

I need to get away from Dad. Take the bus to Lido Key and find the game-players I saw online. The way things are going, I'll be stuck working in the backyard all afternoon.

"Can I take a break for a little while?" I ask.

I already know what he's going to say.

"There's no time," he says, frowning. "I've got people counting on me, Smidge. You want to leave me stranded?"

A flicker of guilt shoots through my chest. "No, it's just . . ." I try to think of something that sounds right. "I promised some friends we'd meet up."

"Oh, really?" he says, like this is hard to believe.

I don't usually go anywhere on Friday. I'm always working for Dad. If I finish early, he'll find more chores to do.

"Yeah," I tell him. "They're waiting for me."

"Where exactly?" he wants to know.

"The park."

Only half a lie.

Not the whole truth.

"What's going on there?" He thinks I mean Pinecraft Park, where the old men play shuffleboard behind the chainlink fence. When he smiles, my chest sinks. Because now I'm going to lie.

"Just hanging out. No big deal."

Dad mops the shine off his forehead. It's not even lunchtime and he's already tired. "Anybody I know?"

I don't have many friends. When I finished school last year, they all drifted away. I used to see a couple of girls from my class working at Der Dutchman, the Amish restaurant on Bahia Vista. After a while, I didn't see them anymore.

"They're friends from school." I can't look him in the eyes. That's the thing about hiding the truth. You tell one small lie. Then you tell another.

"Well, I need you here today," he says.

"Please? Just for a little while." I'm almost begging.

Dad shakes his head. "You've got responsibilities at home. I know it's hard to understand, but that's more important than hanging out with friends."

I knew he'd say this. Still, I can't help wishing I could fly away. Lift out of my skin above the streetlights, beyond the patchwork of houses, even higher than the cars speeding down Bahia Vista.

"Fine," I say, throwing down the cedar plank, letting it topple into the grass. I start walking toward the house.

"Lucy," he says.

I don't look back. It's always about Dad. His rules. Does it even matter what I think? I'm sick of hearing about it all the time. My dad acts like everything he does is perfect. He says the rules are supposed to keep us together, but I can't pretend to care anymore.

I'm not what he wants me to be.

As I head toward the porch, I know something's off. There's a strange kind of quiet. A stillness in the breeze. Then I see the police car parked on the front lawn. Sarasota County Sheriff. A cold jolt rattles through me.

I can't fly away.

Not now.

A woman in dark sunglasses steps out of the police car. She's clutching a 7-Eleven cup rimmed with lipstick stains. In her sneakers and shorts, she doesn't look like a cop, but I can tell by the way she's marching around like she owns the place.

"Hot day, isn't it?" she says, smiling. "Mosquitoes are biting fierce. Guess my blood tastes sweet."

The name on her badge says *Ricketts*. I stare at the gun strapped to her belt and wonder if she's ever shot anybody.

Dad comes marching up the lawn. When he sees the cop, he gets this hard look on his face. He glances at me, then back at Ricketts.

"Can I help you?" he asks.

"Maybe you can," the cop says, steering her gaze in my direction. "This must be your daughter."

"That's right," Dad says, putting his arm around me. "This is my girl, Lucy."

Ricketts stretches out her hand. When I don't take it, she lets it droop to her side. "Nice meeting you, Lucy. Can we talk for a sec? Got a couple questions for you. Won't take long."

"Am I in trouble?"

"I don't know," she says. "Are you?"

Dad takes a step forward. "Hold on," he says, tightening his grip on my shoulder. "You can't just show up, poking your nose where it doesn't belong. This is my property and I've got a business to run. You hear?"

"Yes, sir. I understand," she says, lifting her sunglasses. Her eyes are pale gray, like the Gulf at dawn. "I'm just taking a drive through Pinecraft, talking to your neighbors. That's all."

Taking a drive? The Sarasota police never come around here. Not unless they've got a good reason.

I glance across the street where Mrs. Keller is hanging the wash. She keeps looking over at me and Dad. No doubt, she's wondering why there's a cop car parked on our front lawn. Or maybe she already knows.

"This is about Alice, isn't it?" I say quietly.

Dad frowns. "That's enough."

"Go on, Lucy. We're just having a little chat," says Ricketts, turning to me. "Alice Yoder was your friend?"

*Was.*

Not *is.*

I'm starting to put it together. Mr. Showalter brought Alice's phone to the police. Now they're here in Pinecraft looking for answers.

"Is she okay?" I ask Ricketts. "Did something bad happen to her?"

"I was hoping you could tell me," she says, narrowing her eyes. "That was quite some party on the beach last weekend."

In my mind, I see the Sarasota police marching up and down the sand, waving their flashlights. The Old Order girls in their long dresses, caught in the tide.

"Do you know if Alice was with anyone that night?" Ricketts asks.

"What do you mean?"

"A boyfriend," she says.

I promised not to tell anybody about Tobias. Did I make the wrong choice? Is it a sin if I keep a secret to protect Alice? The truth weighs heavy in my bones, deeper than all the water in the ocean.

"Alice was with me."

Ricketts nods. "Yes, that's what I understand."

What exactly did the Showalters tell the police? It's one thing if I'm in trouble, but if gossip spreads all over Pinecraft, it could hurt my dad's business. He depends on word of mouth to sell what he builds.

"What about Alice's other friends?" Ricketts asks.

"Friends?" I can barely hear what she's saying, I'm so nervous. "There were lots of people hanging out on the beach."

"Amish teenagers, you mean?"

Dad's had enough of Ricketts. "I don't need you trespassing on my property, spouting off nonsense and bullying my daughter. This is Pinecraft. Go back to Sarasota if you're looking for trouble."

"Maybe you'd like to come by the station," she says, taking a sip from her Styrofoam cup. "Answer a couple questions."

This is so wrong. I can't let Dad sink into this mess.

"If I talk to you for a minute, will you leave my dad alone?" I ask her.

Ricketts lets her gaze drift into the backyard, where the gazebo rises behind the mossy oak trees.

"Sure thing, hon," she says, suddenly sweet again.

"Not out here."

"Okay. Where?"

"Inside the house."

Dad holds me closer. "No, Lucy. I won't allow this."

Across the street, Mrs. Keller is watching us. Dad notices, too. And she's not the only one. Mr. Showalter's on his porch, smoking a pipe. Who else is watching behind their windows? It feels like everybody in Pinecraft is watching.

I march up to the front porch.

"Won't be too long," says Ricketts, following behind me.

In the kitchen we settle at the table, like the day Mrs. Yoder showed up, looking for Alice. I sit across from Ricketts in the wobbly chair. Dad never got around to fixing it. Instead, he shoved a piece of wood under the leg—a wedge shaped like a church steeple.

"You're good to your dad, aren't you?" says Ricketts, leaning across the table.

"I try."

On the table, Dad left this week's *Budget*. It's how the Old Order get their news. The pages are spread open to the ads. *Handmade Amish Craftsmanship* it says below a picture of Dad's gazebos.

"Bet it's not easy working for your family," says Ricketts, glancing at the newspaper. "Especially for someone your age," she says, glancing at Mama's sewing basket. It's been on the kitchen shelf so long, I almost forgot about it. "Wouldn't you rather be with your friends?"

I'd rather be in school, learning about the ocean. But that's not something I expect her to understand.

"Your friend, Alice, is a different kind of Amish than you," says Ricketts, surprising me. Most people can't tell the difference between Beachy and Old Order. "She's not allowed to do a lot of things."

"Alice is on *Rumspringa*."

"That makes it okay, right? She was just having fun at that party. Maybe you were a little bit jealous?"

It stings, hearing it out loud. But I won't fall into her trap.

"Let's try this again," she says. "Where did Alice get that cell phone? Did her boyfriend give it to her?"

"I don't know."

"You don't know if he did?"

"No, I meant—"

Too late. I've already messed up. I slump a little lower in that wobbly chair. At that moment, I wish the floor would split open and swallow me whole.

"It must be hard, growing up Amish."

What does she know about being Amish?

"And if her boyfriend gave her a present," Ricketts goes on. "Might be hard to resist something like a cell phone."

I stare at the knots swirling across the pinewood table. A long time ago, it was a living thing, a tree rooted in the earth.

"And the blood?" says Ricketts.

What is she talking about?

"There was blood on Alice's phone?"

Please don't let it be true.

"So this boy your friend met." Ricketts lowers her voice. "Maybe you can tell me about him?"

"Tobias?"

"Is that his name?" She shifts forward in her chair.

For a moment, we're both quiet.

I can't tell her anything about Tobias. He's just some boy Alice met. Where? I don't know. I figured he was a *Rumspringa* boy. A snowbird. He could be from anywhere.

"Are you going to talk to me, Lucy?" says Ricketts.

"I don't know anything, okay?"

"Is that the truth?" she says carefully.

Now I get it.

Ricketts doesn't think I'm lying to protect Alice.

She thinks I'm lying to protect myself.

The front door swings open and Dad storms into the kitchen. I've never seen him so angry.

"You've had enough time," he says to Ricketts. "More than enough. I'm asking you to leave."

Ricketts doesn't move. "I'm not done talking to Lucy."

"Yes, you are," he says, holding the door open.

"We still have a few things to discuss."

"Not without my permission."

"Fine." Ricketts gets up from the table. She drops her Styrofoam cup in our sink, as if I'm going to wash it for her. "I'll be at the station later today, if she changes her mind. And if she doesn't . . ."

I dig my fingernails into my palms. Let the pain take over.

Still, I hear every word.

"How old are you, Lucy?"

"Sixteen," I mumble.

She nods. "We'll talk again soon."

Not if I can help it.

When Ricketts finally leaves, I can breathe again. Dad goes to the kitchen window. I stand behind him, watching the police car drive away. It looks so out of place. A big city thing. Was she telling the truth? It's too horrible to imagine, Alice's cell phone, the sparkly pink rhinestones crusted with blood.

I lean against Dad's shoulder. "I'm scared."

"It's okay to be scared," he says. "But you're safe now, Smidge. This is my house. That sheriff's got no right coming around here, stirring up trouble. What sort of questions did she ask you?"

He doesn't understand why that cop's looking for me. Or why she's asking so many questions. He still thinks I'm good inside. But he doesn't know how deep I've sunk. So low, I may never find the light again.

"She thinks I did something bad to Alice."

Dad blinks. "Alice is like a sister to you. Why would that policewoman think you'd hurt your best friend?"

"Alice's phone . . ." I can barely shape the words.

"What about her phone?"

"There was blood on it."

"Yes," says Dad quietly. "I know."

I can't believe it.

"Why didn't you tell me?"

Now Dad's keeping secrets too?

"Didn't want to upset you," he says. "You've been carrying a big load. Didn't know how big until you got sick in church—"

Sick?

"I wasn't sick."

He's still not listening. "I'm worried about you, Smidge," he says. "There's nothing we can do for Alice now. Nothing except pray."

I can't sit here and do nothing. I need to find Tobias's friends, the boys who were playing that game online. But how can I get away from Dad? He's got me working all afternoon, painting that stupid gazebo.

"It's time we got back to work," he says, grabbing his hat. "Keep your hands busy so your mind can't wander."

In the backyard we lift the cedar planks and fit the pieces together. The roof reminds me of a boat's helm, steering us across deep water. I can't stay in Pinecraft anymore. Not if Alice is in trouble. I have to go wherever she's gone, no matter how far.

I'm the only one who knows the way.

# chapter thirteen

# princesses

L ater that afternoon, Mr. Showalter pulls up in his truck.
"Now what?" Dad mutters.

No doubt, Mr. Showalter noticed the police car on the front lawn. Now he's over here looking for gossip.

"Be back in a minute," Dad says, shaking his head.

Near the workshop he left a stack of paint cans on the lawn. *Snowy pine.* That's the color he picked out for that stupid wedding gazebo. I glance back at Dad. He's nodding at Mr. Showalter, pretending to listen to whatever boring thing he's saying. I need to move fast. The workshop's door is flung wide open. I duck inside, almost tripping over the boards on the floor.

The walls are bristling with hooks. That's where Dad hangs his tools. I scan the saw blades and gleaming hammers. Usually he leaves the screwdrivers there too. He keeps them on a steel pegboard, all lined in a row.

I need something to open one of the paint cans. I yank open a drawer and shove my hand inside, feeling around for a screwdriver. All I find is measuring tape. Carpenter's pencils with square edges, hand-sharpened with a pocketknife. A sand dollar I gave to Dad a long time ago. The shell's crumbled to pieces, but I can't find the doves. I picture them fluttering away, like moths through the window.

"What are you hunting for, Smidge?"

Dad's standing in the doorway with Mr. Showalter. They both stare at me, waiting.

"Sandpaper," I tell him.

"It's on the table," he says, frowning, "right where you left it."

"Oh," I say, like I'm surprised. As I reach for it, I glance at the cabinet above the worktable. Dad's got a bunch of rusty cans on the shelf. He fills the old cashew tins with bolts and nails. And there, sticking out of the farthest tin, is the plastic handle to a screwdriver.

"You're not done sanding?" Dad asks.

"Almost."

Mr. Showalter scratches his beard. "We should let your daughter get back to her chores. Sounds like she's got a lot to handle."

What does he mean, a lot to handle? Does he think I'm guilty, too? I can't stand his high-and-mighty attitude. Or the strange way he's looking at me. I feel like crawling under the worktable with the wood shavings.

"You're right," I tell him. "There's a lot of work to do. We have to finish nailing the roof panels. Then we're going to start painting. Want to help?"

He takes a step backward. "Promised my wife I'd stop by the post office."

Yeah, that's what I figured.

"Well, I best be on my way," he says, heading for the door. He turns to Dad. "Let's talk before I go."

The door bangs shut. When they're finally gone, I reach up and grab the screwdriver. Then I press my cheek against the door.

"We can't have the police showing up here," Mr. Showalter's voice drifts through the pinewood. He's still going off about the police. The way he's talking, you'd think Dad's the one in trouble. Not me.

"They won't be back," Dad says.

"Do you really believe that? It's probably all over the TV by now. And that's the last thing we need."

"My daughter had a talk with the sheriff."

"Oh, she did?" Mr. Showalter says. "Your daughter's friend is the reason the police are driving down my street."

"It's no business of yours," Dad says.

"Actually, it is my business. Both of us. If word gets out that something's not right with the Amish in Pinecraft, you can say goodbye to your fancy gazebos. Because you won't be selling them anymore."

I wince. It hurts to hear Mr. Showalter talk to Dad that way. But I know it's true. We could lose everything. And I'm to blame.

I push open the door to the workshop. The paint cans are hidden in the tall grass near the gazebo. I crouch down on the ground. Slide the flat edge of the screwdriver under the lid. The thing's screwed on so tight, it won't budge.

"Lucy?"

Dad's calling for me. I jam the screwdriver into the paint can. Then I start working my way around the lid. Finally, it pops off. I give that can a good, hard kick and a tidal wave of paint gushes across the lawn.

"What's going on here?" Dad comes walking up the path. When he sees the paint can toppled over, he frowns.

I stare at the ooze in the grass. "The lid came off."

Not exactly a lie.

Dad sighs. "Head in the clouds."

Mr. Showalter's right behind Dad. He glares at me, the no-good girl. "What a waste," he says, like I can't do anything right.

"It's my fault. Let me walk to the store on Bahia Vista. I'll pick up another can."

Dad tugs his hat over his eyes. "Not much left of the day. I'd rather you stayed at home, Smidge. You haven't even had lunch."

"If we don't start painting now, it won't dry in time."

I never argue with Dad, but he knows I'm right. Maybe that's why he finally says, "Be back in an hour."

It's not enough time. I have to take the bus to South Lido Key. That's where Tobias's friends are playing the game today.

"You forgot something." Dad slips me a twenty.

"Thanks."

He gives my arm a squeeze. "Glad to see you smiling again."

I want to sink into the ground, lower than the bones of the ocean.

When I reach the bus stop on Bahia Vista, I'm the only one waiting on the bench. Maybe the last bus came already? In Pinecraft, they stop running after sundown. There should be another on the way.

"Did the bus show up yet?" I ask an Old Order woman who walks up and sits next to me.

She folds her hands in her lap.

Silent.

Ten minutes later, the bus finally shows up. Heads turn as I step inside and search for an empty seat.

When I was little, everyone used to smile at me.

Now they stare.

• • •

South Lido Key is crowded on the weekend. Seagulls hover in midair, as if dangling on invisible strings. Me and Alice used to bait our fingers with saltines and lift them high, holding our breath, until the birds finally swooped down and took what we gave them.

Near the water, dozens of umbrellas tilt in the sand. Kids sit at picnic tables, eating off paper plates. As I walk to the beach, they stare at me. I'm sick of all the stares and whispers. For once, I want to look like everybody else.

I slide the pins out of my hair and take off my prayer cap. Then I shove it in the bottom of my tote bag. My hair spills down my back. I wonder if I look like Alice when she stepped off the bus.

As I pass the seawall, I remember my walk with Faron, our kiss. The sand is littered with cigarettes and empty beer bottles. Strange how things can look so different after the sun rises.

Across from the beach, a hiking trail leads into the pines. Dad would say it's a bad idea, exploring the woods by myself, but I don't have a choice. I turn away from the water and head toward the shade.

In the video online, the boys were in a field. I don't see anything like that here. The pines are so thick, there's hardly any sun. Still, I'm sweating in the late afternoon heat. I tuck a strand of hair behind my ears. It feels strange, letting it sway loose and unpinned.

The trail leads to an open clearing. There's enough space to play a game here, but there's nobody around. I listen, but hear nothing. Not even the ocean's pulse. Then a shout breaks through the quiet.

I spin around.

"Don't move," somebody says.

A boy runs out of the woods and lunges in front of me. He's carrying a stick, like the people in the video I saw online, and wearing some kind of costume, a long, flowy cape decorated with stars.

"You," he says, waving the stick at me. "Intruder, you have passed the forbidden gates of my kingdom. How do you plead?"

This boy must think I'm playing the game. My long-sleeved dress probably looks like a costume to him. Okay. I'll play along.

"I plead guilty."

He looks confused. "You're not going to defend yourself?"

"No."

He pushes up his helmet. "But you're supposed to fight me."

"How?"

"You don't have a weapon?"

I shake my head.

"Not even magic?"

"I don't know how to fight."

"Well, that's no excuse," he says, raising his arm. "Killing blow one. Killing blow two," he yells, whacking me with his stick.

"Stop it." He's not hitting me very hard, but it still hurts.

"You're out," he says.

"What am I supposed to do?"

"Nothing. You're dead."

"I am?"

"Go wait in the dungeon," he says, pointing at a circle of stones near the edge of the clearing.

This game doesn't make any sense. I walk over to the "dungeon," where a girl in a wheelchair is hanging out in the shade, gluing feathers to paper masks. On the back of her chair balloons sway in the breeze like she might take off into the sky.

"Are you dead too?" I ask.

"For now," she says. "But I hope it's not permanent. What character are you playing today?"

"I'm just here to watch."

"Me too," she says. "I'm Crystal, by the way. I haven't seen you at any games before. Are you a newbie?"

"I guess."

"So you've never gone LARPing?"

"What's LARPing?"

She squeezes a bead of glue onto a mask. "It's live-action-role-playing. Kind of like a video game in real life."

I don't play video games, but I think I understand. "You're supposed to kill the bad guys."

Crystal laughs. "Oh, my god. You're hilarious. What's your name?"

"Lucy Zimmer."

"I've never met a Lucy Zimmer. So we're both doing something new." She bends forward in her chair, like a queen bowing on her throne.

Did Alice play this make-believe game up north? I know she wants to be a famous actress in Hollywood someday. She told me there's a drive-in theatre down the road from the Amish craft fair in Maine. At night, she'd sneak out to watch the movies. Alice would memorize all the lines and act out the parts for me. Yeah, she was good at pretending.

I need to find out more about this game.

"Do you make all the costumes?" I ask Crystal.

"Most of them," she says. "I'm going to major in fashion design next year at Ringling. I'm so excited, I can't shut up about it."

When she says, "Ringling," I think she means the art school up in Sarasota. If I could study anything I want, I'd be excited, too.

Crystal grabs a handful of peacock feathers from her bag. "I haven't played since I got killed in the last battle. It really sucks to be eaten by a plant. Especially a Phantom Fungus whose intelligence is mindless."

"That sounds pretty bad."

"It was beyond tragic. But maybe I can get resurrected next time."

"What do you mean, 'resurrected'?"

"When somebody dies, they have a chance to come back to life."

"So they're not dead anymore?"

"If they're lucky," she says. "You're really new at this, aren't you?"

"I was hoping my friends would be here."

"If they're not on the battlefield, they probably flaked out. Don't you hate when that happens? It messes up the whole game."

"Where's the battlefield?" I ask.

"You're looking at it."

I glance at the open space between the pines, where the boys are whacking each other with big wooden sticks.

"What character is your friend playing?" Crystal asks.

I try to describe Alice's costume, the glittery wings on her back.

"So she's one of the fairies. It's a mission, keeping track of those girls. I mean, there's a gazillion of them."

"How many players do you have?"

"Let's see. If you count every state, there's fifty chapters," she says, tapping her fingers.

"That's a lot."

"No kidding," she says. "There's over a hundred players signed up for Blackwoods this year."

Where did I hear that name before? The video Tobias put online. He told Alice they were supposed to play a game at Blackwoods.

"It's going to be epic," says Crystal.

"What happens at Blackwoods?" I ask.

"Oh, just the most amazing battle of the entire year. We drive up to Maine every fall. All the chapters get together and fight for the throne. It gets real atmospheric with the leaves changing and stuff."

I remember the video I saw online. The changing leaves. Tobias in the woods with Alice. The wings on her back.

"Do you know someone named Tobias?" I ask. "He's Alice's boyfriend. She's from Maine too."

"Tobias? You mean Toby?"

Toby.

"Yeah," she says. "Toby does the video every year. He's like, the technology expert."

"So he's not from here?"

Crystal shrugs. "I've only seen him at Agora, back in Maine. LARPing's really big up there. Everybody camps at Blackwoods in Acadia National Park. It's like our own special world. Five days of awesomeness. Nobody judging you. Total escape from reality. Because reality kind of sucks. You know what I mean?"

I know exactly what she means.

"When I'm LARPing, I can be myself. At school, everybody thinks I'm a freak. But at the games, we're all freaks." She laughs.

I can totally imagine Alice playing this game. She always loved to pretend. Why didn't she tell me about it? Maybe she thought her mom would find out. When we were little, Mrs. Yoder never let us play make-believe. "It's like telling lies," she said.

"When are the Agora games?" I ask.

"This weekend, actually. You should go."

The games are a thousand miles away. How can I drive up to Maine? I don't even have a car. But I have a little money saved from my job. Dad usually keeps most of it. There's no way he'd let me go.

Crystal pushes up her mask. Now it looks like her face has sprouted wings. "Excuse me for saying, but your dress is kind of plain."

"Could you make a dress for me?"

"Maybe." She glances at the players on the field. "I mean, yeah. If I had more time. I usually just make stuff for my friends."

I don't see anyone else around here. All this time, Crystal has been sitting in the shade by herself.

"I bet it takes a long time to sew a costume," I tell her.

"That's sort of an understatement."

"What if I helped?"

"For real?" she says, brightening. "You would do that?"

"If you showed me how."

Crystal grins. "Nobody ever asked me before."

"Really?"

"You're the first. So what did you have in mind? I could sew a nice purple bodice for you, real princess-like."

"I'm not much of a princess."

"Of course you are. Maybe you could be a Spellcaster or a Dragon Barbarian. You can be anything you want."

"But I don't know how to play."

"Everybody knows how to pretend. You're already good at it. In fact, you're probably an expert."

She's right.

I'm good at hiding the truth.

And that's why I don't feel very good at all.

## chapter fourteen

# rotten fruit

When the game ends, I steer Crystal's wheelchair into the sunshine and help her pack away the costumes.

Crystal shoves a handful of feathers into a bag. "Want to grab lunch? My blood sugar's going to crash."

"What does that mean?"

"It means bad things happen if I don't eat. Sometimes I get dizzy and pass out. That's the worst, you know?"

I do know.

"Then you should probably eat soon."

"Sooner than later," she says. "Or else I'll turn into a zombie. But if you don't have time, that's totally okay."

"I've got time." Actually, I'm supposed to be back at the workshop helping Dad. But I don't want to go home. Not when I'm having so much fun.

"Where should we go? I'm so broke right now," says Crystal. "Is there, like, a dollar menu nearby? Oh wait. Do you like mango shakes?"

"Mango's my favorite."

"Me too. There's this little fruit stand I keep hearing about. It's in the Amish neighborhood. They're supposed to have amazing desserts. I'm talking homemade cookies and pie and everything."

I can't believe what I'm hearing. "Isn't that kind of far away?"

"Nope. This place is actually super close. I didn't even know we had Amish people in Sarasota."

There's no way we're going to Pinecraft. What if Crystal thinks it's weird? I've never had any friends who aren't Amish. She doesn't know that I grew up without TV. Or that I wear the same boring clothes every day. I've kissed a boy, but I haven't gone further. I think about that kiss a lot. At night, I press my fist to my lips and remember.

"Here we are." Crystal waves at a black van, as if it can see us. The windows are covered with stickers—a dragon gobbling a family of stick figures. On the antenna, a tiny pirate's flag snaps in the breeze. "This is Captain Darkwater, my suburban assault vehicle."

I'm still trying to think of a way out.

Crystal pushes a button on her keychain. The van's door swings open and a ramp lowers to the ground.

"Pretty sweet, huh?" she says, wheeling herself onto the ramp. "Just like magic."

I climb in the passenger seat. No going back now.

"The seatbelt's busted," Crystal says. "But it's all good. I don't speed on rainy days."

"It's not raining."

"Exactly," she says. "This thing is dangerous, right? It's already surpassed another level. Ignore the sand."

Now we're flying down Ringling Boulevard. I haven't been here since the party last Friday, when Faron drove to the beach at sunrise.

"Hello? Earth to Lucy?"

"Sorry. I didn't hear you."

"That's because you were spacing out. Can I turn on some music for our listening pleasure?"

"Okay."

Crystal plugs something into the radio. Drums explode out of the speakers while the singer *ahh-ahh-ahhhs*.

"You like Matt and Kim?" she asks.

"Who?"

"Their last album was epic."

"I don't listen to a lot of music," I say, watching the power lines swoop across the window.

"Are you serious? I am so totally burning you a mix."

We turn onto Bahia Vista, a road I've crossed all my life. Everything feels so far away. Big Olaf's ice cream. The parking lot where the buses pull up, carrying the snowbirds to Florida. The girl in a long dress and bonnet, waiting at the stoplight, holding her daddy's hand.

"This place is so freaking cute," says Crystal.

As we pull up to the fruit stand, an Old Order man steers his three-wheeled bicycle through the intersection. He doesn't even look twice.

"Oh, my god," says Crystal. "Where can I get one of those bikes? You could put me in the basket and push me around. That would be hilarious."

I glance at the Beachy-Amish women at the fruit stand, checking to see if I know any of them. Everybody's waiting in line, all lined up in their pastel dresses, their baskets loaded with strawberries. Behind the cash register, a girl is racing back and forth, trying to keep up with them.

Mallory Keller.

"You can go ahead. I'll wait in the car," I tell Crystal.

"What? Now you're ditching me?"

"Okay, okay." My hand trembles as I reach for the door. If anyone sees me without my prayer cap, I'm going to be in trouble.

Crystal lowers the platform thing and eases her wheelchair onto the pavement. "Those Amish girls must be sweating to death," she says. "It's like, ninety degrees out and they've got long sleeves."

It feels like she's judging me too.

Crystal's talking really loud and everybody's staring. A couple of girls from my old school are right behind us.

"Is that Lucy Zimmer?"

"Why isn't she wearing her *kapp*?"

"Does she think this is *Rumspringa*?"

# chapter fifteen
# breaking the rules

"So that was your dad," Crystal says.

We're at Big Olaf's. Same place where the buses roll up, carrying the snowbirds. *Florida's Finest Ice Cream* says the sign next to a giant soft-serve cone. The sun's high above the palm trees. Not a speck of shade on Bahia Vista Street. I dig my plastic spoon into a cup of Cookies and Cream.

"Yeah, that's my dad," I finally say.

Crystal takes a sip of her shake. She's quiet. No doubt sizing everything up. The brightly painted mural of a horse and buggy on the wall down the block. A man with a bushy Old Order–style beard, towing a boat behind his pickup truck. The girl in a long dress, just like mine, carrying a baby in her arms.

"Does that mean you're one of them?" she asks.

*Them.*

I take a deep breath. Okay. Here it comes. "My family belongs to the Beachy Amish-Mennonite church."

"But you don't look Amish."

Yeah, I've heard that before. But it's more than what you look like on the outside. It's about everybody being the same. That way, there's no pride to get in the way of your path to heaven. How can I explain this to Crystal?

"Mennonites are different from the Old Order."

"Seriously?" Crystal widens her eyes. "What's the difference? Come on. I won't judge you, I swear."

Then the questions begin to roll.

"Do you believe everybody's going to hell?" she asks.

"No." Why would I believe that?

"Are you allowed to go out with boys?"

"Yes," I say, my face tingling with heat.

"I thought Amish girls had to wear bonnets or something."

I scoop the last bite of ice cream into my mouth, but I don't even taste it. Why are these questions so hard to answer? Maybe I'm embarrassed about being different. Or maybe it's because I never tried to talk to someone about it. Not if they're from the outside world.

"I'm supposed to keep my head covered," I tell Crystal. "Usually, I wear a prayer cap. That's kind of like a bonnet. But I took it off."

"Why aren't you wearing it?" she asks.

"I don't want to anymore."

"Because it makes you feel weird, right?" she says, nodding. "I bet people stare at you."

"All the time."

"That sucks," she says.

"Yeah, it does."

I'm surprised. At first, I expected Crystal to judge me. Now it seems like she understands. I mean, really understands.

"Are you in trouble now?" she asks. "Your dad was kind of freaking out."

That's one way to put it.

Crystal doesn't say anything for a minute. "Does this mean you're going to get shunned?"

"No, my church doesn't believe in shunning."

"Is that really a thing? I mean, does it really happen?"

I think about Faron, the scars on his fingers. "Yes, it really happens. The Old Order are a lot stricter than us."

"Sounds like you've got it easier," she says.

"Maybe."

"But you still have to follow the rules."

"We don't really have 'official rules.' It sort of depends on where you live. Here in Florida, the church is pretty relaxed. Everybody kind of does their own thing. I mean, it's not like I'm in a cult or something."

"Sorry," she says, chewing her straw. "I'm all up in your business."

Now I feel bad. "It's okay. You can ask me anything. I don't mind."

"So what makes you different from the Old Order?"

"Mennonites can have modern things like electricity. We're allowed to drive cars and listen to the radio and stuff. That's a pretty big difference."

"What's so bad about technology anyway?"

"It's the electric part that's bad. The Old Order doesn't want the outside world connected to their homes. I mean, they can use batteries and solar power or whatever. Does that make sense?"

"I guess," she says. "What else is different?"

"I'm not allowed to have *Rumspringa*. You've probably heard of that, right?" I know everybody likes to joke about it. I try to put it into words. "It's when you have to make a choice. If you decide to join the church, you have to stay Amish forever."

"That's crazy," she says. "You have to make a big decision like that? I can't even decide if I like Gushers more than Fruit Roll-Ups."

"It's a pretty big deal."

"And what if you don't want to be Amish?"

It's a question I've been thing about a lot lately. In my mind, I see the Old Order girls dancing in Water Tower Park. Alice in her skinny jeans, walking away from me. When we were little, we used to climb the mango trees and share our secrets. But all that's changed now.

"If you don't want to be Old Order Amish, you can't stay in that world anymore. You have to leave everything behind. Your friends and family. It's all gone."

She shakes her head. "Why didn't you tell me?"

"Because people think it's weird."

"Yeah?" she says. "A lot of people think *I'm* weird."

As we finish our ice cream in the sunshine, a pair of Old Order girls zip past on bicycles.

Crystal smiles. "It's like your own secret world."

"Why do you say that?" I ask.

"Everybody's just like you."

I never saw Pinecraft that way before.

"Come on," I tell her. "I want to show you something cool."

At the post office next to Big Olaf's, there's a bulletin board covered in scraps of paper—so many fliers and notes, I can't see what's underneath.

"This is where we leave messages," I explain.

"Secret messages?"

I laugh. "Well, it's not a secret if everybody can read it."

She pushes her wheelchair up to the bulletin board. "This is so amazing. I could make a collage out of all this stuff. Or feathers for a mask. The possibilities are endless." She stretches out her hand and tears off a scrap of paper. "So where's your school?" she wants to know.

"It's next to our church on Honore Avenue. But I'm not in school anymore. My classes only go up to tenth grade."

"You're already done with school? Isn't that against the law or something? What if you get busted by Child Protective Services?"

What is she talking about? "I'm not a child anymore."

Crystal sighs. "Wow. You're so lucky."

That's what she thinks.

"If you're not in school, what are you supposed to be doing?" she asks.

"I work for my dad. We build gazebos and stuff."

"Sounds exhausting."

"It is."

"Don't you miss being in school?"

I watch the Old Order girls on their bicycles. As they disappear under the coconut palms, their long skirts ripple in the breeze.

"I miss it a lot."

"Here's another question," she says. "Would your dad try to stop you from going to college?"

"We never talked about it."

"Well, maybe it's time."

Dad wouldn't like it if I went to college and studied the ocean. Would he push me away? Or turn his back on me, the way Faron's dad had shunned him?

When we're back in the van, I'm still thinking about it. Crystal slows down near the canal in Pinecraft Park. Behind the chainlink fence, the bearded old men are playing shuffleboard, like always.

"Looks like they've been around forever," she says, leaning out the window. "Maybe since the dinosaurs."

"Pretty much," I say, sinking lower in my seat. I don't want anybody to see me. Not after what happened today.

"What about Amish guys who aren't a hundred years old? Are you allowed to go out and have fun?"

I glance at the empty basketball court. "Fun" isn't something I know much about.

"Well, at church, there's the Youth Ministry. That's kind of like Bible study. We mostly just sit around and talk."

"Sounds exciting."

I shrug. "Not really."

"Do you guys party? I mean, do you go out drinking and stuff?"

How much should I tell her?

"The Old Order boys . . . they have big parties here in Florida," I say. "It's kind of a secret, but everybody knows about it."

"How do you find out? You don't have cell phones or computers or—"

"Yes, we do. My best friend, Alice, is Old Order. She's on her *Rumspringa*, so she's allowed to have worldly things."

"So your B.F.F. has different rules. Isn't that weird?"

I never used to think so.

Until now.

"It's hard when you're Old Order. You can't do anything without the whole world waiting for you to mess up. That's why Alice tried to run away."

"Wait. Your friend ran away?"

I want to keep talking to Crystal, but it feels like a betrayal, letting her into my world. At the same time, I'm aching to talk to somebody.

"Last weekend, me and Alice were at a party," I explain. "We were supposed to go to Lido Key and watch the sunrise. But she never showed up."

"Oh, my god. I'm so sorry. If there's anything I can do, just let me know, okay?"

How can Crystal help me? Her life is so different from mine. She's got a car. She can drive wherever she wants. She's going to college next year, studying fashion design, whatever that is.

She's free.

"It really sucks to lose a friend," she says, squeezing my hand. And at that moment, I think she knows how it feels.

Maybe she can help after all.

"Can you give me a ride tonight?" I ask.

It's Friday. There's got to be another party. I could try to talk to the *Rumspringa* boys again.

"Where do you want to go?" she asks.

"Water Tower Park."

Crystal smirks. "Let me guess. You're going to one of those crazy Amish parties?"

"If you'll drive me there."

"Okay," she says. "But you're not having fun without me. I'm coming too."

"You want to go too?"

Now I'm really stuck.

If I bring Crystal, it will mess up everything. The *Rumspringa* boys won't talk. Not if she's with me. To them, she's "English." In other words, she's even more of an outsider.

"Are we doing this or what?" she says.

I nod.

"Oh, my god. This is so happening." Crystal smacks the steering wheel. "Let me give you my cell number."

"I don't have a cell."

"Oh." She blinks.

"I'll call you from the pay phone on Bahia Vista Street. We can meet in the parking lot by the fruit stand."

"That's so old school." She laughs.

Now I'm about to do something I never thought I'd do.

I'm going back to Water Tower Park.

•  •  •

We pull onto Kruppa Avenue and turn onto my block. Mr. Showalter is on his front porch, smoking a pipe. As we slow in front of my house, he gawks at Crystal's van. I want her to keep driving, but he's already seen us.

Crystal parks on the lawn, which Dad just mowed. My dresses are hanging from the clothesline, all in a row. It's kind of embarrassing.

"Almost forgot," she says. "You can borrow my iPod. Let me know what songs you're into. I'll make the best mix ever." She unplugs the iPod and snaps it into a case decorated with grinning skulls.

"Thanks. I never had a mix before."

"No problem," she says, handing it to me. "It would be an honor to create your first playlist."

I shove the iPod into my tote bag. "See you tonight."

Crystal waves as I get out of the car, lugging the can of paint. Mr. Showalter is still watching us. Doesn't he have better things to do?

I start walking toward the front door. Then my feet take me in the other direction. I haven't seen Mrs. Yoder since last Saturday, after she showed up at my house. Did Alice's mom go to the police and blame me? Is that why Ricketts came to my house, asking questions? That's what I need to find out.

The screened-in porch is empty. All the windows are covered up with storm shutters. They're supposed to keep you safe from hurricanes, but it must be really dark inside. My hand is shaking as I knock on the door.

To be honest, I've always been scared of Alice's mom. One time, Alice found a paper clip on the ground and twisted it into a ring. Mrs. Yoder pried it off her finger so fast, the scratch didn't heal for days.

I knock again.

No answer.

In my head, I'm saying things like, "Please don't hate me. It was wrong to leave Alice alone at that party. I can't go back and change what I did."

If only I could.

"She's gone."

Mr. Showalter is standing behind me.

"The widow's gone," he says.

Mrs. Yoder isn't here?

"I came over to return her daughter's cell phone," he says. "But there's no one around."

"So you took it to the police."

"That's right," he says, glaring.

"Then why did you blame me and Dad after the police showed up?"

"It's your fault the police are in Pinecraft. You and those *Rumspringa* boys."

"What about Mrs. Yoder?" I ask, trying to keep my voice calm. "Where did she go?"

He shakes his head. "It makes no sense. If my girl was missing, I'd be turning over every stone."

Maybe she was sick of everybody talking about Alice. Or maybe she was ashamed. He's right. It doesn't make sense.

Is Mrs. Yoder keeping secrets too?

"Why did she leave?"

"You tell me, Lucy Zimmer," he says.

I shove past him.

Mr. Showalter grabs my arm. "You and Alice went to that party together. Why did you go to the beach without her?"

I tug against his grip, but he's too strong.

"Where is Alice?"

"I don't know."

"Really?" he says. "If you're such good friends, why don't you know? Tell the truth for once."

I pull away from him and run across the street. I'm moving so fast, I don't even pay attention to where I'm going. I just want to get away from Mr. Showalter and his questions. Away from everything.

I keep running until I reach Pinecraft Park. Behind the chainlink fence, the basketball court is empty. The *Rumspringa* boys are gone. Tears burn behind my eyes. Just last weekend, I was here with Alice, talking about the party.

I never imagined it would be the last time.

*April 25*
*Smyrna, Maine*

*Dear Lucy,*

*The Rumspringa boys are playing baseball in the cornfield. I can hear them shouting behind the barn. Last year, the bishop tried to shut it down. He says it's too worldly, the way they get fired up over that game. My mom says he's right. If you fall in love with worldly things, you're never getting into Heaven. What's so bad about running outside in the sunshine? I think the Lord's got bigger things to worry about than baseball.*

*Me and Lisa Engel tried to sneak onto the field. The boys told us to go home. We were messing up their game. I want to play too, but they won't let me. Same thing as church. The men always stand up front and talk with the bishop, while the girls sit still and listen. That's the way it's always been. But that doesn't make it right.*

*I know things are different in Florida. You have church in a real building, not somebody's house. And you go to Sunday School, where everybody talks about the Bible, how those old stories fit into the world today. Wish we had something like that. I'm supposed to keep my mouth shut, but that doesn't stop the questions from popping into my head. Do you know what I mean? Feels like things are never going to change around here. I'm counting the days until summer.*

*The red mare went missing again. It's been raining like the Great Flood. I can't imagine where she goes. I mucked out the stalls and opened all the windows. (The water trough's frozen solid. Can you believe it?) By the time I got done, she snuck inside the barn, all by herself. Well, that was a surprise!*

*Lucy, it's been months since your last letter. I'm sure you're real busy, but I miss our "paper conversations," as you say. It's so lonely here sometimes (I know that sounds strange because I'm never really alone). All I want is a little space to breathe. Then I'd sit under the willow tree at sunset. Watch the deer nibbling sweet-fern and sumac in the backyard. As soon as I quit my chores, Mom finds more work to do.*

*When I dragged the mare out to pasture, she rolled in the mud. Guess I should've known better. That's what she does. EVERY. TIME. Yet I fell for it like a stone in the river. I really wish she could talk. Then I'd know where she wanders off.*

*Wish I could go too.*

*Tomorrow I'll take the colt to the market. The Rumspringa boys will be there, showing off their hogs and steers (if you asked me, I think they're a perfect match). Do you want to marry an Amish boy? He'd probably just boss you around all day. Who needs that? Not me. That's for sure.*

*Have you kissed anybody yet?*

*It's kind of embarrassing, but I wanted to tell you. A couple months ago, I kissed this boy, Andrew Becker. He tasted like Wintergreen Lifesavers, the kind that spark between your teeth.*

*I haven't seen Andrew for a long time.*

*He ran away to a safe house.*

*At least, that's what everybody says.*

*A safe house is just a bunch of ex-Amish renting a place together. If you walk away from the church, there's nowhere else to go.*

*It must be really hard, leaving home.*

*Scary, too.*

*I think about it a lot.*

*Now my mom's calling. I've got to finish my chores before she notices I've snuck off. If I forget to unlock the henhouse, I'll find the chickens hanging outside the coop, waiting for me. Don't they ever want to go somewhere else? Or are they too stupid to see? The door was open all along.*

*140 days until Florida!*

*Alice*

## chapter sixteen

# dents and scratches

After I get home, I help Dad finish painting the gazebo. He doesn't say much as I stand on the ladder, rolling my brush across the cedar beams. Why can't I have friends who aren't Amish? Everybody else gets to hang out on the weekend. Go to the beach. Kiss boys.

How am I supposed to act like an adult?

I'm not allowed to be one.

Sometimes I try to imagine what it would be like. My real life. The place I want to be. I'll study the ocean in a real school. I can almost picture it. Me in jeans, not a stupid dress. Hair down. Maybe I'll even learn how to drive a car. I'll drive it far away from Pinecraft and never look back.

All Dad cares about is work. He won't let me have my own world. In a way, I guess he's trying to keep me safe. He's scared because I went to that party with Alice and now she's missing. But he can't keep me locked inside this house forever.

When the sun goes down, Dad finally decides it's time to quit. "Get cleaned up," he tells me. "I'll set the table."

It's the most he's said for hours.

We eat dinner in silence. I almost wish he'd yell at me. At least say something. But Dad just keeps scraping his fork on the plate. He won't even look up.

"Can I be excused?" I ask quietly.

"Get the dishes done first."

That's all he says.

I rinse the pots in the sink and go straight to my room. Alone on my bed, I listen to Crystal's iPod. I play the same songs over and over. It's like chewing a piece of gum until the flavor's all gone.

I need to meet up with her and find that party tonight. But it doesn't look like I'm going anywhere.

Dad pushes open the door. He doesn't even knock.

"You hiding in here, Smidge?"

I shove the iPod under my pillow.

When Dad takes off his straw hat, he looks tired. His jeans are splattered with paint and his face is sunburned. He sits on the bed and I fall against him, as if the whole world has tipped.

"Let's talk about what happened today," he says.

"Okay," I tell him.

Except I don't get to do much talking.

Dad gives me a speech about "walking the Lord's path" and not following the crowd. The world is a wicked place. That's why we should keep ourselves as far from it as possible.

"That girl I saw you with today . . ." He doesn't finish his sentence.

"Her name's Crystal."

"Never seen her before. Is she from around here?"

It's pretty obvious that Crystal isn't Amish. Is that why Dad's so nervous?

"She's my friend."

That's all he needs to know.

He reaches under my pillow and takes out the iPod. "This doesn't belong to you," he says. "Tomorrow I want you to give it back."

"But she let me borrow it!"

"Understand?"

I stare at the wall.

"Did you hear me, Lucy?"

"Yes, I heard."

"Good." He hands it to me. "It's wrong to take things that aren't yours," he says, reaching into his back pocket. He pulls out the screwdriver. "Found it in the grass," he says. "Wonder how it got there?"

"It must've got lost," I say in a small voice.

"And from now on," he adds, "I don't want to see you hanging around that girl."

This is so wrong. Does he think I'm two years old?

"You can't choose my friends for me."

"True," he says. "But you need to start acting a little more grown-up."

Dad grabs his hat and leaves the room.

When he's gone, I plug myself into the iPod. I play my favorite songs until the battery goes dead.

• • •

I stay awake for hours, waiting for Dad to go to sleep. Finally, the light winks out in the hallway. I wait a couple minutes. Then I sneak into the kitchen. My sneakers are in a heap by the door, the word "Reebok" blacked out with magic marker so nobody sees the brand. I cram my feet into the shoes without tying the laces.

As I move past the orange trees, I catch sight of somebody in the backyard—a man in a straw hat, standing under the gazebo in the moonlight. Dad. What's he doing out here? I can't let him see me.

Too late.

"Not sleepy, huh?" he says.

"Just wanted some fresh air."

Dad nods like he understands. He looks up at the gazebo and smiles. "Got me thinking about your mother," he says, rubbing his eyes. "Our wedding day. Your mother planted those trees," he says, staring at the orange grove. "Right before you were born."

"I don't remember her."

It's not easy, saying this out loud.

Dad doesn't say anything. Then he gives me a hug. "I'll remember for both of us."

When somebody's gone, they never really leave. There's always a piece that stays behind. The trees in our backyard. Or the recipes in Alice's dusty old cookbook. All the gospel hymns we sing together in church, lifting our voices as one.

We go back inside the house. Dad takes his time getting ready for bed. I listen to him splashing at the bathroom sink. I feel bad about sneaking out, but I don't have a choice.

The Sarasota police can't bring Alice home, no matter what they do. They can push buttons on computers. Drive around Pinecraft in their big city cars. They don't know the Old Order. And they'll never break through those walls.

I'm the only one who saw what happened. Alice in the back of that truck, looking for an escape. Why didn't she talk to me? Did she think I was going to judge her? Or that I wouldn't understand?

*This isn't fun anymore.*

*Then leave.*

The house is quiet when I lace up my sneakers. As I reach for the door, I hear Dad coughing in his room. A small thread of guilt wraps around me. Yeah, I'm angry about what happened today. Still, it feels wrong, going behind his back.

I walk all the way to the pay phone on Bahia Vista. Cars stream back and forth like minnows in a pond. What if Crystal doesn't show up? I'm already late. I mean, really late. Maybe she got tired of waiting. Or changed her mind. I bet she thinks all this Amish stuff is weird. Not that I blame her.

I drop my quarters into the slot.

*Please pick up.*

The phone rings and rings.

Finally, there's a click.

"Lucy?"

"Yes, it's me."

"On my way," Crystal says.

Minutes later, a pair of headlights sweep across the road. Crystal's van pulls up to the fruit stand. I yank open the passenger door and climb inside. As we drive past the empty lot, I stare at the blackened stumps in the front yard.

"That used to be a mango farm," Crystal says. "Can't believe they burned down all those trees."

"When did it happen?" I ask, staring out the window.

"Last weekend," she says. "Maybe some kids did it. I don't know. It seems kind of evil, if you ask me."

If someone set the fire last weekend, it must've happened after I was there. After me and Alice met up in that empty lot.

We take the next exit and pull off the Tamiami Trail. Crystal slows onto the dimly lit street near Water Tower Park. No cars in the lot. It's completely dark.

"You're sure there's something happening tonight?" she asks.

I glance at the parking lot. It was a mistake coming here. I should've known the *Rumspringa* boys wouldn't come back. Not after last weekend.

"Hold on," I tell her. "I'll take a look around."

She nods. "Whatever you say, sensei."

I climb out of the van and start walking. The park feels different now. Bigger. And lonelier too. The empty picnic tables. Spanish moss swaying in the breeze. Strange how a place can change without really changing at all.

When I reach the bridge above the canal, I lean against the railings and look down at the muddy weeds. The snowbirds aren't going to let me into their world. They're good at keeping secrets. And I'll never be one of them.

Headlights brighten the oaks. A car makes a turn on Royal Palm Avenue, spilling light onto the grass. It pulls up to the bridge, moving real slow. The door swings open and Faron gets out.

My breath catches in my throat. What's Faron doing here?

Somebody's moving behind the trees—a skinny boy with a backpack slung over his shoulder. When he reaches the truck, they climb inside, just like me and Alice, the night she disappeared.

I turn and start running back. If I don't get to Crystal in time, the boys will drive away and I'll never find them again.

When I reach her van, I yank open the door.

"We have to leave. Now."

"Hold on. Where's the party?" she says.

"There is no party."

"So where are we going?"

I don't know where.

But we better move fast.

• • •

Faron's truck speeds past a row of trailer homes. Then he pulls into a driveway. The front yard is filled with junk—rusty car parts and smashed-up pieces of furniture.

"No way," says Crystal, shaking her head. "I'm not going in there."

"Fine. I'll go by myself."

When I get out, the damp heat crushes me like a fist. The trailer is only a few miles from Pinecraft, but I'm beginning to realize how far I've gone.

There's a group of boys smoking on the front porch. Their cigarettes glow and disappear as I walk toward the house.

"You again."

Markus is leaning against the railing, blocking the way in. When I see him, my stomach churns.

"Is Faron around?" I ask.

He tosses his cigarette in the dirt. "What are you? His girlfriend?"

"Please. I just want to talk to him."

"Faron's inside," he says, jerking his head toward the open door.

I don't want to go in there. The trailer smells like beer and sweat. A dirty bed sheet hangs over the window. Empty bottles are scattered on the floor where a couple of boys are stretched out in front of a giant television. They're so into their video game, they don't notice me. They shout at the screen, fingers twitching, faces blank. The pictures on the TV aren't real, but it makes me sick, watching them pretend to kill people.

"Lucy?"

A hand brushes against my arm.

"What are you doing here?"

I can hear the shame in Faron's voice. I want him to pull me into a hug. Make the pain go away.

"This is a safe house, isn't it?" I say.

"Something like that." Faron glances at the boys playing their video game. "This ain't a place for you."

"Because I'm not Old Order?"

"Don't even go there," he says.

The *Rumspringa* boys are staring big-time, but they don't say anything as I walk inside the trailer. It's so dark in here, I can barely see. The skinny boy with the backpack is slumped on the couch, looking lost.

"That boy," I whisper, glancing across the room. "You were helping him run away, weren't you?"

Faron turns his head away. "That's right."

"Why didn't you tell me about this place?" I ask, holding back tears.

"Didn't think you would understand. Things are different in the real world. It ain't Pinecraft. Not everybody's your friend."

The front door swings open and Markus steps into the trailer. He yanks down the visor of his baseball cap like he's hiding from the dark.

"You guys look real cozy," he says, glaring at me and Faron. "Maybe you should take it somewhere else."

"Sounds good," says Faron, grabbing my hand. He pulls me toward the dim hallway.

"Where are we going?" I glance up at Faron, but he's looking straight ahead.

"Have fun," Markus calls after him.

Faron tilts his head next to mine. His warm breath is close to my neck. "No worries," he says. "We can talk easy in here."

He leads me into a bedroom. There's a mattress on the floor, circled by piles of dirty clothes. The only light is a candle in a glass, the same kind my dad burns during a hurricane.

Faron closes the door. "I'm sorry, *fehlerfrei*," he says, sinking down on the edge of the mattress.

I sit next to him. It feels strange, being alone in the dark with a boy. "Sorry about what?" I ask, smoothing my skirt over my legs.

"All of this," he mutters.

We're both quiet. I can hear the boys shouting at their video game, making a big deal about killing the bad guys. Maybe the good guys too.

"The Sarasota police were at my house today," I tell him.

"The police?" he says, leaning closer.

"Yeah, a lady sheriff."

"Why? You didn't do nothing."

"Because Alice is my friend."

"They think you know where she's at?"

"No." I swallow hard. "They think I'm the reason she's gone."

"I don't get it," he says. "You and me were at the beach that night. Alice took off by herself."

"The police don't know that. They think it's weird that me and Alice didn't leave the party together."

Faron rubs his eyes, as if he can't stand to look at the world anymore. "Never thought we'd be in so much trouble, just giving some kid a ride."

"How did Tobias know about the safe house?" I ask.

"Word gets around," says Faron. "There's no place to go. Nobody who gives a damn. We pick someplace to meet, like the park tonight. They pay and I drive."

"But what if Tobias isn't Amish?"

"You're thinking Alice met him back home?"

"Maybe," I say, glancing at the quilt on the mattress. It's an Old Order–style pattern, crisscrossed with yellow and blue squares.

"What makes you say that?"

Might as well tell the truth.

"Alice had a secret life."

"That goes for all of us," says Faron.

"It's more than that," I explain. "Alice used to play this game with Tobias. A fantasy game where you can be somebody else."

I'm thinking hard. I saw Tobias in the parking lot that night, bragging about the car he wanted to buy.

*. . . soon as I'm up north . . .*

Did Tobias steal her money and go back north? I think about the fantasy games, how it's easy to believe in something that's not true. Did he trick her into believing he was for real?

There's only one thing left to do.

"I have to go north and find Tobias."

Faron shakes his head. "You'd be wasting your time."

I'm the only one who understands those two worlds—Old Order and English. Nobody else can float between them. Not the way I can. If I go north, looking for Alice, I'll be leaving everything behind. Everything I've ever known. A girl from Pinecraft doesn't just get up and walk away. I'm supposed to sit quiet and still. Keep my mouth shut. Follow the rules.

I glance at the floor. That's when I notice it. A palm frond sticking out of a mason jar. I remember that night when we stood on the bridge in Water Tower Park. Faron daring me to fetch the leaf. He kept it all this time.

Somebody knocks three times, startling me.

Markus hollers behind the door. "You keeping that girl all to yourself?"

Faron doesn't look at me. His face etched in shadow, half lit by the candle, but I can tell he's ashamed.

"You shouldn't be here," he tells me.

"Because of Markus? I'm not scared of him."

Faron smiles. "I know. But maybe you should be," he says, squeezing my hand. "I'll walk you out."

I follow him through the door. Markus is waiting in the hall. He shoves his arm in front of me.

"Going somewhere?"

He's wasted. I can smell the beer on his breath. This isn't good. When I try to step around him, it's no use. He won't budge. Then Faron gets in front of me.

"Move."

"Not until I get a turn," says Markus, stroking my hair.

"I said move."

Faron swings back his fist. It happens so fast, I can't believe what I'm seeing. Markus slams against the wall, groaning. He sort of crouches down, holding his head, like he's going to stand up again.

He doesn't.

"Come on," says Faron, pulling me through the hallway.

When we reach the front porch, I search the road for Crystal's van, but it's not parked there anymore.

She's gone.

Now I've lost another friend, just when I needed her most. I bet she got scared and took off. Not that I blame her. This place is strange to me too. The boys in the safe house, playing their killing games. The way Markus grabbed me like I was nothing more than a joke. Faron's right. I don't belong here.

Neither does he.

As we walk to the truck, he glances back at the house, watching the boys on the front porch. They're watching us too. And they look angry.

"Why are they staring at us?" I ask.

"Come on, Lucy," he says, looking over his shoulder. "Get in the truck."

I stare right back at those boys. "Were you at that party?" I shout. "Did you see what happened to Alice?"

"They're just kids. They don't know anything," says Faron.

The boys mutter at each other in Deitsch. One by one, they toss away their cigarettes and drift inside the trailer.

When the door finally closes, Faron jingles the keys on his belt. "I'll take you home. Pinecraft is only a couple miles from here."

"Because that's what you do. Drive people around."

He shrugs. "Or you could walk."

"Fine."

I've had enough of those boys. Let them sit on that porch until it collapses.

The truck's faded red paint is scratched, making me think of Faron's scars. His hands will always remind him of the pain, no matter how hard he tries to forget. He unlocks the passenger door and I climb inside.

"You got some nerve, talking back like that," he says, but even in the dark, I can see him smiling.

The lucky rabbit's foot dangles from the mirror. I reach up and pinch it between my fingers. It's not soft like I imagined. Sharp bones poke through the brittle, tie-dyed fur. It's just a dead animal's foot.

Nothing magic about it.

## chapter seventeen
# ashes

On the way home, we drive past the empty lot. The stumps are in a heap by the road.

"Can you pull over for a minute?" I ask Faron.

"You really want to go back there?"

I nod.

My heart is pounding as we get out and walk through the charred grass. There's a pile of concrete bricks stacked for a new house. They've already dug a swimming pool. The shallow end is flooded with dirty rainwater. Steps tilt into the muck, going nowhere.

Faron shines his flashlight across the lot. "These fancy new houses take up a lot of space. Wish they'd all burn down." He picks up a rock and throws it at the pile of concrete. "You've got broken glass everywhere," he says, nudging a beer bottle with his sneaker. "Then they chop down all the trees. No more shade and a lot of dry brush. That's an accident waiting to happen."

I stare at the ground, where a chain of footprints stamps the dirt. The pattern reminds me of a leaf threaded by a ribbon. Where have I seen it before?

"It wasn't an accident."

He looks at me. "What's that?"

"Somebody set the fire on purpose."

"You saw them?"

I didn't see. All I have is faith to go by. Yet I know what I believe is true.

I take a deep breath. "It was Tobias."

Faron is quiet.

"I didn't think you'd believe me."

"Come on, Lucy. I'm just trying to understand."

"I'll show you."

We walk across the lot. "See? His sneakers left tracks in the dirt."

"What makes you so sure it's Tobias? Could've been the workers."

"They don't wear fancy sneakers like this. Besides. He never cared about Alice. All he cares about is money. At least, that's what it sounded like."

"What do you mean?" asks Faron.

"I heard him talking that night. And I heard you too."

He blinks. "When was this?"

"You were in the truck, waiting for me and Alice at the drugstore. Tobias was talking about cars. You said it's not worth driving if you can't go fast."

I watch his face. He's confused. Maybe a little scared. "Did you talk to Tobias? He told you, right? That's how you know." He still doesn't get it.

"You said I was the quiet one."

Faron shakes his head. "Yeah, well I was wrong about that."

I'm still not sure if he believes me. But for now, his smile is enough.

As we walk to the truck, I take a closer look at that pile of concrete. The bricks are clean. They weren't damaged in the fire. I remember the burning smell, the morning after Alice disappeared.

"Do you think Tobias came back here after the party?" I ask.

Faron shrugs. "Why would he do that?"

"He was looking for Alice. She told me they got in a fight. When I left the party, he was trying to find her. What if Tobias came back here?"

"Makes sense," says Faron. "This is the last place they were together."

"He was really wasted," I say, remembering how angry he was that night. "What if Tobias came back here and set the fire?"

We're both quiet for a moment.

"Lucy," he finally says. "Why are you so damn smart?"

"I'm not that smart. I just read too much."

"Says who?"

"My dad."

"Well, he's wrong."

• • •

Sunlight dribbles through the orange trees in my front yard. It's early, but Dad's already working outside. He's pushing the wheelbarrow by the tool shed, his face shielded by a straw hat. I sink down a little lower in the truck, hoping he doesn't see me.

"That's your dad, right?" says Faron.

I nod.

"Want me to talk to him?"

"No," I say, shaking my head. "It would only make things worse."

I'm in so much trouble right now. More trouble than I've ever been. Dad must be so disappointed in me. I feel bad because I hurt him. But I don't feel ashamed about staying out all night. That's the confusing part.

"Your dad's a carpenter, huh?" says Faron. "My dad too."

"How did you guess?"

"The gazebo in the yard. Looks pretty solid," he says. "Good Amish craftsmanship, right?"

"We built it together. Me and my dad."

"You?" he says.

"Got the calluses to prove it," I say, lifting my hands.

"Man, you're something else. I never met any girls like you before."

"You mean Amish girls?"

"No," he says. "You're different from any girl I've ever known."

"Is that a good thing?"

"That's a very good thing," he says.

I don't say it out loud, but Faron's different too. He's not like the *Rumspringa* boys in the safe house. He's stronger than all of them.

I just wish he believed it.

He puts his hand on my knee. "When can I see you?"

I need to think of a plan. Dad isn't going to let me leave the house. That's for sure.

"Can we meet up tonight?" I ask.

"Where?"

"Pinecraft Park."

I figure the park is safe enough. It's not that far from my house. Most of the time, it's empty at night. And that's a good thing. In Pinecraft, there's always somebody up in your business.

He squeezes my hand. "I'll be there."

When I climb out of the truck, Dad doesn't say anything. He marches in front of me, blocking the way.

*Please God. Don't let him get too mad.*

Why am I talking to the Lord?

He's probably mad at me too.

Dad watches the truck speed down Kruppa Avenue. "Must be nice having no responsibilities."

"It won't happen again."

This isn't the first time I've made that promise. But it's the second time I've broken it.

"You're right. It won't happen again," Dad says. "Because I won't have you chasing after a *Rumspringa* boy."

It's so unfair, the way he's judging me.

"Faron's not on *Rumspringa*. He's not even with the Old Order anymore. That's why he's been shunned."

"Either you're Amish or you're not. You can't pick and choose."

"I thought *Rumspringa* was supposed to be a choice."

"You are not on *Rumspringa*, Lucy. And you're old enough to know right from wrong. Do you want to end up like your friend, Alice?"

Now he's judging her too?

"You're talking like the Old Order is messed up and we're so perfect."

"No, we aren't perfect," Dad says. "But let me tell you something, Lucy. We are different from the Old Order. We have rules."

"What if I don't like the rules?"

He frowns. "You want to run that by me again?"

"I can't stay in Pinecraft forever."

I've finally said it.

I wait for Dad to start yelling. Instead, he sighs. "Fine. You've got time to decide."

He doesn't say *choose*.

All this time, I've been holding my dream inside. Keeping my mouth shut. Watching from a distance, quiet as a ghost.

I'm not going to be quiet anymore.

"Dad, I've already made my decision."

"And what's that?"

"I want to go to college and study the ocean."

He shakes his head. "The ocean's right here. What do you need school for?"

Dad can't understand why I spend hours at the library. He says I'm filling my head with lies. He doesn't believe in a world that changes and grows. That's not how the Lord made it. But I think the Lord's too big for a world that small.

"It's not just about school. I want to keep learning new things. But I can't do that if I stay here."

"You are hurting me, Lucy," he says, rubbing his eyes. "I was up all night, thinking the worst. Does it even matter to you?"

Yeah, it matters.

A lot.

"Nothing happened," I say, lowering my head.

"And you expect me to believe you?"

"Please. Just listen."

"I'm done listening."

Right then, I wish Dad would hit me. At least the pain would be quick. Instead, it's hidden deep inside where I can't get away from it.

"Come with me," he says, walking behind the house.

This is going to be bad.

I follow him into the shade of the orange grove. All the trees are lined up in rows, as tidy as stitches on a quilt. Dad crouches beside my favorite tree. There's an axe buried deep in its trunk.

"Can't save it, once the canker takes hold," he says, passing the axe to me.

"Not that one."

He shrugs. "It's got the sickness."

"But that's my tree."

"I'm sorry, Lucy. It has to be done."

"Please don't make me do this." I'm begging him.

Dad's already walking away. "Better cut it down. Or else the canker will spread to the others."

The axe is heavy in my fist. I stare at my favorite tree, the branches so thick with fruit, they sway toward the grass. It doesn't look sick at all.

I press my hand against the tree one last time.

"I'm sorry," I whisper.

I blink away my tears. Then I swing the axe into the trunk. Chips of bark fly against my skirt. Over and over, I slam the blade into the wood, all my anger and sadness. My dress is soaked with sweat. The sun disappears behind the clouds, hinting at rain. Still, I keep hacking until my blisters crack and bleed.

After what seems like forever, the trunk begins to lean. I back away, coughing as dust mazes the air. The tree seems to fall in slow motion. Branches swoop across the sky and smash into the ground. All that's left of my favorite orange tree is a stump.

I've cut down plenty of trees with Dad. It never was this hard. How can something so big disappear into nothing? The smell of sap and citrus lingers in the breeze. In a couple months, I would've picked that fruit. We always gave away oranges for Christmas.

I kneel beside the stump and count the rings.

It was the same age as me.

## chapter eighteen
# chain of stitches

I rinse my hands at the kitchen sink. I'm so exhausted, I don't even notice the plate of leftovers until I sit down. The cold chicken and potato salad is just stuff I'm shoveling into my mouth, keeping me alive.

On the table, there's a wicker basket. It used to be Mama's, a long time ago. Inside it, I find her sewing needles. I close my eyes and try to imagine her in this chair, stitching a quilt.

"You never learned."

Dad's in the kitchen, tugging off his work gloves. Ever since I was little, I always thought my dad was strong. Now he looks tired and worn-out. For the first time, I notice the gray staining his beard.

"Maybe you just need a little practice," he says, sitting across from me.

"Sewing isn't really my thing," I tell him.

"That doesn't mean you can't try."

Dad reaches into the sewing basket and pulls out an Amish-style quilt. The blue and yellow squares are so beautiful, I'm afraid to touch them.

"It's an old pattern from Lancaster County," he says, unfolding the quilt on the table. "This one's called Sunshine and Shadow. We've got to deal with both in our lives, Smidge. The good and the bad. But that's what makes us strong."

When I hear him say this, my eyes sting.

He folds his hand over mine. "Maybe someday you'll finish that quilt. You got your mama's long fingers."

I can't hold back anymore. Hot tears slide down my chin and splat on the table. It feels like everything is lost. All the breath I've got left.

"You're scaring me, Lucy," he says. "I don't know my own daughter anymore."

He doesn't understand.

I'm more *myself* than before.

"What's happening to you?" Dad stares out the kitchen window, as if the answer is hidden in the ponds, the Spanish moss, the orange trees. Even the sky looks darker now.

I don't want to stay still. I'm not like the oak trees in our backyard. I'm more like the Gulf, shifting back and forth. Or the sandhill cranes that swoop across the marshes in winter, too many to count.

"So you met an Old Order boy," he says quietly.

I swallow hard. "Yes."

Dad's been waiting for this. All he wants is for me to "get settled." But I can't think about settling down. Not when there's so much I want to do.

"It's one thing to have an Old Order friend," Dad tells me. "But their world is very different from ours." He says it again, louder this time. "Very different."

"Faron is different."

He's not like the *Rumspringa* boys on the basketball court. Maybe he grew up Old Order, but he chose to walk away. And if you grow up Amish, it's supposed to be your choice. It's not about the clothes you wear. Or if you're allowed to drive a car or watch TV. It's not about the outside world.

It's about the way you look at it.

Dad grabs my hand. "Feel like talking?"

I do.

Once I get going, I can't stop. I tell Dad about what really happened in Water Tower Park the night Alice disappeared.

I finally tell the truth.

"Me and Alice got in a fight," I say, my voice shaking. "She didn't want to go home. So I left without her."

"You made a bad decision," he says. "But so did Alice. You both have to take responsibility. It's done now. Can't go back and change it."

He gets up and puts his arms around me. Now I'm sinking against him, letting it all pour out. The weight of my secrets. All the hurt I've carried inside.

I glance at the calendar on the kitchen wall. A horse and buggy plowing through a snowstorm. I've never tasted snow. Never petted a horse. The only buggy I've seen is a mural outside the diner on Beneva Road.

"There's something I want to tell you," Dad says.

I'm listening.

"When I was your age, I had an Old Order friend. We were close, like you and Alice. He came down to Florida on *Rumspringa*. Got himself a real nice car. Drove all over Sarasota in it. Always wanted to go fast," he says, shaking his head. "Too fast."

At first, I don't understand. Then I get a shivery feeling. No wonder Dad never lets me drive anywhere.

"How come you never told me?" I ask.

"It's in the past now," he says.

. . . *that's where the past belongs* . . .

"Did your friend run away from the Old Order too?"

"You can't run from trouble, Smidge," he says. "It will find you, one way or another."

I feel scooped out and empty. I can't even cry anymore. If me and Dad are trading secrets, there's more I need to say.

"Dad I'm not going to . . ."

I can't get out the words.

"Not going to do what?" he asks.

"I'm not going to get baptized."

Silence.

I wait for him to say I'm making a mistake. Instead, he sighs.

"Tell me why."

"Because . . . I just . . ."

What am I supposed to say?

"I'm not sure."

"About baptism?"

Dad thinks I've lost my faith. But he's wrong. I'm supposed to follow the rules. If I do everything right, I'll be okay. Keep my mouth shut. Don't think too much. Stop asking so many questions.

"I don't want to stay in Pinecraft. I can't get baptized now. I want to go to college and study the ocean."

"College is a lot of money. More than we can afford."

"I know. That's why I've been applying for scholarships."

"What? You did this without telling me?"

Now I've told the truth. If Dad's going to start treating me like an adult, I need to be honest with him.

He sighs. "Lucy, why do you love the ocean so much?"

In my mind, I see the Gulf at sunrise. The Old Order girls in their long dresses, laughing in the surf. The poison in the water. The tide, how it gives and takes away.

"The ocean is everything to me."

"Well, it's too late to be making this decision," he says.

It's not too late.

"What if I get accepted? The school's real close. I could work at home and take classes at night."

Now I've done it.

"You already have work to do," he says. "And that work is here."

Dad thinks school is all about getting a job. But it's a lot more than that. He doesn't want me taking classes. He thinks it's dangerous because I'm filling my head with lies.

The ocean is dangerous too.

But that doesn't mean I'm going to hide from it.

All this time, I've been wishing for my own *Rumspringa*. I was jealous of Alice's freedom. The things I couldn't have.

I don't need *Rumspringa*.

I can make my own.

"I'm waiting for that letter," I tell him. "And if it comes, does that mean . . ." I can't say it out loud. Would my dad push me away? I mean, would he *shun* me?

He blinks. "Lucy, I don't want to lose you. But if that school says yes, we're going to cross that bridge together. Let's talk about it later," he says, getting up from the table. "Tomorrow's a big day."

Tomorrow.

My baptism.

"I'm not going to church tomorrow."

Dad turns around. "And why is that?"

"Because I won't be here." No more sneaking around. Dad needs to know the truth.

"What do you mean?" he says, horrified.

"I can't go through with it, Dad. It's not my choice. It's yours. All this time, I've been trying so hard to be perfect for you. I was afraid of messing up. Scared of doing the wrong thing. But how am I supposed to learn if I don't make mistakes?"

"This is the biggest mistake of all," he mutters.

I've never stood up to Dad before. I get the feeling he's having a hard time, learning how to listen.

"It's my decision."

"So that's it? You're running away?"

He's wrong.

I'm not running from something.

"I'm going to find Alice."

"How?"

When I don't answer, he says, "You and that *Rumspringa* boy?" Dad shakes his head. "I won't allow it, Lucy. You're pushing too far."

"I can't stay here, Dad. Not if she's in trouble."

"Yeah? Well, *I* need you here."

"What if it was your friend? Wouldn't you do the same for him?" I'm almost shouting.

Now it's Dad's turn to stay quiet.

The house is quiet too. All the backyard noises drift into the kitchen, filling up the empty spaces. Cicadas buzzing in the oaks. The breeze scraping their branches across the roof. Music I've heard so often, it's become part of me, like the sound of my own breath.

The quiet doesn't last long. I recognize the sway of those branches. It means the rain's about to let loose. And then it does.

Dad races outside. He heads straight for the workshop and I follow, running as fast as a girl can run in a long skirt. The paint hasn't set on the gazebo. All that work, gone in minutes. It's too late to save it, but Dad's hauling out the blue tarp.

"Help me," he says, as I grab the other end.

Together we yank the plastic tarp over the gazebo. Dad doesn't need the ladder. He's tall enough to snap it over the roof. I help him spread out the corners, blinking as the cold, hard drops plunk into my eyes. Still, Dad won't give up. He keeps pulling that tarp in every direction, trying to make things right.

"It's no good now. We have to start over." Dad throws the tarp on the ground in a crumpled heap. I've never seen him so worn out. It's like he's been tugging on a rope and finally let go.

I fold the tarp like a blanket, pulling the corners to the middle. Gently, I lift it up and pass it to my dad.

"Don't do this to me, Lucy," he says.

Dad stands under the gazebo, his face slick with rain. He watches in silence as I turn and walk through the orange grove.

• • •

In Pinecraft Park, the streetlamps glow above the basketball court. Nobody's behind the chainlink fence tonight. The storm has slowed to a drizzle. I stand under an oak tree, shivering as raindrops leak off the branches. Minutes pass. After a while, I'm starting to wonder if Faron's going to show up. Then I see him walking toward me in the rain. He's got his hood pulled up and his face is lost in shadow.

My dress is soaked, the skirt clinging to my legs. I'm suddenly aware of my body, the rise and fall of my chest. It feels strange, meeting a boy in the park at night. But there's nobody here to see. No eyes to judge us.

"I thought you weren't coming." When I smile, he doesn't smile back.

"They wouldn't listen," he tells me.

"Who?"

"I told them you're one of us."

He's not making any sense. "What happened?"

"I got kicked out."

"They kicked you out of the safe house?"

"Something like that."

I remember the way those Old Order boys looked at me. The stares from the porch as we walked to the truck. "This is all my fault."

"It ain't nobody's fault." Faron shakes his head. "I can't stay down in Florida anymore. I got no money left."

"What are you going to do?"

"Go back home, I guess."

I'm stunned. "But I thought you were . . ."

He stares at his hands. "If I go crawling back north, I'll have to ask Dad for my old job at the sawmill."

I know this isn't what he wants. It would kill him inside.

"What if I go with you?" I ask.

"Lucy, you don't get it. Things are different up north. *We're* different."

I never thought he'd say that.

"You don't want me to go."

"Of course, I do. But you've got to understand. Up north, it ain't like Pinecraft. It's the real world."

"I don't even know what that means. What's real?"

"This," he says, leaning in.

As we kiss, there's the familiar tug of electricity. That's all we are. The world is made of invisible things following secret rules, like seagulls and the tides, and all the things we feel but can't see.

I feel it now.

We walk to Bahia Vista Street. Every car is speeding fast. If I tried to count their headlights, I'd lose my place. Just disappear. I think about Tobias, the way he smiled when Alice showed him that money. The make-believe games about death and blood.

I explain about the video Tobias put online. "It's more than a game to them. It's like their own secret world. No wonder Alice got caught up in it."

All the LARPers will be camping at Blackwoods in Acadia National Park this week. Crystal's going to be there. She can help us.

If she ever talks to me again.

"How long will it take to drive there?" I ask.

"A couple days, if I punch it."

"What if I drive too?"

"You want to drive the truck?"

I nod.

"Lucy, you're something else," he says, laughing.

"I want to learn."

"You will. It just takes time."

The truck is parked on the side of the road. I'd hardly notice it, except for the frayed piece of rope holding the broken pieces together.

"How did you learn to drive?"

Faron shrugs. "Taught myself."

"Yeah, but you're like a car expert or something."

"Nah. It ain't hard," he says, putting his arm around me.

There's another question burning in my mind. Something I've been wondering, but too afraid to ask.

"Where did you get the truck?"

Faron's smile fades. "I already told you. Built most of it from scrap."

"But how?"

"See this?" he says, crouching next to the fender. "It's from another old truck. So is the engine. The brakes too. All from the junkyard."

"So you put it back together."

"That's right," he says, a little too quickly.

"What about the rest of it?"

Faron looks at the ground. "What about it?"

I don't want to ask this question. But I'd rather know the truth than keep pretending it's okay.

"Did you steal the parts for this truck?"

He doesn't answer.

"Did you?"

"Yeah, I did," he says, lowering his head.

It hurts, hearing him admit this out loud.

"But you know what? Who gives a damn about a broken-down truck? After I got hurt at the sawmill, I couldn't work no more. Believe me, Lucy. I tried. Got shot down every place I went." He stares at his hands. "Nobody wants to hire the stupid Amish kid."

"You're not stupid."

"Tell that to my dad," he mutters.

I want to take away the hurt. Fix him.

But I can't go back in time.

"It's in the past," says Faron, like he's eavesdropping on my mind. "I already told you, Lucy. I've done a lot of stupid things. No use lying. But I want to do better."

He's not the only one.

"I'm sorry I let you down," he says. "You probably hate me right now."

"I don't hate you."

Headlights cut across the park. There's a car moving real slow, turning around the block. It cruises next to us and the window rolls down.

"You guys okay?" a voice calls out.

Ricketts.

What's she doing here? She's not in a police car like last time. Maybe she's driving around Pinecraft, looking for trouble.

Or looking for me.

"Kind of late to be in the park," says Ricketts, glaring at me. "What do you say I give you a ride home?"

"It's not too far to walk," I say, but she still doesn't leave.

"All right, Lucy," she says. "I remember."

I bet you do.

The window rolls up halfway. "Be safe now," she adds, driving away. I watch the headlights fade behind the oak trees.

"Let me guess," says Faron. "That was your friend, the sheriff?"

"She'll go after my dad next. This could really hurt him. I mean, he could lose his job, the house . . . everything."

"Then we better move fast."

As we head to the truck, there's a rustling above us. The green parrots. I watch them flicker through the branches. Then I notice someone coming toward us. Just by the slopey way he's walking between the trees, I know it's Jacob.

"Your dad said I'd find you here," he mumbles.

"Go home, Jacob."

He glances at Faron. "So it's true. You and him."

"This is none of your business."

"Why are you doing this?" he asks. "There's nothing out there for you, Lucy. Nothing you can't find here."

What makes him so sure? He's never been far from Pinecraft. As far as I can tell, he's never going to leave. That's his choice. Not mine.

"Please," I tell him. "This is something I need to do. I know you don't understand."

Jacob gets in front of me, blocking the way. "I used to think you were smart," he says. "But I was wrong."

It hurts, the way he's talking so mean. He probably thought we'd end up together. But here's the cold honest truth: Jacob would be a lot happier with a Mennonite girl from Pinecraft.

I push ahead of him.

"You're no better than anybody else," he shouts at me.

I never said I was better. Just different, that's all. And I'm smart enough to know I don't belong. If I stayed here, I'd always be wondering. Always questioning. And that's why I have to leave.

When Faron starts the engine, I'm almost ready to walk away. Turn around and walk home, where nothing ever changes. I march right up to that truck and grab hold of the door. Then I scoot next to him.

Faron stares out the windshield at the drizzly rain. "You sure about this?"

The lucky rabbit's foot swings back and forth, the keys winking in the streetlight. If only we could stay inside the truck forever, while the traffic swirls around backyards so empty, even birds don't rest there. I want to hold the Gulf in my fist, let the salt water rinse away the past.

"Yeah, I'm sure."

He reaches across the seat and kisses me. "You're a brave girl, Lucy Zimmer."

# quilts

All night, Faron drives. I crack the window and breathe in the smells of new places. Every so often, I spot a fish camp on the side of the road. Brightly painted shacks rising on stilts. Plywood signs for mangrove snapper and smoked mullet. Hours pass and I don't say a word.

"Ever been this far from Pinecraft?" Faron asks.

"Never."

"It's kind of scary, right?"

Yeah, I'm scared.

In the morning, Dad's going to wake up to an empty house. He won't understand why I'm gone. He'll probably think I've run off like Alice.

He won't understand what I'm looking for.

"First time I left home, I couldn't sleep," Faron says. "It takes some getting used to."

"What does?"

"Being on your own," he says, looking at the road.

A siren wails in the distance. All of a sudden, a flood of blue and red light swells inside the truck. I turn around, squeezing my eyes against the brightness. I can't stop thinking about what Faron told me. This truck doesn't belong to him. I don't care if he built it from scrap.

"You never got caught," I say quietly.

Faron watches the police car swerve ahead of us. "That don't make it right. Is that what you're saying?"

"I didn't say it."

"But you're thinking it."

"What if someone finds out?" I ask.

"They can't tell, just by looking. Nobody knows what I did."

"And what happens if we get pulled over?"

"Then we're both in trouble," he says, cutting into the next lane.

Near the highway a billboard rises above the straggly trees. A girl, her red mouth. Then another girl. Bleached hair and smiling teeth. The woods are filled with billboards, their silent faces zipping past us, one by one.

When Alice stepped off the bus in Pinecraft, I couldn't imagine I'd be on the road looking for her. Everything's different here. I've never seen buildings that tall, their jagged shapes filled with light, yet somehow so empty.

As we speed across a bridge, I study the cables slanting above us like a rib cage. That's all that keeps us from falling.

"Are we still in Florida?"

"Jacksonville," he says. "About an hour from the border."

Already I'm so far from home. Even if we turned around, it feels like I'm never going back.

• • •

The sky is still dark, though morning's coming soon. Faron's been driving for hours. When I look through the windshield, I can't tell where we're headed.

North.

That's all I know.

My eyes burn from lack of sleep. I can barely keep them open. Then the truck begins to drift into the next lane, sparking a round of honks, and I know that Faron must be tired too. More than tired.

"We've got to pull over," he says, jerking the wheel. "Or else I'm going to wake up in a ditch."

"Where?"

"Somewhere not in plain sight."

I squint at the field beside the road. Picket fences, arranged in a circle. There's no place to hide the truck, so we keep driving. A couple minutes later, we pass a silo on a hill. Maybe it belongs to a farmer. I've never seen a real farm. Only the pictures in Alice's old recipe book.

"Over there?" I say, pointing at the woods.

He shakes his head. "The sun's going to rise pretty soon. We can't take a chance on a farm. They might already be up."

We get off the highway at the next exit. Faron steers the truck down a dirt road, searching for a spot that looks good. A sign says there's fifty acres for sale. All those pine trees, ready to be chopped down and turned into *Luxury Homes* with *Spectacular Lake Views*.

"What about there? Does that work?" I ask.

"Works good," he says, cutting the headlights. We cruise real slow, bumping our way through the vacant lot. Branches scrape against the window. I can barely see the "spectacular view." It's more like a shimmer behind the trees. A promise of something better. Or a wish that you know won't come true.

I climb out of the truck and the cold slams into me. When I tried to imagine someplace that wasn't home, I didn't picture this muddy patch of land. I thought it would be bigger somehow. And I always thought I'd be alone. I'm not sure why. It's just the way I'd always been.

"You cold?" says Faron, unzipping his backpack. He takes out a quilt. It's a Morning Star pattern, crisscrossed with blue and yellow squares. "This used to be my mom's," he tells me, unfolding it in the truck bed.

"It's beautiful," I tell him. And it is.

"She made this quilt. I've had it since I was little."

"I have one too."

"Yeah?" he says, smiling. "Did your mom sew it for you?"

It's strange, but I didn't realize until now. Mama probably stitched that quilt for me a long time ago. Maybe before I was born.

"She's gone now," I say, watching him spread out the quilt.

"I'm sorry," he says.

"She died after I was born. That's what Dad told me. Fever or something."

Faron is quiet for a moment. "That doesn't mean you can't miss her."

He's right.

In a way, I do miss Mama, though I never knew her. Most of all, I miss the conversations we never had. As much as I love my dad, it's not the same thing. I can't tell him my secrets. Or ask him questions. At least, the kind I've had lately.

I stare at the quilt in the back of that truck. A rush of heat floods through me. Of course, we're sleeping together. I mean, side by side. I want to act like it doesn't mean anything. No big deal. But I've never been this close to a boy. Never done more than kissing.

"You go first," I say.

Now Faron's the one who seems nervous. He reaches up and pushes back his hair. "I'm going to take my jeans off, okay?"

I nod.

He turns his back to me. It's sort of sweet and ridiculous at the same time. I mean, it's not like I can't see him. Slowly, he tugs off his jeans. He unzips his hoodie and shrugs out of the sleeves. Then he yanks his T-shirt over his head. Maybe he can feel me watching, but I don't look away.

I remember Alice talking about the guys back in Maine. One time, Alice told me she liked looking at their arms. The muscles in their legs. That's all. She said kissing was fun, but she couldn't imagine sleeping with a boy. The way she talked about it made me wonder if I'd ever want to. But I like looking at Faron.

All of him.

"Come on, Lucy," he says, climbing in the back of the truck.

When I slide under the quilt, he doesn't move. He's right there, looking up at the stars. I listen to the rise and fall of his breath, wishing he'd turn over and hold me.

I reach under the folds of the quilt and find his hand. He squeezes my fingers and I squeeze back. If I were Old Order, I'd wear a "night dress." Alice used to talk about *bundling*. When a boy likes somebody special, they stay awake in bed, holding each other until sunrise. The girls wear fancy clothes—long, colorful "night dresses."

Well, I'm not wearing anything fancy tonight. Just my plain old cotton dress. It's strange, feeling the warmth of Faron's body next to mine, his warmth so close.

Strange in a good way.

"Everything's so quiet," I whisper.

"That's why I couldn't sleep when I left home," he says. "All that noise inside my head."

"What do you mean?"

"You hear the cars, right? City noise. Back home, it's noisy too. Never had any space to myself. Now I'm free. Nobody bossing me around. But it's kind of empty without my mom and dad."

"You miss them."

"A lot."

Faron tells me about Maine. The ice on the river, the way it shudders when it thaws. The mossy smell of the fields. In Pinecraft, I never saw the seasons change. He makes it sound like a new beginning, a fresh start.

"But you still wanted to leave home."

"I spent my whole life hearing no," he tells me. "All I wanted was a yes. Once I got down to Florida, it felt like I had to hurry up and try everything. Looking back, it's pretty obvious I was going nowhere."

"I wanted to leave home too," I whisper. "But I was too scared."

"You?" He laughs. "Lucy Zimmer, you're the bravest girl I ever met."

Maybe I am brave.

"But not like Alice. She's the brave one."

"That's because you're her friend," he says.

I never saw it that way before.

Did Alice look up to me, the way I'd always looked up to her? Maybe we looked up to each other.

I want to ask Faron more questions, but it feels like we've already gone too far. "Is it weird, being up north again?"

"This ain't north." He kisses my forehead.

"Alice said it got so cold in winter, her eyelashes froze. She used to wash her hair in a bucket."

"Yeah, it's hard, growing up Old Order," he says. "One time, my dad killed a chicken right in front of me. Just swung it over his head, real fast, and snapped its neck. Then he made me yank out the feathers. The whole time I'm in the barn, thinking, What if there's nothing else? We die and go into the ground. That's it."

At night, I close my eyes and try to picture it. The emptiness. It scares me more than any hell I can imagine.

"I was just a little kid," says Faron.

When his voice cracks, I know he's fighting back tears. I reach for him under the quilt and we're kissing again. His mouth is warm against mine. All the space between us has closed up.

For now, it's enough.

## chapter twenty
# blackwoods

I'm shivering in the truck, huddled under a blank sky at dawn. It's so cold, my breath is steaming. The trees take on a hazy shimmer, like my backyard after it rains. In the field, there's a goose staring back at me.

"Look." I nudge Faron. The grass is swarming with them. "What are they thinking?"

"Breakfast. Same thing I'm thinking."

"Why haven't they left yet?"

"You mean south?" he says. "They'll fly when they're ready. I always wondered how they know where to go."

The geese are travelers, too. Every year, they head south along an invisible path in the sky.

"They see things we can't see."

That's how they know.

When we pull onto the highway, the sun's coming up. The air inside the truck is thick. I lean back against the seat and roll down the window. I didn't sleep much last night. I felt the road unwinding, the way you can still feel the ocean long after it pushes against your skin.

After a while, we stop at a gas station. I'm starting to wonder if we can reach Blackwoods tonight. What if Tobias isn't at the games? Maybe we're driving all this way for nothing. But it's a chance I'm willing to take.

"Want to stretch your legs?" says Faron, climbing out of the truck. "I could use a Coke."

"Okay." My dad never let me drink soda.

We walk to the vending machines, where a boy in a puffy jacket is slumped on a bench, smoking a cigarette. He seems nervous for some reason, bouncing his leg and looking around, like he's not sure what to do.

"See that kid? He's on *Rumspringa*," Faron says.

"How do you know?"

Faron shrugs. "I just do."

The boy watches us plunk quarters into the slot. His eyes meet mine, and I quickly look away.

"Are you really going to talk to your dad?" I ask Faron.

"That depends on whether he'll talk to me."

Inside, I'm churning. Faron can't go home. He doesn't belong with the Old Order.

What's going to happen if he tries?

We get back in the truck. When I look out the window, the boy is still on the bench, watching us speed onto the highway.

• • •

By the time we reach Maine that night, it's so dark, I can barely see the farms beside the road. The woods are filled with secret things. Treehouses, no longer hidden by leaves. A swimming pool draped in a blue tarp. Horses leaning over a stream.

"Where are we?" I ask.

Faron tugs up his hood. "North."

I glance at the mountains, the way they chisel into the horizon. "Tobias was here with Alice last summer."

"That's in the past. What makes you think he's here now?"

"Because it's his safe house."

The LARPers have their own secret world, just like the *Rumspringa* boys. They need somewhere to belong. When they couldn't find that place, they made one.

We're following the signs to Acadia National Park. Faron is driving fast, cutting ahead of the trucks on the highway.

"So what kind of game is this anyway?" he asks.

I try to think of how to describe it. "You can make believe you're somebody else. It's like pretending."

"What do they pretend?"

"Battles, mostly."

"Never heard of a game like that," he says.

The park is so big, I don't know where to look for their campsite. Soon we find the sign for Blackwoods, and Faron pulls over. He reaches into his backpack, takes out a heavy wool coat, and slides it over my shoulders. It's an Old Order–style coat. No buttons. The lining smells like cedar and smoke.

"Aren't you cold?" I ask.

"I never get cold."

He fumbles with the hooks, latching it tight. "There you go," he says. "All you need is a pair of boots."

If somebody looked at me, they wouldn't know my family's Amish-Mennonite.

Maybe they wouldn't know I'm a girl.

• • •

It's cold when we get out of the truck. Colder than I've ever been in my whole life.

Faron grabs my hand. "You ready for this?"

I nod. "More than ready."

Together we march up the trail. Branches snap against my chest. I stumble along, tripping over things I can't see. Rocks and fallen logs. I listen to the night noises swirling around us. The crunch of our sneakers. Crickets sawing away.

A shout breaks through the quiet. Faron pulls me along the trail, aiming his flashlight at the woods. We run toward the sound, winding our way through the bone-white trees. The clearing ahead is dotted with tents. Flags snap in the breeze.

"This must be their camp," I tell him.

Somebody darts between the trees. On her back is a pair of glittery wings, reminding me of Alice's costume. I can't let her get away. Not after I've come so far.

"Lucy," Faron shouts.

I take off, running after her. The girl races ahead, her wings bouncing as she zigzags through the brush. She swerves off the trail and disappears into the woods.

When Faron catches up with me, he says, "Don't go running off like that." He blinks. "Is that how you play the game?"

I aim the flashlight at the ground. The girl is face-down in the dirt, her wings splayed out, as if she fell from the sky.

She lifts her head.

"Do you guys have a healing potion?" She squints into my flashlight. "I really hate being dead."

"Sorry," I tell her.

"That's okay," she says, standing. She wipes the dirt off her face. "What dimension did you guys come from?"

"Florida."

The dead girl blinks. "For real? I knew we had a lot of chapters but . . . you came all that way to Blackwoods?"

"We're not actually here to play," I explain. "I'm looking for Tobias. Have you seen him?"

She frowns. "You know Toby?"

I don't know if I should say more. When I mentioned his name, she didn't look happy. If Tobias got himself in trouble with this girl, she's not going to talk to us.

"He's supposed to be here with his girlfriend," I say.

"You mean Sarah?" she says.

I'm so surprised, I can't answer.

Who's Sarah?

Just then, a boy stumbles out of the bushes. He's wearing a long, black robe decorated with stars. His pointy hat keeps slipping over his glasses.

"Am I too late?" he says, gasping for breath.

"You were supposed to save me, Ben." She rolls her eyes.

"Sure thing, my lady. Hold on." He reaches into his knapsack and flings something into the air. "Healing potion," he yells, as sunflower seeds rain down on us. He pops one in his mouth and chews. "Good thing my magic is environmentally friendly."

"Be serious, okay? I just got ransacked by pirates."

He stares at me and Faron. "Are you here for glorious battle?"

"We didn't do anything," I tell him.

She shrugs. "They're looking for Toby."

"Everybody's looking for that kid. But he flaked out this year," says Ben. "It's totally messing up the game. All our Plot Members are gone now."

"Where is Tobias?" I ask.

"Tobias? That's his real name?" Ben says, laughing. "We used to battle it out online, playing *World of Warcraft*."

"So you played games online?"

"That's how I know Toby. We didn't hang out much I.R.L."

"What does that mean?"

"You know. In real life."

Is that how Alice met her boyfriend? They played games online? If that's true, I'm even more scared for her.

Maybe Alice doesn't know Tobias "in real life" either.

They probably started talking online last summer. Maybe she thought he could help her escape the Old Order. I remember Alice standing outside the basketball court, watching the *Rumspringa* boys, the way her eyes shined.

"Toby was always starting fights," says Ben. "He's got anger management issues. No joke. When I invited him to Blackwoods last summer, I didn't even know he had a girlfriend."

"Is her name Sarah?" I ask.

"Yeah, I think so. This girl was super cute. Don't know why she's going out with Toby. I mean, she could do so much better. Anyway, I tried to get him into LARPing. I thought it would be more fun than gaming, you know? Get out some aggression. And it was fun, at first. Then Toby starting freaking out."

"What happened?"

"Like I told you. That kid's got problems. He always has to win. And if things don't go his way, he freaks out."

The dead girl nods. "One time, he pushed this girl so hard, she fell and twisted her ankle or something. All because of a stupid game."

"Of course, he says it wasn't on purpose," says Ben. "Nobody believes him. So we kicked him out."

"That's why he's not at Blackwoods? He got kicked out of the game?"

"Yeah," says Ben. "We tried to give him a second chance, but the whole thing's pretty messed up."

"When was the last time you saw him?" I ask.

"I think he was down in Florida or something. He just got back a couple days ago. Took a bus home or something." Ben digs around inside his knapsack. "He left this at my place," he says, taking out a video camera. "Toby was supposed to film the battles tonight," he says. "That's all he's allowed to do. But obviously that's not happening."

"Let me do it."

All my life, I've hidden myself from cameras. Now Ben is showing me how to work the GoPro. "This thing is so sweet. He was going to strap it on his helmet. Are you sure you can handle it?"

I nod. "I'll do my best."

"Awesome. If you find Toby, you can give it back. Many thanks, my lady," he says, bowing so low, his hat flops into the grass.

• • •

"I didn't know mountains were so big," I tell Faron as we head through the woods back down the trail.

"That's why it's hard to move them," he says.

"What if Tobias is hiding out somewhere? I mean, he could still be at the games, right?"

Faron shakes his head. "It doesn't sound like anybody really knows him."

"Ben said Tobias left that camera at his house a couple days ago. That means he's here in Maine."

"Yeah, but if Tobias is Old Order, why does he have a video camera?"

"Maybe he's on *Rumspringa*."

"That's what I thought," says Faron. "But there's something about Tobias that doesn't make sense. Did Alice say how they met?"

"I'm not sure," I say, looking up at the sky. All those stars. "She said they were hanging out last summer."

"That's when he played *Warcraft* online with Ben."

"So?"

"It's not like a real friend," he says.

"Maybe that's how he met Alice."

"You think she met this guy online?"

"Yes."

"Then she's in a lot of trouble," says Faron.

If Alice met her boyfriend online, he could be anyone. When I thought Tobias was Old Order, I wasn't so scared. He was one of us. Now I'm wondering how many girls he talked to online.

Did he really care about Alice?

Or was he just pretending?

When we reach the campsite, there's nobody around. The tents are circling the bonfire, the air laced with smoke. There's a flag with a skull and crossbones dangling from a tree. It gives me the shivers, just looking at it.

Faron pokes his head into one of the tents.

"What are you doing?"

"You'd rather sleep in the truck?" he says, climbing inside.

"Don't you think we should ask first?"

"Ask who? Everybody's in the woods, pretending to kill each other."

"Okay," I tell him. "But if we get caught, it's your fault."

"Deal," he says.

I shove my way inside the tent. He's right. It's a lot better than sleeping in the truck. Warmer too. I stretch out on the blanket next to him.

"Still got that camera?" he asks.

"Yeah. But I don't know how to use it."

"Easy," he says. "Just start pushing buttons."

I don't see any buttons. When I touch the screen, it brightens into a picture. A crowd of girls dancing in the woods. Oak trees and Spanish moss. The water tower, rising above it all.

"It's Water Tower Park."

The picture goes dark. Nothing else to see.

"Can you make it start at the beginning?" asks Faron.

I press the screen again. The picture melts into a blur, racing backward. Now we're at the party, swaying in the crowd. Music thudding. All the girls in their bonnets, smoking behind the trees. I scan their faces, searching for Alice.

Two girls slip out of the woods. One in a tank top and jeans. The other, dressed plain.

*"This isn't fun anymore."*

*"Then leave."*

It's like looking through somebody else's eyes.

Me and Alice, fighting about going home.

You can't erase the past. But I get the feeling that's exactly what Tobias tried to do.

The camera goes dark. For a second, I think I've seen everything. Then I hear Alice crying. She's in the backseat of a car, her face streaked with tears.

"Stop it," she says. "You're hurting me."

Somebody's laughing in the background. I know that laugh. It's been with me since the night of the party.

"Get over here," says Tobias.

She reaches for the door handle, but he's too fast.

"I said get over here."

He slams her head against the window. Alice's body slumps forward, knocking the camera off the seat, and there's nothing else to see.

*July 18*
*Smyrna, Maine*

*Dear Lucy,*

*I met a boy.*
*His name's Tobias.*
*We just started talking, but I know he's perfect. When he smiles, I'm flying. He makes me laugh. And he's got the most amazing eyes. I can't stop thinking about us together. I know it's going to happen. I just don't know how.*

*It feels like the whole world has changed color. Even the sky is bluer. I was so busy staring at it this morning as I walked to the Amish Market, I dropped my quilts in the mud. I must've looked ridiculous, standing there, giggling. I just couldn't help it! Mr. Lapp came by in his buggy. "Only the devil laughs all the time," he said. Then I laughed even more. You should've seen his face!*

*Promise not to tell anybody about Tobias, okay? You've always been good at keeping secrets. That's for sure. I hope you meet a boy soon. Then you'll understand how awesome it feels. I pray it happens soon.*

*I can't sleep tonight. I wonder if he's thinking about me too. If my mom found out, she'd put my name in the bann. She wants me to marry an Amish boy. But I can't even imagine a life like that. It doesn't matter what she says. I would do anything, if I could see Tobias again.*

*In a couple weeks, I'll be down in Pinecraft. Fingers crossed, Tobias will be there too. And then we'll be together.*

*I won't let anything stop me.*

*56 days until Florida.*

*Alice*

## chapter twenty-one

# luck

All night, the pictures tighten their grip. Alice in the backseat of that car. Her head slamming against the window. The fear in her voice as she begged Tobias to let go.

When I open my eyes, it's dark outside. I stick my head out of the tent. It's quiet. The campsite is empty. Then a firecracker soars above the pines.

A group of boys run past, waving their foam-padded swords. All of a sudden, the LARPers are everywhere.

I shake Faron. "Wake up. They're coming."

"Who?" He yawns.

"The battle is starting. We have to get out of here."

Faron grabs my hand and we race out of the tent. Shouts echo through the woods as the LARPers charge into battle. I know they're just pretending, but I hold onto Faron a little tighter.

We plunge through the crowd of people in their costumes. There's so many fairies, just like Crystal told me. They rush past us in their glittery wings, moving ahead of the boys and their swords. It's amazing to see girls take action like that.

"Let's go," says Faron, tugging me away.

In the distance, smoke threads the lights in the parking lot. We run toward it, stumbling down the trail. When we reach the truck, Faron shoves his key in the door. I jump inside and he cranks the engine.

"Wait," I tell him.

"What's the matter?"

"The camera. I left it in the tent."

"Forget it," he says. "We can't go back now."

Snowbirds

As we pull away from Blackwoods, I watch the campsite grow smaller. Fireworks sizzle above the mountain, leaving trails across the sky. We drove a thousand miles, looking for Tobias, and he isn't at the games. But that doesn't mean I'm giving up.

If he did something bad to Alice, he can't run away from it.

I won't let him.

• • •

At sunrise, we're on the road.

"It feels like we came all this way for nothing," I tell Faron.

I want to go back to the campsite. There's got to be somebody there who knows Tobias. Or knows where to find him.

We pass a diner on the highway. The parking lot is filled with cars. Most are topped with bright yellow kayaks or bikes. There's a giant SUV parked up front. On the antenna, a tiny pirate's flag snaps in the breeze.

"That's Captain Darkwater!"

Faron looks at me. "You must be hungry. Now you're seeing things."

"Pull over," I tell him.

"Okay," he says, jerking the wheel. "Besides. I could use some breakfast."

He swerves into the parking lot. I'm out of the truck before he can turn off the ignition. So Crystal made it to the games, after all. Will she talk to me? Or have things changed, now that I'm in her world, not the other way around?

Faron sits on a bench outside the diner. "You go ahead," he says, taking out his pack of Reds. "I need a smoke."

I head straight for the door and push it open. This place reminds me of Der Dutchman back in Pinecraft, only messier. The gritty floor sticks to my sneakers as I head inside.

The waitress is leaning against the counter, talking on a cell phone.

"What do you mean, I never call?" she says, frowning. "I'm calling right now." She puts the phone down on the counter. "Can I help you?" she asks me.

I study the maze of tables. Crystal's wheelchair is tucked in a corner of the room, a bouquet of silver balloons swinging from the armrests.

"I think I see my friends," I tell her.

I take a deep breath.

Then I start walking.

The LARPers at Crystal's table are still in their costumes—long robes and pointy hats. Their swords are tucked under their chairs, as if they might go into battle, right in the middle of the diner.

Ben is here too, sitting next to Crystal. For some reason, she's wearing a fuzzy hat. It reminds me of a stuffed animal, complete with whiskers and pointy ears.

"Dude," says Ben, tugging on her hat. "Why do you have a teddy bear on your head?"

"For your information, I'm not a dude," she says, laughing. "And that's not a bear. It's a snow tiger."

When I reach their table, Ben waves at me. "Hark now, fair maiden."

Crystal widens her eyes. "Oh, my god. Lucy, what are you doing here? You made it all the way to Blackwoods."

I smile. "Yeah, with a little help."

"You mean, a little help from your boyfriend?"

"My what?"

"If you were spending the night at his place, why didn't you tell me? For real. I wouldn't have judged you."

"What do you mean?"

"I saw you guys together." She smirks.

"You did?" This is so embarrassing.

"Yeah," Crystal says. "You're not mad, right? We're still friends?"

"Of course." I sink next to her wheelchair and give her a hug.

"Good. Because it would really suck if we stopped talking."

In Pinecraft, I never had a lot of friends. Now I'm starting to wonder why. It always feels like everybody's watching you. Judging. Waiting for you to mess up. All this time, I thought Crystal was judging me too. Maybe I shouldn't be so quick to think that someone's looking down on me.

I dig inside my tote bag and find the purple iPod. "You're probably looking for this," I say, handing it to her.

Crystal presses it into my hand. "It's yours now. That's my old one anyway," she says. "And look. It matches your dress."

I laugh. "Can you show me how to charge it?"

"Your dress?"

Now we're both laughing. It feels good to laugh like that. I mean, really laugh, like nobody's watching.

Ben picks up a butter knife and whacks my arm. "What magic hast thou brought us?"

I stare at him.

"Did you get a lot of good footage?" he asks.

"Not exactly."

"You still have the camera, right? Don't tell me you lost it."

"I left it at Blackwoods."

Ben puts his head on the table. "This is so not cool."

"I'm sorry."

"Whatever," he says. "It's not my camera."

"It's mine, actually," says the girl sitting across from us. Another one of the fairies, judging by her wings. She's so thin, the bones in her wrists look sharp and painful, like they might cut you.

"Sarah?"

The fairy-girl nods. "That's me."

"How do you know Tobias?"

"Me and Toby started talking online last summer," she says, staring down at her empty plate. "At first, he was really sweet. You know. Different."

*Not like other boys.*

"Then he starting acting mean," she says, wiping her eyes. "It was like he changed into somebody else."

I think about Alice trapped in the backseat of that car. The tears streaking her throat.

"So you met him online?"

"It's not as lame as you think. I mean, we had these amazing conversations," she says, looking away. "You're totally judging me right now, aren't you?"

Why would I judge her? When I read Alice's letters, I always felt like she was right there, whispering in my ear. Sometimes it's easier, sharing secrets with someone who's far away.

"When did he stop writing to you?" I ask.

"I don't feel like talking about it," she says flatly.

"Please. If you can tell me anything—"

"Toby said we could go someplace. Get away from here. Yeah, it sounds really stupid. But I actually believed him. Why do you even care?"

"Because that's what he told my best friend."

Sarah looks at me. I can tell she's really embarrassed. "I knew he was hooking up with other people. But I didn't want to believe it."

For a minute, I think she's going to start crying. I almost feel sorry for her.

"I haven't seen him online for a while," she says. "Toby was going down to Florida to see his grandparents. This was like a week ago. I thought that was kind of weird. I mean, it's not even

Thanksgiving break yet. I keep signing onto *Warcraft*, hoping he's online. Pretty lame, huh?"

"So he hasn't been online?"

"Yeah," she says. "There's nothing on his Facebook page either. It's like he doesn't exist anymore."

*If you're not online, you might as well be dead.*

"I can't believe he played me like that," she says, rubbing her forehead. "And it sucks because he owes me money. A lot, actually."

"You gave him money?"

Sarah chews her lip. "This is so awkward."

"What did he need money for?"

"He said it was an emergency."

Ben laughs. "And you actually believed him?"

"Shut up," she says.

"It's not like he doesn't have a job. Toby works at this canning place up in Gouldsboro."

"Where is that?" I ask.

"It's about an hour off US-1. But I wouldn't bother driving there," he says. "That place is insane. There's no way they'll let you in."

"If you see Toby, tell him it's over," says Sarah. "I don't ever want to see him again. And tell his new girlfriend to watch her back."

"Why?"

"Because she's going to be sorry."

I'm scared now. But it's not going to stop me from looking for Alice. If she's in danger, there's nobody else that's going to help her.

Crystal reaches for my hand. "You're not really going, are you, Lucy?"

"I have to."

"But why?" she asks.

Because me and Alice are sisters.

That's why.

I leave the table and head outside. If Sarah is telling the truth, then Alice is in more trouble than I ever imagined.

Faron is waiting on a bench outside. "How did it go?"

Before I can answer, the door swings open. Crystal pushes her wheelchair into the sunshine. She whips off her furry hat and tosses it at me.

"For luck," she says.

"Thanks," I say, tugging it over my head.

Faron smirks. "Thought you didn't believe in luck?"

"I do now."

"Well, it will keep your lid warm," she says. "And here's a doggy bag for the road." She hands me a Styrofoam carton soaked with grease.

I pry it open. Inside is a mess of pancakes slathered with oatmeal and eggs.

"Oh well," says Faron, popping a strip of bacon into his mouth. "It all goes down the same hatch."

Crystal laughs. She pulls my sleeve and whispers, "Your boyfriend is pretty awesome. And he smells yummy too."

After two days in the truck, I doubt either of us smells yummy.

"Call me when you get back to Florida," she says. "We need to hang out. And I'm totally going to make that princess dress for you. Remember?"

I remember.

"And Lucy . . . be careful, okay?" she says. "That guy you're trying to find . . . he sounds like a freak. I mean, he could hurt you."

I give Crystal a hug. "I'll be careful."

"Good," she says. "Or else I'll hunt you down."

Did Tobias use Sarah's money to get to Florida? He tricked her into believing he was for real. Alice too.

How many girls believed his lies?

If Tobias is here in Maine, I'm going to find him.

I climb back in the truck. Another hour of driving and no guarantees. But we've come this far. I can go a little further.

"So where are we headed?" asks Faron.

"Gouldsboro," I tell him.

"What for?"

"Because that's where Tobias is."

If I'm lucky.

## chapter twenty-two
# fish bones

The faded plywood sign rises above the cannery, so tall it almost reaches the power lines. It's carved into the shape of a fisherman in a yellow rain jacket. Between his giant hands, he clutches a lobster trap.

"This must be it," says Faron as we walk to the docks.

The oily stink of fish makes my stomach clench. Do the cannery workers ever get used to it? Or do they take three or four showers once they're home?

A woman in a plastic hairnet and overalls is talking on a cell phone outside the cannery. She watches the lobster boats as they bob on the harbor. I get the feeling she's watching us too.

"I'm on break right now. Ask Nana to get it for you. No, we're out of mayonnaise," she says, stretching out the word: *may-uh-nayze.*

"Hello, ma'am," I say in my extra polite voice.

She turns around. "You folks lost?"

"We're looking for Tobias."

"Tobias? You mean that boy, Toby Granger?" She flicks her cigarette in the water. "He works the Slime Line, yeah?"

"Can we talk to him?"

"Not until five," she says, snapping on a pair of gloves. "If you can wait that long."

"Doesn't he have a break or something?"

"Toby can't get a break," she says, shoving past me. She stomps ahead, the planks creaking under her rubber boots.

Faron looks at me. "What now?"

"Only one thing to do," I say, sitting on the edge of the dock. We wait.

• • •

All afternoon, we wait. Nothing to see except boats and buoys drifting with the tide. That gets old real fast.

Good thing I'm good at waiting.

"You think he's going to talk to us?" asks Faron.

"I'll make sure he does."

He's been talking to a lot of girls.

Now he can talk to me.

Faron stands up and looks at the horizon. "There's a harbor seal," he says, pointing.

"It's a sign."

"There you go again, talking about luck." Faron squeezes my shoulder. "You cold yet?"

"I thought you never got cold."

He shrugs. "Let's wait in the truck. Warm up a little."

"What if Tobias comes out and we miss him?"

"It ain't quitting time yet."

"I know. But we're getting close."

"Won't be gone long," he says, walking away. "Holler if you get lonely."

I sit on the edge of the dock, swinging my legs over the slate-gray water. The beaches are different here, more rock than sand, but the same birds whirl in the sky—sandpipers and gulls. They didn't leave for the winter. They'll stick it out a little longer.

So will I.

At last, the workers begin to spill out of the cannery. Most are women with raw, windburned faces. They're all wearing plastic hairnets. I squint at the crowd, searching for Tobias, but I don't see any boys.

As they leave, I reach into my bag and take out my prayer cap. Carefully, I pin my hair inside it. I wait for the last cannery worker to slip out the door. It's the woman I saw on the docks. Mayonnaise Lady. She's on her cell phone, walking straight ahead, gripping it like a compass. Back and forth she paces outside the door. Will she ever get out of the way?

Now she's yelling into the phone, spitting words I'd never say out loud. I feel bad for whoever is putting up with that. Still, she won't move away from the door. Slowly, it begins to close.

I can't wait anymore.

So I run.

"Hey! You can't just waltz in there," she shouts.

The door swings shut.

I lean against the wall, my heart thudding in my chest. There's a glassed-in booth at the end of the long corridor. Maybe it's some kind of security desk. As the workers leave, they stop and talk to the man inside. I stumble along with the others, like I'm supposed to be there.

The floor is slick with fish guts. My stomach tightens and I almost throw up, right in front of everybody. I'm not dressed like the cannery women. But I've got my hair tucked under my prayer cap. I slip into the crowd and keep moving.

In the next room, fluorescent lights gleam off rows of metal machinery. I stare at the conveyor belt, the sardine heads gaping, their pointy mouths open in surprise. I can't help looking at their delicate bones, the empty skulls and rib cages, like a piece of sculpture, and the bones inside me too.

In the back of the cannery, there's a door marked MEN'S. I really don't want to go in there. Gritting my teeth, I push my way inside.

There's a row of sinks and only one stall. I tap it with the heel of my sneaker and the door bangs open.

Tobias looks up at me, his eyes blank. "What the hell are you doing here?"

He's wearing the skeleton T-shirt, only now it's smeared with bloodlike splotches. The toilet lid's down and he's sitting on it, snapping pages in a comic book. We both stare at each other.

"Get out," he yells.

"I want to talk to you, okay?"

"You're Alice's friend."

"That's right," I tell him, stepping closer. "We've been friends a long time. Best friends."

"I hate that girl," he says flatly.

This isn't what I expected to hear.

"Why do you hate Alice?" I ask, trying to stay calm.

"Because she lied." He tosses the comic book on the floor. It lands with its pages flopped open—girls shooting bullets out of their eyes.

"Please. Just talk to me."

Tobias rubs his face. For a second, I think he's going to start crying. "She lied about everything."

He gets up and shoves past me. If Tobias disappears inside the cannery, I'll never find him. I race after him, but he's already out the door. My feet pound through the hallway, skidding on bits of bone and fish guts.

I stumble into the room with the metal tables. There's nowhere to go except outside. Tobias is ahead of me. He ducks under the conveyer belt and lands on his knees. I run to the other side, blocking his way out.

"Where is Alice?" I shout at him.

Tobias slumps over like he's been shot. He groans and rocks side to side. "I didn't do anything to her. Just leave me alone."

"I saw what you did."

He wipes his hands on his jeans. "What are you talking about?"

"It's on Sarah's camera."

"You're friends with her?" he says, wincing. "That's why you're coming after me?"

"I want to know where Alice is."

"Well, obviously she's not here." Tobias inches toward the door.

When we leave the cannery, the sky is blank. It's even colder outside than it was before. Across the parking lot, Faron is leaning against the truck.

Tobias makes a face. "You again."

"It's okay," says Faron, like he's trying to convince himself. "You're okay," he says, moving closer to us. "Everything's okay."

Actually, nothing is okay.

Tobias glances over his shoulder. The workers are smoking on the docks. One of them dumps a bucket into the water. The seagulls swoop down and wrestle over the mess, screaming and jabbing each other.

"Just leave me alone," he mutters.

"Not until you start talking."

"I didn't do anything."

When somebody says, "I didn't do anything," you can bet they're lying.

"What if I get us some beer?" Faron asks. "Then maybe you'll feel like talking?"

"We can't drink at my house."

"Fine. Just tell us where to go."

"I'm not going with you," Tobias says. He's got this damaged edge to his voice, like people have been shouting over him for so long, he's given up.

"What about a hotel?" Faron asks. "You could take a shower, drink a couple beers. Does that work?"

"We're getting a six-pack, right?" Tobias says.

Faron nods. "I'll stop at a gas station."

Tobias stays quiet for a minute. He looks at the workers, then back at us.

"Deal," he finally says.

When Faron pulls out the keys to the truck, Tobias stares at his hand. "You're lucky. There's this girl at the cannery who cut off her thumb," he says, hoisting himself into the truck bed. "I couldn't hear her screaming 'cause they make us wear earplugs."

"You don't have to ride back there," Faron says.

Tobias hangs over the side like a dog. "I can be the lookout."

"Lookout for what?"

"If the cops start chasing us."

Faron glances at me. I know what he's thinking. We have to get rid of the truck. Not now. But soon.

As we speed away from the cannery, I look at my sneakers, their laces soaked in fish grease.

They will never be clean again.

## chapter twenty-three
# from away

"**A**bsolutely not," says the guy at the front desk. "Everything's booked. I've got nothing open."

I glance around the hotel lobby. A faded painting of a lighthouse hangs over a sagging leather couch. Beside it, a potted plant droops against the wall, its plasticky leaves flecked with dust.

"You're sure about that?" I ask.

"Positive," he says, smoothing a strand of hair off his forehead. I get the feeling he's been here longer than the furniture. "Besides. I can't book a room for someone your age. Hotel policy. You need a parent or guardian's permission."

Now we're stuck. I need to think of something. Fast.

I grab Faron's hand. "He doesn't know," I whisper.

"Know what?"

"He doesn't know we're married."

The man blinks. "Aren't you two a little young for that?"

Faron takes out his driver's license and slaps it on the counter. "I'm twenty-one. It says so right here."

"And how will you be paying?" the man says, putting on his glasses. He squints at the license, then at us.

"Here." I reach into my bag and shove what's left of my money at him. Everything I've saved up from my job. All gone.

The man stares at the pile of cash. "Let me check. Sometimes we get a last-minute cancellation." He pushes buttons on a computer. "Looks like there's a single open," he says after a minute. "King-sized bed. Is that okay?"

My cheeks sting. "Yeah, that's fine."

Tobias is waiting for us in the truck. As we walk back to the parking lot, Faron smirks. "Good thinking, Lucy," he says, squeezing my hand. "I should've thought of that, you know. The marriage thing."

"Why?"

"Because my family's Old Order," he says, staring at the highway in the distance.

Is Faron really going to try and make peace with his family? I know this is important to him. I should be praying they welcome him with open arms.

But I can't.

• • •

As soon as we're in the room, Tobias pulls out a beer. "Nice," he says, trying to wrestle off the cap. "How did you manage to score the six-pack?"

Faron snatches the bottle out of his hands. "Two words. Fake ID."

"That's four words, actually," Tobias says, looking around the dingy room. "Man, this is awesome." He grabs the TV remote and clicks on a fishing tournament. I am definitely over fish at this point.

"Here you go." Faron hooks his lighter under the cap and pops it open. He passes it back to Tobias. "King of beers."

Tobias gulps it so fast, he almost chokes. "Thanks, man," he says, flopping on the bed. He doesn't even take off his dirty sneakers.

"Does anybody want to take a shower?" I ask.

"With you? Sure." Tobias grins.

Faron yanks him by the shirt so hard he almost falls off the bed. "You better start talking. And I mean fast. Got it?"

"Yeah, I got it," he says in a small voice.

"Good." Faron lets go.

Tobias glances at me. "You first."

I don't want to leave, in case he says something important about Alice. Maybe he'll talk more to Faron, man-to-man. I close the bathroom door and let the shower pound my back. When I come out, Tobias looks wasted. He's already finished off two beers.

"I need another round," he says, reaching for the six-pack.

"All right." Faron's eyes meet mine. "You okay, Lucy?"

I nod.

He leaves me there.

Alone.

I sit next to Tobias on the flowery bedspread. "Are we going to talk about Alice now?"

He grabs the TV remote. "That girl totally played me," he says, slurring a little.

"What happened?"

Tobias keeps his gaze on the flickering screen. "Didn't you hear me the first time? I already told you. She lied."

"You haven't told me anything."

"Listen. This is between me and her."

"I was at that party, too."

He looks at me. "Alice wanted to get away from her mom," he says, clicking channels. "Her family's Amish. You know that, right?"

"Yes. So is my family."

"For real? You sure don't look it."

"What about you?" I ask.

"Me? Hell no." He stares at the commercial on TV. *If you've moved to Maine 'from away'* . . .

All this time, I thought Tobias was running away from the Old Order. Now he's saying it isn't true.

"How did you meet Alice?"

"We started talking online last summer. When she told me about the Amish stuff, I thought she was making it up. I mean, come on. I met this girl playing *World of Warcraft*."

"So when did you get together in real life?"

"I got Alice into LARPing," he says. "Then she had to go and kill me off."

He's talking so fast, I can barely keep up. "What do you mean, Alice killed you?"

"She cast an Elemental spell on me. Basically, she froze time so I couldn't move." He shakes his head. "I can't believe she betrayed me like that."

I remember the video Tobias put online. The anger in his voice. *"I'll make up my own rules."*

"After I got kicked out of the games, I didn't see her for a while," he says. "A couple weeks ago, I get this email from Alice, saying we should meet up in Florida. The Amish have this thing called *Rumspringa*. It's kind of like spring break."

"I know."

"Alice's mom was pressuring her to join the church. And you know what that means. I'd never see her again." He gulps the beer, tipping his head back. "I tried to help her. But she was just using me."

My heart is thudding so hard, I wonder if he can hear it. "I thought you were running away together."

"We were supposed to go the bus station after the party, right? But Alice got so wasted. I mean, she was really out of it. Then I find her sleeping in this guy's car. I tried to get her out. But she wouldn't listen."

"I saw what you did."

"You weren't there, okay?" Toby's upper lip is dotted with sweat.

I wait for him to blame Alice.

And he does.

"It's not my fault she got so wasted," he says. "I mean, I'm not in charge of her life or anything."

"So you just left her in the park."

"Isn't that what you did?" he says.

I flinch.

It's not the same thing.

That's what I keep telling myself.

"Where did you go after the party?" I ask, looking right at him.

"I got a ride to Lido Key. Didn't stay long. The cops showed up and kicked everybody out."

I remember the crowd leaving the beach. The Old Order girls in their long dresses and bonnets. The red and blue lights fanning across the sand.

The Showalters found Alice's cell phone on Lido Key. Broken. How did it end up on the beach? And what about the money inside that plastic bag? All those bills, rolled tight.

"You stole Alice's cell phone."

He takes another gulp of beer. "I gave her the damn thing. And then she goes and breaks it."

"Did you steal her money?"

"Alice's money? We were supposed to go to the bus station in the morning. Alice had this stupid idea about going to California. She was going to be in the movies or something. I mean, this girl had no concept of reality. There wasn't enough money to get out of Florida, much less California."

"But you took it anyway. And then you walked back to the empty lot in Pinecraft."

His eyes widen. "How did you know that?"

I stare at his sneakers dangling over the edge of the bed.

"Whatever," he says, wiping his mouth on his T-shirt. "Alice ditched me. I went back there, trying to find her."

"You weren't trying to find Alice."

He squirms. "I was looking for her."

"You were looking for the rest of her money."

Tobias swings back his arm and I flinch. For a second, I think he's going to hit me. Then he slowly lowers his fist. He glances at the bathroom door. The shower is gurgling away. I need to keep pushing for answers before Faron comes back.

"You were talking to a lot of girls online," I say. "You lied to them. And you took their money. Did Alice mean anything to you at all?"

"You know what?" he says. "I don't even care."

"Please. Just tell me if she's okay." I'm shouting now. Begging him to tell the truth. But Tobias won't look at me.

The bathroom door swings open. Faron steps out in a haze of sweet-smelling steam. When he sinks onto the bed, Tobias moves away, like he's afraid of sitting too close. He pulls another beer out of the six-pack.

One more beer turns into two.

Then three.

Tobias curls up on the floor like a little kid, the empty bottles scattered around his head.

He won't be talking anymore tonight.

"Did you get anything out of him?" Faron whispers.

I'm holding back tears. "He doesn't know where she is."

"You think he's lying?"

"I don't know. He stole Alice's money. But he didn't find all of it. She must've hid the rest. That's why he went back to the empty lot after the party. He was trying to find it."

"Alice did the right thing."

"She was probably hiding it from her mom, too," I say, remembering how Mrs. Yoder wouldn't let Alice keep her money from the craft fair.

"Where's her mom now?" he asks.

"Mrs. Yoder didn't stay in Pinecraft. She went back to Maine."

"Do you know which town?"

In my mind I see Alice's letters. The old-fashioned handwriting in the top left corner. Never a complete address. Just the name of a post office.

*Smyrna, Maine.*

Faron nods. "That's what I thought," he says.

"Why?"

"Because I'm from there, too."

"You're from Smyrna?"

"We're from the same *Ordnung,*" he says, meaning the bishop's rules you've got to follow. "There's a lot of Amish up in the mountains."

"How far is that from here?" I ask.

"About a couple hundred miles north. If we're going to make it, we need to get on the road early tomorrow."

"You're still going back home," I say quietly.

He closes his eyes. "Don't have a choice," he says. "But I made a promise to you, Lucy. We're going to keep looking for your friend."

The TV brightens and dims, throwing shadows above the bed. I stay awake a long time before falling asleep, thinking about what Tobias said. Did he even care about Alice at all?

The morning sun dribbles through the blinds.

I glance at the empty bottles on the floor.

Tobias is gone.

## chapter twenty-four
# tides and currents

His blanket is rolled like a snail in a corner of the room. It smells so gross, I don't want to touch it. Empty bottles are tipped on the carpet. The TV has switched to cartoons—a mouse smacking a cat with a frying pan.

"He can't be too far," says Faron. "We could drive back to the cannery. He's got to show up for work."

I shake my head. There's only one place left to go. Somewhere I've only heard about but never seen. A cold place up in the mountains. When I try to imagine it, I shiver.

The widow's home.

"I don't know, Lucy. You're stirring up a lot of trouble." He gets this far-off look, as if he's drifting to another place. "The Old Order . . . we're good at keeping secrets."

"Are you keeping secrets too?" I ask.

"Yeah," he says. "But not from you."

He heads for the bathroom and shuts the door.

I'm alone again.

How did I end up so far away from home? I stare at the painting framed above the bed. Another lighthouse. Seagulls hovering over a red-roofed cottage. A sailboat leaning into a swell of dark water.

Did Alice have doubts about running away? Is that why she hid the money? As long as I can remember, she wanted to leave the Old Order. She told me in her letters. What happened after I left the party that night? Tobias got her drunk and stole her cash. He broke her cell phone so she couldn't ask for help. Then he left her in the park. Alone.

When I knock on the bathroom door, Faron is at the sink, dipping his razor under the faucet.

"Hey." I smile at him.

"Hey yourself," he says, smiling back.

"You look different."

"Thanks." Faron's smile quickly fades. He gets back to work, shaving his upper lip, but leaves the rest alone.

I reach into the sink and pinch a loose strand of hair. "Why aren't you shaving it all off?"

"Makes things easier," he says, splashing his face.

"What's easier?"

He doesn't answer.

I know he will blend in, once we reach the Amish up in Smyrna. But there's another reason for the beard. Something I don't want to think about.

"You can't go back to the Old Order. Not after they shunned you."

"That's right," he says. "I can't go back home. I'll never be Amish again. Don't want to be. But if I'm working for my dad, it's easier this way."

"Easier to give in."

"Is that what you think I'm doing? Giving in? Lucy, you have no idea. I've got no choice."

"So it's about making your dad happy."

"There's no place where I fit in. Nowhere left to go. I'm telling you. I've got nothing."

"There's me," I say in a small voice.

"Yeah, there's you." Faron pulls me into a hug. "The smartest girl I ever met. There's good stuff in here," he says, stroking my forehead. "I don't care what your dad says. You're going to study the ocean."

We hold each other for a long time. I don't want to let go. But I know that Faron has to make his own choice.

"Don't you want to be free?" he says.

"Of course I do. But how?"

"I'll tell you how," he says. "You go to the library. Get on the computer. Look up that fancy school in St. Pete. Find out what it takes to go there. And trust me. You're going to make it happen. I believe it."

"So I've got a choice and you don't."

"Lucy, you're so smart," he says, lowering his head. "And I'm not."

"Don't say that."

"It's true."

"No, it's not. You're just running away again."

"I'm done running," he says. "Things will get better. You'll see. If we rush ahead, we'll just mess it up. And I'm not going to let that happen."

"I don't want you to leave."

"It won't change what we've got," he whispers. "Me and you, we're in this together."

Everything changes.

The whole world is made of change.

That much I know.

"I'll wait for you," he says. "*Fehlerfrei*. Look at me."

I look.

Faron's eyes are wet. He kisses me gently. "I'll wait."

We will find a way to be together. I believe it, the way I know the tide will tuck in its edges and swell again. The way I believe in snow, although I've never seen it, and the moon's grip on the ocean, and us too.

I believe with my whole heart.

## chapter twenty-five

# mittens

It's cold in the mountains. As we pull off the highway, we pass a yellow traffic sign with a picture of a horse and buggy: SHARE THE ROAD. Up ahead, the pavement is dotted with piles of manure like beads on a chain.

"Welcome to Smyrna," says Faron.

He's already changed back into his plain clothes. His long-sleeved cotton shirt and jeans are for Amish men who work long hours outdoors. He looks so different now. When I hear him talking in that slow, easygoing voice, it's almost startling.

"Do you think the Amish craft fair is still open?" I ask him.

"It's more of a summer thing," he says. "In the winter, a lot of places shut down. Most people take a break and go south."

Yeah. I know.

In Alice's letters, the craft fair is a pretty big deal. Everybody gets together to eat and gossip, just like at our church picnics back home. She never mentioned anything about working during the winter. By then, she and her mom were in Florida.

"If it's open, maybe somebody knows Mrs. Yoder," I say. "They might even know where she lives."

"Maybe," says Faron. "But you're forgetting something, Lucy. There's no chance they're going to tell us."

"Only one way to find out."

"I'm serious. They're not going to talk to us."

"What are we supposed to do? Turn around and go home?"

"No," he says quietly. "I can't do that."

He's scared. Why didn't I see it before? Coming back to Smyrna is like trying to cross a bridge that's been burned. When you're shunned, you're already living in hell. And the Old Order will do everything it takes to remind you.

We park the truck on the side of the road. Faron doesn't want to bring attention to himself. I'm making it worse, just by being here. The Old Order won't care for the way I look. Even my prayer cap is too worldly.

"Want your coat back?" I ask Faron.

"Nah. I'm good."

"You're not cold?"

"Never," he says.

My breath is steaming as we get out of the truck. "I need my own coat."

"True. But our money's all gone."

I'm so exhausted, I can barely walk. The path winding up the hill is steep. I don't spot any cars on the road. Only wheel tracks in the dirt. The U-shaped stamp of a horse's hoof. A pair of mittens dangling from a tree branch, as if somebody peeled them off and disappeared into the sky.

When I see the horses lined up in orderly rows, I get a little nervous. Dozens of buggies fill the parking lot at the Dyer Brook Amish Craft Fair. It's like looking through a window into another time.

So they're here after all.

The craft fair is inside a long, barn-shaped building. A sign tells us to REJOICE IN THE FELLOWSHIP OF THE LORD THIS AUTUMN HARVEST. I wait for a minute outside the door. Then I grab the handle and push it open.

This place is just like the fruit stand in Pinecraft, only bigger. Not to mention, crowded. Bearded old men in dark blue shirts and suspenders are huddled in the corner, drinking coffee, while the Old Order women dart back and forth in their stiff black dresses and bonnets. The tables are loaded with fresh-baked cookies and pies, along with paperbacks about living a godly life.

As soon as Faron walks through the door, everyone turns and looks. It's more than the usual stares and whispers. This time, the Amish are judging us too. In Pinecraft, it was different. We were one big family. Here, it's pretty obvious I don't belong. And Faron? He's invisible.

I bet a lot of these people used to be his friends. Now they're making a big deal, shoving past him in line as if he doesn't exist. No handshakes or hellos. They just keep talking to each other like he's not even there.

"I'm sorry, Lucy," he says. "I never should've brought you here. I knew this was going to happen."

I can hear the hurt in his voice. "Don't let them treat you like that."

"They're not going to talk to us."

"Fine. Then I'll talk to them."

I make my way through the crowd. Heads turn as I push toward the long rows of tables. It's probably even busier in the summertime. Right now, it's mostly about food. They've got everything from pickled red beet eggs in jars to hunks of beef wrapped in brown paper. I don't see many crafts. But there's an Old Order girl in a heart-shaped bonnet selling Amish quilts. She's humming softly. A gospel tune. Some things don't change no matter where you go.

When I stand next to her table, she looks up.

"Your quilts are really beautiful." I smile.

"Thank you," she mumbles.

I've already made a mistake. I shouldn't have mentioned the beauty of her quilts. Now she's going to feel uncomfortable.

I unfold a few more quilts from the pile. They're all so perfect, it's hard to believe they were stitched by hand. I gently trace their blue and yellow patterns.

"I think this one's called Sunshine and Shadow?" I ask.

She blinks in surprise. "Yes, that's right."

"It's my favorite."

"Mine too," she says, blushing. "Are you visiting Smyrna?" Her voice is slow and easy, like Faron's.

"I'm from Pinecraft."

"Oh, you're from the Florida gang?" she says.

That's what the Old Order call the Beachy Amish-Mennonites, as if we're all friends.

If only that were true.

"I'm looking for Alice Yoder. She makes quilts too. Her mom sells them here sometimes."

"Alice?" There's a flicker of recognition. "No, I haven't seen her in a long time. Not since last summer."

Is she lying?

"What about Mrs. Yoder? Does she still work here?"

"I wouldn't go around asking questions about the widow. Most people don't like strangers coming here, stirring up trouble. Especially if you're with Faron Mast," she says, glancing over her shoulder.

"Please. My friend Alice is in a lot of trouble. I'm really scared for her."

The Old Order girl leans closer. "I don't know what happened to Alice," she says carefully. "But if you're looking for her mother, I'd talk to John Lapp. His family's got a store off Duck Pond Road. That's where we sell our quilts at Christmas."

I follow her gaze across the room to where a tall, bearded man in glasses is drinking coffee with a group of older men.

"Thanks," I tell her.

She blushes again.

I feel like I should buy one of her quilts, but I don't have any money left. And I have something else in mind.

"Do you make clothes too?" I ask.

"Yes, but I didn't bring any dresses today."

"What about a coat?"

"I might have one," she says. "Especially for someone who came all the way from Florida. I imagine they'd be needing a winter coat."

What can I give her in exchange? I reach into my tote bag. I'm not carrying much except Crystal's purple iPod. When I slip it under the table, the girl's smile grows bigger. Does she know how it works? If she's a *Rumspringa* girl, I'd say yes.

"You like music?" I whisper.

She looks at me. Understands.

Without a word, she takes off her coat and offers it to me. It's a little small. The sleeves don't cover my wrists. But it will keep me warm.

"Almost forgot," she says, tugging off her black mittens. No doubt, she knit them herself. I can't help thinking of the pair I saw earlier, dangling from a tree branch.

As I turn to leave, she says, "I pray the Lord brings Alice home safe."

The Lord always forgives.

That's what I've been taught.

What about liars?

Does the Lord forgive them too?

• • •

As I walk back through the crowd, I notice an Old Order boy staring at me. I thought the coat would help me blend in, but, so far, it's not helping. We make eye contact and it's like I've broken some unspoken rule. He glares and turns away.

So this is what it feels like to be shunned.

"Well, look at you," says Faron. "You're a proper Old Order girl now."

"I wouldn't say that."

"Does this mean I can have my coat back?" he asks.

"Only if you're cold."

"I don't get cold," he says, shrugging into his coat. Once again, I'm struck by how different he looks. Almost as if he never left the Old Order. Still, it makes no difference to the old men huddled in the corner.

I stare back at the men. "Do you know them?"

He nods. "And they know me."

The younger man in glasses walks across the room. He stops in front of an Old Order woman and lifts a baby from her arms.

"What about him?" I whisper.

"John Lapp."

"His family sells the Yoders' quilts. Maybe he can help us."

"Don't count on it," says Faron. "Nobody's going to talk to you, Lucy. They'd be putting their whole lives in danger."

"Why?"

"If they speak up, it's only asking for trouble."

"But why is it dangerous?"

"They're afraid."

"Afraid of what?"

"Everything," he says, looking over his shoulder.

A group of Old Order women slip past us. They keep their heads bowed toward the ground, almost faceless in their stiff black bonnets. I can't imagine Alice trapped in this world. She'd do anything to escape, no matter how dangerous.

"I don't care if they're afraid," I tell him. "They can't stop me from asking questions."

I move toward the row of tables in the back. Faron is right behind me, ignoring the stares of the bearded old men.

When John notices us, his face turns pale.

"Faron Mast. So the prodigal son returns," he says, balancing a plate of apple fritters in one hand and a squirming baby in the other. "Your dad's going to kick a fit."

"Ain't that the truth, John."

They start talking in Deitsch. The words fly back and forth. There's no way I can keep up. At first I expected John to ignore us. After all, Faron's been shunned. But this is a public place. Maybe that's the difference. Still, I get the feeling that we aren't exactly welcome here.

"So you're from Pinecraft," John says, turning to me. "Bet you've never seen snow." He flashes a mouthful of big white teeth. "Do you know what happens when it melts?"

"No."

"Your feet get wet."

John smirks. He isn't much older than me. The skin around his eyes is smooth and his arms are strong like Faron's.

"The Lord's been good," he says, kissing the baby's forehead. "Got another little one on the way this spring."

Faron nods at the Old Order girl slumped at the table. All this time, she hasn't said a word. I can't help thinking of the Old Order girls in the surf at sunrise, how free they looked there.

"Still got that old Ford?" John asks.

"Yeah, it's still running."

"Maybe we should go take a look at it," he says, lowering his voice. "I could use some fresh air."

John passes the baby into his wife's outstretched arms. I know why he wants to leave. He doesn't want to get in trouble. Not with so many eyes on us. I used to think it was hard living in Pinecraft. Everybody watching. Just waiting for you to mess up. That's nothing compared to the Old Order Amish in Maine.

As we head for the door, a dozen faces turn. The bearded old men twist around in their chairs, shifting their enormous bellies. I glare back at them. Go ahead. Take a picture. It lasts longer.

I'm almost thankful for the cold once we're outside. At least it's easier to breathe. There's a horse and buggy coming up the road.

The boy at the reins is wearing a faded red sweatshirt. The girl is bundled in a dark shawl and bonnet. They look straight ahead as the buggy rolls past. I stare at the safety triangle on the back, so bright and out of place.

Faron watches in silence. I try to imagine him in that boy's place, steering a buggy on a dirt road.

"Never thought I'd see that again," he mutters.

"And I never expected to see you," John says. "It's like talking to a ghost, returned from the dead."

He's right.

We are ghosts.

"Don't have much time," John says, looking back at the road. "Whatever needs saying . . . better say it quick."

He's nervous. If someone catches us in the woods, they'll think we're up to no good.

"You want to check out the truck?" I remind him.

John hesitates. He takes off his glasses and wipes them on his sleeve.

"Come on," says Faron, marching ahead.

His truck is at the bottom of the hill, parked under a tree. The red paint stands out against the overcast sky.

Faron brushes a leaf off the windshield. "My dad used to dump out the gas tank. He'd get so fired up."

"That's one way to put it," says John. "You'd go tearing down those country roads. Almost got yourself killed, racing that thing."

I glance at Faron. He never mentioned this before.

"Well, it's still in one piece," he says.

"You or the truck?"

Just then, a crow swoops above us. It calls out once, twice. Three times. I search for it in the branches. There's nothing. Only the skeletal trees.

"I can't help you, Faron Mast. Whatever trouble you're in, it's time you faced it on your own."

John looks so smug, like he's never made a mistake. Never had to fight for himself. Yeah, he's got it all figured out.

"I'm the one who's in trouble," I tell him. "Not Faron."

"Is that right?" John says, turning to look at me. "What sort of trouble could a Beachy girl from Pinecraft get into?"

"My friend Alice is missing."

He takes a step back. "Alice Yoder?"

I nod.

"That's no surprise," he says. "Alice has been running around for a while. She's got boys on her mind. I'll tell you that much."

He's talking like she deserves to be missing. But she didn't do anything wrong. What's so bad about wanting to kiss a boy? Or dreaming of faraway places like California, where it's always sunny and warm?

What's so bad about wanting to be free?

"So the Yoder girl ran off," he says, like it's no big deal. "That's no business of mine."

If a *Rumspringa* girl disappears, it's somehow her fault. I can't help feeling that things would be different if Alice were a boy.

"Your family sells the Yoder quilts," I say to him. "I'm thinking you might know where Alice's mom lives."

"The widow?"

"That's right."

He squints like he's trying to remember. But I know he's only putting on a show. "The widow hasn't come around lately."

"I didn't ask if you've seen her," I say, gritting my teeth. "I asked if you know where she lives."

"Now why would I know that?" John leans against the truck and crosses his arms. At that moment, I want to scream at him. He can't tell me he doesn't know where Mrs. Yoder lives. He only cares about saving his own skin.

"What about Alice's dad?" I just blurt it out.

"Her dad?"

"Yes."

He frowns. "Sam Yoder's been gone over ten years."

"I heard there was an accident."

"Well, that was a long time ago," he says.

"What happened to him?"

"He was out on Cochrane Lake. I guess probably he was fishing for trout. You can't trust the ice that early in the season. You'll sink like a stone and never come up again."

I shiver.

Alice said her dad was hurt in an accident. She told me he was dead. I never questioned her. Never wanted to make her sad. Now John's saying it's true.

"The water's not deep, but it's mighty cold," he adds.

I believe John's telling the truth. Or rather, he thinks it's the truth. The two aren't always the same.

"The Yoder family's been through a patch of darkness," he says, shaking his head. "A shame to lose one more."

*One more?*

The way he's talking, you'd think Alice is dead too.

"What do you mean?" I ask.

John's already walking away. "You don't belong here. Both of you," he says, looking at Faron. "Better get on the road. Head south where you belong."

"Please. Can't you tell me where Mrs. Yoder lives?"

"The widow doesn't need you poking around. Leave the past alone. She's known a lot of suffering."

"I just want to talk to her. That's all."

"You got a big voice, Lucy," he says, heading up the hill. "But you need a bigger backbone."

All the electricity inside me is burning. If I listen, I can hear it, like dipping your head underwater. It doesn't matter that Alice is in trouble. As far as the Old Order is concerned, she's gone.

She's not even a ghost.

# chapter twenty-six

# snowflakes

We've been driving for hours, trying to find Cochrane Lake. I stare out the window. All I see are pine trees so thick, they blot out the fading sunlight.

"You never drove up here?" I ask Faron.

"Never," he says, gripping the steering wheel. "Once I got the truck, I was gone. Couldn't get away fast enough."

No wonder the Old Order families feel safe, traveling by horse and buggy. It keeps them from going too far.

We haven't passed any farms. Only dirt roads that lead to nowhere. If the Yoders live close to the lake, why haven't we seen anything yet? Not a single roof jutting above the road. No chimney smoke threading the pines.

"I'm telling you, Lucy. You can't believe everything that comes out of John Lapp's mouth."

"He's telling the truth. At least, the way he sees it."

"Yeah, but we've been driving in circles forever."

"Why can't you just have faith?"

He grabs my hand and squeezes. "I'd hate to see you get hurt."

"Too late," I mutter.

"Lucy. Remember what I told you. We're in this together."

Silence.

"Remember?" he says again. Louder, this time.

I still won't look at him.

Faron slows down and pulls over. He cuts the ignition. Unhooks his seatbelt. Kicks the door open and climbs out.

The keys dangle next to me, swinging back and forth.

From the truck, I watch him disappear into the woods. Now I've done it. I wait a few seconds. When he doesn't come back, I grab the keys and hop out.

The ground crunches beneath my sneakers. I can feel my breath curling like steam around my face. The late afternoon sky is a smear. Hardly any sunlight left. I turn a corner, following a hint of smoke in the breeze.

Faron is looking at the mountains. I'm not used to them yet. I keep checking to make sure they haven't moved.

"It's snowing," he finally says.

"Where?"

"Everywhere."

All around us, snowflakes spin in midair. I stare at the specks gleaming in my hands.

"They have patterns?"

"Of course they do." He laughs.

I laugh too.

We walk to the truck and everything's okay now. The snow paints the road with a brightness purer than the sky.

It's like starting all over again.

• • •

Walking back through the woods, I think about Alice. This is her home. But I don't feel her spirit here. I slide the pins out of my prayer cap and let my hair swing loose. Still, it's not enough to keep me warm.

Faron grabs my arm. "Somebody's in the truck."

Behind the windshield, there's a flicker of movement.

"I've got the keys," I tell him.

"Did you leave it unlocked?"

Maybe I did.

"Wait here," he says.

When Faron reaches the truck, he yanks open the passenger door. Somebody is inside, crouched on the passenger seat. And that somebody is a little girl in an Old Order bonnet.

"It's okay," I tell her, walking up, real slow. "Nobody's going to hurt you."

Tears leak down her chin. She's got this scared look on her face, like we're going to eat her alive. Her pale eyes dart back and forth.

"What's your name?" I ask softly.

"Emma Farber."

"How long have you been hiding in there?"

She lunges for the door, but I move in front of it, blocking her way out.

"Please don't tell my dad," she says, sniffing. "I just want to go home."

"You live around here?"

"Not too far," she says. "Just off Smokey Hollow Road."

"Ever been to Cochrane Lake?"

"Sure. Lots of times."

"Then you probably know the Yoders," I say, glancing back at Faron. "Can you show us the way?"

"You mean the widow's place?" she says, blinking at me.

"That's right. Do you know where she lives?"

Emma lowers her head.

She knows. But she's scared. This is a really big deal for her, talking to us. I bet she's never been in a car before.

How can I get her to trust me?

"What if we drive you home?" I ask.

Finally a hint of a smile.

"Here's the deal," I tell her. "If we give you a ride in the truck, will you help us find the widow?"

"She won't talk to you," Emma says flatly.

"Why not?"

"The widow doesn't talk to no one. Especially if you're . . ." She struggles with the words. "If you're not from around here."

Faron gives me a look.

"Tell her." I nudge him. "Only say it in Deitsch."

He does.

Emma's mouth drops open. "*Kannscht du Pennsilfaanisch Deitsch schwetzer?*"

"Yah, I can speak Deitsch," he says, climbing behind the wheel. "Been speaking it all my life."

For a minute, they go back and forth, talking fast. I stand next to the truck, feeling a little left out.

"Okay," says Emma, sliding over. "I'll show you where to go."

• • •

The road winds through the mountains. By now, the sun has faded away. We pass row after row of plain white farmhouses. In every window, a tiny candle burns, keeping watch.

"The widow's place is that way," Emma tells us.

There's a dirt path up ahead. No telephone poles or street lights. Just a clearing in the pine trees.

"You follow that trail," she says.

Faron jerks the wheel, pulling off the road.

"No. Please don't take me there," Emma says, grabbing my arm so tight it burns.

He slams the brakes.

"Please," she says again. "I can walk home by myself."

"You sure about that?" he asks.

She nods. "It's not far."

I push open the door. Emma is right behind me, scooting down from the truck in her long dress. She looks so out of place.

Not to mention, really scared. It doesn't seem right, leaving her alone, but she's already disappearing into the woods.

"Emma, wait."

I call her name, but the Old Order girl doesn't turn around. She's a dark shape, floating between the pine trees, until finally, she is gone.

## chapter twenty-seven
# old ways

The Yoder farm is hidden at the end of a dirt road. Faron parks the truck and we get out and walk. Unlike the other farmhouses I saw earlier, this place is rundown and neglected. Most of the shingles have fallen off the roof. The front porch is sagging as if it's about to collapse, and the paint has blistered like dead skin.

A dog trots out from behind the barn, whipping his tail. He lopes up to me and slams his paws on my shoulders.

"Looks like you two are old friends," says Faron.

"This is Alice's dog. His name's Shepherd," I say, scratching his ears. I remember from her letters. And the cornfield where the boys played baseball. It's empty now. Just a smear of brown stalks dappled with snow.

Shepherd crouches at my feet and whimpers. If he could talk, he'd tell us: *Somebody is nearby.*

The widow.

She's marching up the dirt road, carrying a stack of firewood. When she sees me, the logs tumble to the ground.

I stand in front of Mrs. Yoder, waiting for her to get angry. Scream at me. But she doesn't say a word. She bends down and gathers up the firewood like nothing ever happened.

"Lucy Zimmer," she finally says. "Are you just going to stand there catching flies?"

Slowly, I walk toward the pile of twisted branches. I scoop up as many as I can carry. Mrs. Yoder doesn't even glance at me.

"Come along," she says, disappearing inside the farmhouse.

I can't decide what to do.

The door hangs open, swinging on its hinges.

As I step onto the porch, the boards creak under my sneakers. It's dark inside and smells like old things. The kitchen is lit by the sickly glow of an oil lamp. There's a long pinewood table, like the kind my dad built. I wonder if Alice's dad made it.

Mrs. Yoder is hunched near a wood stove. I drop the armload of firewood on the floor. Still, she doesn't move. It's like I'm not even there. She tosses a branch into the fire and the air sharpens with smoke.

"Sit down," she says.

I sink into the hard wooden chair.

Faron doesn't sit at the table, although there's plenty of room. He stands in the corner, head bowed, looking at his hands.

Mrs. Yoder looks too.

She takes her time, peeling off her snow-crusted boots. It's so strange, the way she's acting, like I haven't come all this way, hoping to make things right. After a minute, she flicks her gaze at me.

"Where's your *kapp*?" she says.

Without thinking, I reach up and touch my hair.

She frowns. "Are you on *Rumspringa* now, too?"

I don't say anything. Mrs. Yoder knows I'm from Pinecraft. I'm not allowed to have *Rumspringa*.

"And the Mast boy," she says, glaring at Faron. "His name's been put in the *bann*. He's not supposed to be here. But it doesn't really matter. He can't work. Not with those broken hands. Nobody cares about him anyway."

Faron closes his eyes.

"Isn't that right?" she snaps.

"Leave him alone," I say, getting up from the table. "Faron hasn't done anything to you."

She motions for me to sit down. "What's happened to you, Lucy Zimmer? You were always such a strange little thing. We'd go to the beach and you'd dig up fish bones. Carry them home in a bucket, stinking like the devil. Always the one with the oddest questions. 'Do starfish come from the sky?'"

I remember those trips to Lido Key. The crowd of people on the sand, watching me and Alice—a pair of Amish girls digging for shells.

"A strange little thing," Mrs. Yoder says again. She nudges the rug on the floor, pushing it back in place. "Your father's heart must be shattered. Did he give up on you?"

"Did you give up on Alice?"

Mrs. Yoder flinches. It's the first hint of a reaction I've seen from her.

"That's a fine one, coming from the Beachy girl who left my daughter alone in Water Tower Park," she says. "There's nothing to be done with Alice. Not unless you go back in time."

What does she mean, go back in time?

"I'm sorry," I tell her. "I should've stayed with her."

"You went home," says Mrs. Yoder. "Isn't that what you said?"

The lie tightens its grip.

I can't hold on anymore.

"Yes, that's what I said. But it's not true."

I glance back at Faron. He's still looking at his hands.

Mrs. Yoder goes over to the wood stove. She tosses another handful of sticks in the fire. When she turns around, her eyes are shiny.

"I know," she says.

I'm stunned. How does she know?

She eases into a chair. Now we're sitting across from each other, just like the day after the party. This time, Dad isn't here to protect me.

Mrs. Yoder stares out the window. "Alice is dead," she says, watching the snow tap against the glass.

My head is spinning. I can't breathe in that too-close room. Can't make sense of what the Old Order woman is saying.

"She's with her father now."

When I hear "father," I think she means the Lord in heaven. Then I remember what the *Rumspringa* boys told me in Pinecraft Park.

*"She ain't no widow. That's just what Alice tells everybody. Her dad's still alive. He went missing too. Long time ago."*

Alice's dad left the Old Order. That must be the truth. Not those rumors about him falling through the ice on Cochrane Lake.

"Alice's dad is in Maine, isn't he?"

Mrs. Yoder doesn't answer.

"Alice is in Maine, too. And so is her father. He's not dead like you've been telling everyone. Why did you keep it a secret?"

She gets up and stands near the window.

Silent.

Alice's mom isn't going to tell me anything. Faron's right. This isn't Pinecraft. I'm an outsider. My dad is Beachy Amish-Mennonite. But I haven't been baptized.

In her mind, I'm not Amish at all.

"You shouldn't be here," Mrs. Yoder says, turning away.

When I was little, Alice's mom used to braid my hair, Old Order–style, and sing my favorite hymns in Deitsch. It was like digging up a secret, like the doves hidden inside a sand dollar. We sang together, walking home from Lido Key, our buckets full of shells.

I used to think we'd always be friends. Me and Alice. But that's when the world wasn't so big. Now I know it's made of yarn and thread. Many stitches, tied together. One square of tattered cloth, holding on to the next. All different, though they might look the same.

There's room enough for all.

"If you don't tell me where Alice is," I say to Mrs. Yoder, "I'll tell everybody that you lied about her dad."

Mrs. Yoder turns around. "And why would they believe you?"

"Because I'm going to find him," I tell her. "And then everybody will know you lied."

"Why would I lie?" she says, a little too quickly.

"Because you're scared. You didn't want to lose Alice. It's like she never had a chance. Never got to see anything, except what you wanted her to see. But now I'm starting to see different too."

The snow taps against the glass like a wind chime.

I ask the question again.

"Tell me where Alice is," I say, getting up from the table. "Or I will tell everybody the truth."

"The truth?" Her sharp little face turns toward mine. "Here's the truth, Lucy Zimmer. You talk high and mighty, but you don't know wrong from right. You think there's no harm in making up your own rules. Not following the Lord's path. Hard work. That's the only thing that counts in this world."

"The Lord gave us brains, didn't He?"

Mrs. Yoder glares. "You're a Pinecraft girl. Your idea of hard work is walking on the beach."

"Hard work doesn't make you a good person."

"Is that right?" she snaps. "You're an expert on goodness, now? What makes you so perfect?"

"I'm not perfect," I tell her. "But as far as I can tell, the Lord doesn't care about the length of your dress. Or if a girl wears a skirt or jeans. I'm sure He's got better things to worry about."

"That's enough." Mrs. Yoder opens a drawer and hands me a knife. "Go on. Make yourself useful."

There's a heap of potatoes in a bowl next to the sink. I start peeling them, but my fingers won't stay still.

Faron stands behind me and holds the knife steady.

"Thanks," I whisper.

Mrs. Yoder puts on her coat and slips outside. I have no idea what she's doing out there. The snow is falling heavier now, piling on the windowsill. After a minute, the door swings open, letting in a gust of cold.

"That truck parked by the road. Does it belong to you?" she asks.

I glance up at Faron. He slices even faster, peeling one long curlicue.

"Yeah, it's ours," I say.

"Must've cost a lot."

The knife clatters on the floor. When I pick it up, the handle is speckled with blood.

Mrs. Yoder snatches it away from me. "You're no good in the kitchen," she says, wiping the knife. "Probably can't even set the table."

"Yeah, but I can build one," I mutter.

Faron laughs so hard, Mrs. Yoder spins around. She drags a chair into a corner of the room and he sits down without a word.

All this time, Mrs. Yoder hasn't said anything to him. She hasn't even looked at him. Not once.

So this is what shunning feels like.

It's even worse than dying. At least when you're dead, you leave a memory, like a fingerprint on the earth.

Shunning is like you never lived at all.

"Come along, Lucy," she says, handing me a lamp.

I follow her through the hallway to a door near the stairs. Mrs. Yoder pushes it open. It's so dark, I can hardly see the steps disappearing into the basement.

*Please don't make me go in there.*

"Get yourself cleaned up," she says, as if I've made her house dirty, just by breathing in it.

The damp air smells like the roots of sleeping trees. I hold the lamp in both hands as the door slowly closes behind me. There's a washtub at the bottom of the steps. Alice used to carry a tea kettle for hot water in the winter. I remember from her letters. Mrs. Yoder doesn't give me a kettle. Only a sliver of soap, thin as a fingernail.

I rinse my face over a bowl near the tub. The water's so cold, my hands are numb within seconds. Is this where Alice scrubbed her hair in a bucket? I try to imagine her in this house, trapped with her secrets.

Alice must've known that her dad is still alive. She had to go around, make believing he was a ghost.

The longer you tell a lie, the closer it feels to the truth.

I need to find out more about Alice's family, but I'm running out of time. Mrs. Yoder isn't talking. She just wants me to leave. Only the snow is keeping me here. In the morning, it will be gone. And so will I.

When I climb upstairs, the table is already set. Two lonely plates. Faron is still in a corner of the room, slumped in a chair.

"For the boy," says Mrs. Yoder, handing me a plate of chicken and boiled potatoes. Is she really going to make Faron eat by himself?

In church, everybody's always going on about forgiveness. Turn the other cheek. Love your neighbor more than yourself. They make it sound so easy. How can you believe those words and treat somebody so bad? Doesn't Faron deserve a second chance? What about the rest of us? Alice. Her dad.

Don't they deserve forgiveness too?

I put Faron's plate on the table.

"Not there," says Mrs. Yoder.

I don't move. "Why isn't he eating with us?"

"You know why," she says.

"Lucy." Faron's eyes are pleading with me. "Leave it alone. It's just the way things are done."

"Well, maybe it's time to change the rules," I say, looking at Mrs. Yoder.

"Rules? What do you know about rules, Lucy Zimmer?" she says. "You were spoiled in Pinecraft, running around, free as you please. As far as I can tell, your father didn't teach you anything."

It makes me sick, the way she's talking about Dad. Maybe he's not perfect. But my dad would never treat anybody like this.

"The *bann* doesn't teach you anything," I say.

Mrs. Yoder frowns. "It teaches you not to stray from the Lord."

"The Lord doesn't care about the *bann*."

"So you're talking about the Lord now?"

"The Lord doesn't care if my head is covered. Or if my dress is too short. It's just a bunch of rules that somebody made up."

"The rules are in place for a reason."

"And what's that? Why is my dad allowed to drive a car in Florida? And why do the Old Order girls in Maine go around in buggies? Or roller skates? It's not like it's written in the Bible. I mean, does it even matter?"

I know the answer. It's not about electricity. If you're Amish, it's about letting the world into your home.

"Don't you question the rules," says Mrs. Yoder. "They're what's keeping us safe together."

"Did the rules keep Alice safe?"

Mrs. Yoder slaps me so hard, I stumble backward.

Nobody's ever hit me before. Dad never laid a hand on me, no matter what I did. This is a different kind of anger, leaking its poison into Mrs. Yoder like the hole at the bottom of the ocean. And she's been holding on to it for a long time.

Faron rushes over to me, but Mrs. Yoder moves between us.

"You will sleep in the barn," she tells him. "I want you both gone before the sun rises."

"He'll freeze out there," I say, but she's already climbing upstairs, taking the steps two at a time.

Faron grabs the lamp off the table. I follow him through the kitchen door into the yard, where he stands in the faint light, staring up at the sky.

There's the cold and nothing else.

Still, we look.

*September 5*
*Smyrna, Maine*

*Dear Lucy,*

*He says he loves me.*

*Last night we kissed in the field behind the barn. My heart was beating so fast, I thought it was going to explode. I never felt a kiss like that before. Then I looked up and a star crackled across the sky. It was a sign. I just know it.*

*I've been saving up my money from the Amish Market. Tobias says he's going to need LOTS of cash, if he's taking the bus to Florida. I keep it hidden real good so Mom won't find it. There's a loose board under my bed. It wiggles like a rotten tooth. That's where I hid the money.*

*I hope it's enough.*

*Lucy, I'm on my way out of here. And once I'm gone, I'm never coming back. I'm sick of working all day. "Chicken chores" Mom calls it. Throwing scraps at the hens before they bite off my fingers. Sweating over the stove all day, making jam. (Why can't we buy a jar at the store once in a while?) By the time everything is done, it's time for bed.*

*I'm working on a plan so me and Tobias can be together. I can't tell you everything yet. But it's going to be so perfect. Once*

*I get down to Pinecraft, I'll figure out a way to escape. Will you help me?*

*Remember when we used to climb the mango tree behind your house? You told me that we'd always be friends, no matter what. And I believed you. It didn't matter that we lived so far away. Or that our families are so different. All that mattered was our amazing friendship.*

*When I said you're like a sister to me, I meant it. You're the only one I can trust. I always felt like I could tell you anything. You never judged me. Not even when I told you that I'm not sure if I believe in God anymore. It's hard to believe in something you can't see.*

*The red mare is missing again.*

*I don't think she's coming back.*

*Seven days until Florida.*

*Alice*

## chapter twenty-eight
# thin ice

In Alice's bedroom, I shiver under her quilt. This is where she wrote letters by candlelight. It's where her dresses still droop from their hooks. And it's where she dreamed of escape. But the pinewood walls can't trap me inside this lonely farmhouse.

The house is listening. Floorboards creak as I slip out of bed, holding my breath, in case it hears that too. I head downstairs, where an old-fashioned clothes wringer sits in a corner near a row of dresses hung to dry. They sway on the line, delicate as the skins of living things.

I duck under the clothesline. Almost there. My coat is by the front door, hanging above my muddy sneakers. But Mrs. Yoder's shoes aren't there.

She's gone.

I shove my feet in the sneakers and yank the laces tight. When I pull the door open, the wind blasts through me. The more I think about Mrs. Yoder, the way she treated Faron, the colder I grow inside.

The Yoder's barn is on the hill. I run toward it, flinching against the snow. By the time I reach the top, I'm out of breath. The barn reminds me of the pictures in my dad's Amish calendar—a tall, red building with a pointy roof. A wooden star nailed to the door. I wonder if the Old Order men in Smyrna got together to build it, a long time ago.

"Many hands make easy work," Dad told me.

He said the barn raisings are about bringing people together. One big family. That's what the Amish are supposed to be.

I push the double doors open.

Alice's dog is curled up on the floor. He thumps his tail and whines.

"Don't say anything," I whisper.

I pull myself up the ladder and pray I don't fall. If I wasn't so scared, I might think the loft is a cozy place to sleep. The bales of sweet-smelling hay are stacked so high, they almost touch the rafters.

Faron is huddled under a blanket, shivering. I nudge his shoulder.

"Wake up. Mrs. Yoder knows about the truck," I tell him.

He lifts his head. "Lucy? What are you talking about?"

"She's in the woods. We have to leave. Now. Before she comes back."

We climb down from the loft and head outside, where a gravel path twists through the pines behind the barn.

"That's probably where she went." I point to a light shining on the hill.

"It's the neighbor's house," he says. "I bet she goes over there to borrow their phone."

A wave of sickness crashes over me. "Mrs. Yoder is there right now, calling the police. She waited until you went to sleep."

"Are you sure? The Old Order aren't like that. I mean, she wouldn't do that to me," he says, as if trying to convince himself.

"Don't you get it? She doesn't care if your family's Old Order," I tell him. "Because you're not anymore."

Faron glances over his shoulder. The truck is parked near the road, the windshield covered in snow and dead leaves. Now he's got to choose. He can trust me. Or put his faith in the Old Order, the family who turned him away.

He takes out his keys.

After tonight, he'll never drive that truck again.

• • •

We're driving real slow through the woods. Ahead of us is the lake, surrounded by dozens of smashed-up cars, their parts scattered on the ground as if they fell from the sky. All the trees are thin and silvery. In the distance, the water gleams in the moonlight.

"This is the lake," I tell Faron.

"You really think Alice's dad is still alive?"

*She's with her father now.* That's what Mrs. Yoder told me. If Alice skipped stones on this lake, it was a long time ago.

"Mrs. Yoder's been lying all this time. She's been telling everybody that he's dead. And it isn't true."

"But why?" he asks.

"Something bad happened here," I say, glancing at the cool surface of the lake, so still and silent.

I can't go back and make things right.

The past is in the past. That's where it belongs.

"Alice is with her dad," I tell Faron. "If we find him, we'll find her too."

"What if he doesn't want to be found?"

He's right. What if Mr. Yoder's changed after all this time? Maybe he's gone rotten inside. There's no telling what happened to him.

My throat's so dry, I can't swallow. Can't even gulp a breath. I lick my lips and stare out at the lake. "We have to find him. But first we're ditching the truck."

Faron shakes his head. "You're sure about this?"

"Mrs. Yoder's got the police looking for us."

"So how are we supposed to find Alice's dad on foot? You can't get far if you walk. Not if it keeps snowing."

I don't know how we're going to find Alice's dad, but one thing's for sure.

We'll be together.

I get out and start walking. Dozens of abandoned cars are all around us. Weeds twist through the metal frames, shooting up through piles of snow. Their empty husks are scattered in the woods like crab shells picked clean of their meat.

"It's nothing but a graveyard," says Faron.

I blink.

"A graveyard for cars."

Some are just empty husks, like bones chewed and spit out. The broken pieces seem to float in the darkness. They're just things that men built out of rubber and metal and steel. They aren't alive and they can't hurt me.

We look back at the truck.

"Okay," he says. "Start pushing."

I shove my weight against the bumper.

It doesn't move.

"We need to get some speed going," he says, slamming both hands on the truck bed.

Slowly, the tires crunch over things in the dark. When the truck begins to roll, Faron jumps in the driver's seat, but we've already lost steam. I'm pushing as hard as I can, but the wheels won't spin any faster. I try again and slip on the icy ground.

Faron gets out and helps me push. When he's back inside the truck, it rolls to a stop like it knows what's coming next.

"This ain't working," he says, climbing out. "Got a better idea?"

"You push. I'll drive."

He shakes his head. "It's too dangerous."

"I can do it."

"Yeah, I know you can. But I won't let you."

"It's my decision."

"No, Lucy," he says.

I look away. "Why don't you trust me?"

"It's my fault we're in trouble," he says. "No going around it. And now I've got to make things right."

"Maybe it's your fault. But you don't have to live with it forever. You deserve a second chance."

Doesn't everyone?

Faron is quiet as I get in the driver's seat.

"Let me do this," I tell him.

He kisses my forehead. "I trust you," he says, but I already know.

I lean back against the seat. "Now show me what to do."

"Leave the key here," he says, jamming it in the ignition. His hands are shaking. "Turn everything off. Now put the clutch in. You can coast while it's not in gear."

"Got it."

I jerk forward as he begins to push. Then I grip the steering wheel and put the clutch in, like he told me.

As the truck rolls toward the lake, I'm not scared anymore. I'm still thinking about water—how it changes from one thing to another, yet stays the same.

"Let the clutch off," Faron shouts.

And I do.

A spray fans over the hood like wings. I sit pressed against the driver's seat, hypnotized by the waves plunging toward the windshield. Below the mirror, the lucky rabbit's foot swings and bounces.

I push myself out of the truck and hit the ground hard. Pain zings through my chest as I roll onto my side, gasping for breath. The truck dips below the surface of Lake Cochrane, sinking lower and lower, surrounded by ropes of foam. Then Faron is stroking my face, saying things from far away.

"It's all right, Lucy," he says. "You did good. Real good."

I stare out at the lake. Where the truck floated, there's only water, as flat and still as a quilt.

• • •

The sun is cold. We make our way through the woods, shivering in the pale morning light. The smashed-up cars are hidden behind the pines, twisted and forgotten. When we reach the highway, Faron grabs my hand and squeezes.

"Think it's safe out here?" he asks.

The truck's gone. But I don't think we're safe. Not if Mrs. Yoder is telling everybody in Smyrna about us. There's a diner just off the interstate—a slate-gray building with a faded Coca-Cola banner in the driveway.

I squeeze back. "Let's take a chance."

"Okay," he says. "Can't hide in the woods forever."

Cars speed past us, blaring their horns as we wait to cross. Some of the drivers slow down to take a look. I'm just a girl in a dirty coat, walking beside the road.

We head inside the diner and find a booth near the window. This place smells like coffee and bacon grease. I'm way too nervous to eat. I rip open a pack of sugar and dump it on the table, dragging my finger through the sparkly grains, tracing a heart.

"I'm running on fumes," says Faron. "How much money we got left?"

"You can eat for me," I say, plunking a handful of quarters on the table.

"That much, huh?"

My shoulder aches from where I fell. All the muscle and bone. The parts you can't see. That's what hurts the most.

Our waitress comes over with the menus. She's a little older than me, but she's already got creases in her forehead.

"I hate the hillbilly music they play in here," she says, dumping ice in my water glass. "It's not real country."

Her tongue is pierced with a tiny metal pearl. It looks so painful. How does she take it out? Maybe she never takes it out.

"What can I get started for you guys?" she asks. "My name's Sadie, by the way."

"I want the eggs any style," says Faron, pointing at the menu.

"Okay." She waits.

When he doesn't say anything, it hits me. He's probably never ordered food in a restaurant before.

"How do you like your eggs, hon?" she finally asks.

He looks confused. "The fancy kind with the yellow sauce. And toast."

"Sure thing. What kind of bread?"

"Toasted." He gets up and leaves the table.

I bite my lip and try not to laugh. Sometimes I want to strangle Faron, and sometimes he's the funniest person I ever met.

"Your boyfriend's kind of different," says Sadie.

"He's just tired."

"When he said 'fancy eggs,' did he mean hollandaise?"

"Sounds fancy." I glance across the diner, where a silver-haired couple is sharing a muffin, sliced in half.

One slice.

That's all they need.

"And you?" Sadie asks.

"I'll skip the fancy eggs."

"Plain works for me too." She winks.

Sadie goes away and I'm alone again. I'm still thinking about the frozen lake, the way it keeps its secrets hidden. What happened there long ago?

When Faron comes back, he looks a little better. He must've shaved while he was in the bathroom. His face is smooth, and when he kisses me, I go back to our first night on the beach. How much has changed in a short time.

"Back to normal," he says, brushing his face against mine. "Maybe we should test it out?"

"Test what out?"

"The difference."

He smiles and I can't help smiling back.

Across the room, the silver-haired man and his wife are getting up from their table. The man looks back at us like he's remembering something. Then he takes his wife's hand and walks away.

I stare at their empty table. Nothing left but crumbs and a newspaper. It's a local paper, like *The Budget* back home.

Maybe there's a chance.

Once you've been with the Amish, they will always be part of you. That's what I'm thinking when I grab the newspaper and bring it to our table. I spread the pages like a map. All those ads for "gently used" hockey skates and sewing machines. The scattered bits and pieces of someone else's life.

"Maybe someone wants to buy a truck," says Faron.

"Too late now."

"Yeah," he says. "That old Ford is swimming with the fishes."

"I didn't see any fish in that nasty water."

He smirks. "You're something else, you know that?"

"Thanks."

"Come on," he says. "I'm just trying to make you laugh."

"Well, try harder."

I'm still looking through the newspaper, scanning every page. On the back, there's a row of ads. *We treat your car like family* says the banner floating above a man's head.

He's got a gray-stained beard that curves around his smile. Blue jeans hitched up with suspenders. A straw hat pulled down low over his forehead.

"All right, honey. Here you go."

The waitress slides a plate in front of me. The greasy smell of bacon and eggs yanks me back to the present.

"How far away is this place?" I jab my thumb at the man's picture in the newspaper.

"Oh, just down the road a piece. Sam Yoder does good work. His prices are always fair. As honest as they come."

Sam Yoder.

"Do you know Mr. Yoder?" I ask.

"He's a good guy. Fixed my brother's pickup last summer. Got it back in action, same day."

I squint at the address in the paper. "Can we walk there?"

"Well, I guess you could, if you're up for walking. But I'm telling you, hon. It's nippy outside. You got car trouble?"

"Something like that."

"My shift's about to end. I could give you a ride, if we move fast. Want me to box that up?" she says, grabbing my plate.

"I can move pretty fast," I tell her.

Sadie laughs. "Well, let's get going."

## chapter twenty-nine

# hearts like flint

We're speeding down Smokey Hollow Road, passing every car. Sadie's got the windows open, though it's "colder than a dog's nose."

"This would be a mighty long walk," she says, taking a bottle of nail polish out of her purse. "Where's your car at? Did it break down on the highway?"

I twist around in my seat. Faron's in the back, trying to balance a Styrofoam container on his knees. He mops up the fancy eggs with a wedge of toast and shoves the whole thing in his mouth.

"Our truck's near Cochrane Lake," I say.

Not exactly the truth, but close enough.

"Well, it picked the right spot to die." Sadie plops her hand on the steering wheel and dabs a glob of sparkly black polish on her thumb. "I've been hiking up that way, and I'm telling you, there's a patch of woods that's a graveyard for cars. Wouldn't be surprised if there's cars at the bottom of that lake," she says, fanning her hand back and forth. "Gives me the willies, just thinking about it."

"Did anybody ever drown there?" I ask.

Sadie blinks. "Yeah, we've had a few drownings. Lots of people go out walking on that ice, thinking it's safe. Next thing you know, boom." She thumps the dashboard. "They're gone." She looks at me. "Why do you want to know?"

"I'm just wondering. I mean, it seems pretty dangerous."

"No kidding," Sadie tells me. "Five minutes in that water and you've got no strength left. That's how cold it is. Ever go swimming in the Atlantic?"

The Gulf's not the same thing. But I nod anyway.

"Well, it's a heck of a lot colder," she says. "Actually, there was a little girl who drowned in that lake. Maybe ten years ago."

I sit up straight. "Was the little girl from an Amish family?"

"As a matter of fact, she was. Her father couldn't save them both. That's the saddest part."

"What do you mean, 'both'?"

"There were two little girls who sank through the ice."

"Two?"

"Only one made it."

I'm thinking hard.

All this time, I thought Alice was alone, like me. We were sisters. That's what she always said.

In my mind, I see the frozen lake. Two little girls in dark dresses and bonnets walking on the ice. A man in a straw hat and suspenders. He's calling out, but there's nothing he can do as they drop through the ice, disappearing into cold water.

We slow down and make a left turn. The auto repair shop is on a hill sloping near the road. It reminds me of a farmhouse with an extra big garage. A stack of tires is heaped on the curb, where a jack-o'-lantern sits on a bale of hay. The sign in the driveway says:

MUFFLERS, JOINTS, BRAKS.

Sadie giggles. "Looks like they ran out of *e*'s. Well, this is the car place. You guys all set?"

If it's true that we're mostly made of water, I'd say the tides inside me are churning, hurricane-style. Is Mr. Yoder going to talk to us? Does he know that Alice is in trouble? What if he really isn't her dad?

"Good luck, hon." Sadie wiggles her sparkly fingers as I climb out.

All my molecules are spinning as I head across the road. Sadie honks like we're old friends. Now she's making a U-turn. She must've gone out of her way, driving us here. I'd never expect her to do that. Not even if she was from Pinecraft.

Faron marches right up to the garage. He peers inside the window. "Check out the old cars."

I press my face against the glass. "That one looks like a boat," I say, pointing at a convertible with fins sprouting out of the fenders.

"It's a fifty-seven Thunderbird," he says. "Man, I wish I could get under that hood."

"Why does it have fins?"

"Those are called skegs. It's just for show," he tells me. "They won't make it go fast."

I look up at him. "This is your world, isn't it?"

"Not even close," he says.

Just then, someone calls out, "Can I help you folks?"

We both turn around.

There's a man in a straw hat walking toward us. He's tall and clean-shaven, with a belly straining against his belt. I search for Alice in his face. They've got the same wide-set eyes, as if those blue eyes started off closer together, then drifted apart.

"Mighty pleased to meet you," he says, offering his hand. His fingernails are a little dirty, the ridges caked with grease, but I don't mind. "So what brings you folks here?"

I can't lie to Mr. Yoder. If I say that I'm looking for Alice, what's he going to do? Will he get angry at me?

"I'm a friend of your daughter," I say, looking right at him.

Mr. Yoder crosses his arms. "How did you find me?"

"I knew where to look."

Faron gives me a smile that says keep going. Don't give up. Not after we've come all this way.

"Where is she now?" I ask.

"Home."

There's something in that word, *home*. I get a shivery feeling, like I'm walking on the ice with Alice and her sister, praying the lake won't let go.

"I've been waiting for Alice to come home," says Mr. Yoder. "But you know what they say. The road home's never too far."

"Can I talk to her?"

He frowns. "I'm not sure if Alice is up for company."

"Please. Just tell her I'm here."

"I didn't catch your name."

"Lucy Zimmer."

"My girl's been through a lot," he says, rubbing his forehead. "But she's a tough little knot. You know that?"

I know.

"Hearts like flint."

Mr. Yoder stares at me. Then he murmurs the words in Deitsch.

*"De mad mit dika boka.*

*Hen Hartsa we do woka."*

"Well, Miss Lucy," he says. "Cold day, ain't it? The weather guy says it's going to be a balmy thirty-eight degrees. Let's get the heck inside."

He unlocks the door and we follow him into the office. Hubcaps glint across the wall like hunting trophies. There's a portable radio on his desk with a coat hanger for an antenna. Over the faint hiss of the radiator, a gospel tune plays a song about a love so deep, it could drain the oceans.

"You wait here," he says, putting on his coat. "I'll go have a little chat with my daughter."

Waiting is one thing I'm good at.

Mr. Yoder marches out of the office. I stand near the window and watch him cross the road. He probably lives nearby. I think of Dad's workshop behind our house in Pinecraft.

Faron puts his arm around me. "Is he telling the truth? I mean, is he really Alice's dad?"

Only one way to find out.

After what seems like forever, the door swings open.

"She's on her way," says Mr. Yoder.

I don't know what to say, except, "Thank you." It's the best I can do. Then nobody says anything for a while.

"You got a lot of nice cars," says Faron, breaking the silence. "Is it okay if I check out that fifty-seven convertible?"

Mr. Yoder smiles. "You like old cars, son?"

"Are you kidding? That Thunderbird is a classic."

The two of them disappear into the garage. They're giving me time alone. And that's exactly what I need.

When Alice said she was running away, I never thought I'd find myself in Smyrna, Maine, talking to her dead father. I didn't count on meeting Faron either. Not a *Rumspringa* boy. Or an Old Order ghost. They're something in-between. Both on the outside, looking in.

That's something I understand.

Now I'm alone in Mr. Yoder's office, staring at that door. There's a chain of bells looped around the handle. It jingles whenever somebody breezes in or out, and that's exactly what it does when Alice walks through.

• • •

All this time, I've been looking for my best friend, thinking she's dead. And now she's standing in front of me. I'm still angry at her, which feels so wrong. How can you be angry at a ghost?

She's all bundled up in a denim jacket. The cuffs are studded with tiny metal hearts. Definitely not an Old Order–style coat. When Alice looks at me, her face doesn't change. It's like she doesn't know me anymore.

"Lucy?" she says, turning her head in my direction.

Now she's seeing me, really seeing. All the noise inside that room fades away. The hiss of the radiator, the dull hum of traffic on the highway, my heart slamming against the bones in my chest.

Alice throws her arms around me. "I can't believe you're here," she says, breaking into a sob.

We hug each other for a long time.

Then I let go.

As much as I'm glad to see Alice, I'm still angry.

"You look different," she says, wiping her face. "I mean, in a good way. Dresses are kind of boring, right?"

"Sometimes," I say.

"Well, you always had the prettiest colors. I was so jealous."

Alice was jealous of me?

"But I'm still in plain clothes."

"There's nothing plain about your hat, Lucy. It's kind of amazing," she says.

I lift my hand and touch the furry ears. My snow leopard.

"Thanks," I say. "It's a present from a friend."

"I don't have a lot of close friends," she says, looking at me. "Just one."

"Do I know her?"

"You might," Alice says, smiling. "She's a really cool girl. There aren't many friends who would drive across the country, just to find someone who left without saying goodbye."

"Well, maybe her friend had a good reason for leaving."

"You probably thought I hated you or something," she says.

"No, I didn't."

"But you're still mad."

I look at the floor.

"Yeah, that's what I thought," she says.

"Are you going to tell the truth now?"

Alice sighs. "Where do I start?"

"How about the beginning?"

"Okay."

Alice shrugs out of her jean jacket. She collapses into the chair across from me, like she can't hold herself up anymore.

"That night at the party, I got a little wasted." She takes a breath. "This is so embarrassing. Please don't hate me."

"I don't hate you."

There's more I need to say. "I waited on the beach. What happened to you?"

Alice lowers her head.

"Why can't you tell me?" I shout, but she won't even look up. After all I've been through, don't I have a right to know the truth?

She owes me that much.

"Fine," I say, buttoning up my coat. "I can't believe you used to be my friend."

"Lucy, wait," she says, like that's going to make me stay. "Just give me time to explain."

"You've had enough time," I say, marching across the room.

Alice follows behind me. "Please don't go."

She's changed. That's for sure. I turn and study her face. The tiny gold hoops pinching her ears. A softness in her voice that wasn't there before. Her jaw clenched tight.

I've changed too. I steered the truck into cold water. Slept in a boy's arms under the stars. Walked away from my baptism. Dad. The orange grove and the oaks thick with Spanish moss. All I knew back home in Pinecraft.

Everything around us has shifted like the tide. Maybe that's what friends do. We move and flow in different directions. I'll never stop caring about Alice. It's not like she tried to hurt me, yet our friendship will never be the same. I feel the dull ache of sadness sweeping over me. But I also feel relief, as strong as the ocean's pulse.

As I reach for the door, she's crying.
Still, I don't turn around.
I leave.

## chapter thirty
# over the mountain

The road outside the garage is dappled with snow. I don't know where I'm headed. It doesn't matter, just as long as it's away from Alice.

I can't believe she did this to me. The whole world turned upside down when she disappeared. At least, that's what it felt like. And I still don't know the truth. Why is she hiding at her dad's? Is it really so awful, she can't talk about it?

We used to tell each other everything. I think about the empty lot in Pinecraft, the mango trees we used to climb. Long days at the beach, digging for sand dollars. It didn't matter that our families aren't the same. The world was small enough for both of us. But it's not so small anymore.

I never thought I'd be this far from home. Never believed it was possible. Yeah, I used to wish for it. When Alice gave me that book about the ocean, I almost gave it back. Why bother wishing for something you can't have?

Now I'm farther from the Gulf than I've ever been. When I was little, I used to dream that the surf went on forever. It was easy to imagine the tide drifting into the horizon. One day it will disappear. The water will pull away from the shore. Oceans will fade into sand.

When I built the gazebo with Dad, I noticed the knots in the wood, swirling patterns like a fingerprint. The tree used to be alive. Then it turned into something else. If I buried it in the ground, another tree might grow out of it.

The world is a living thing that changes and grows.

It will keep changing and so will I.

"Lucy?"

I hear Alice calling. Yeah, like I'm going to turn around. She's had enough chances. Too many, if you ask me.

"Please," Alice says, running up the path. "You probably want to skin me alive."

"You're right," I mutter.

"I totally understand why you're mad."

"Then leave."

As soon as it pops out of my mouth, I realize what I've said. The same words Alice threw at me, the night she disappeared.

Alice must remember too. When I finally turn around, I see the tears dribbling down her neck and I feel bad all over again.

"Let's go back inside." I stretch out my hand. For a moment, I'm not sure she's going to take it. Alice stares at it, then grabs hold. Together we walk back to her dad's garage, our footprints stamping the path.

The garage is warm. Almost too warm as I sink into Mr. Yoder's big leather chair.

Alice sits across from me, wiping her eyes. "Thanks for giving me another chance. I know you're really angry."

I was angry.

"When you didn't show up on the beach, I thought you were dead."

"I know," she says quietly.

"You know? Well, here's what I don't know. Why have you been lying all this time about your dad?"

I need to know the truth.

That's all I can ask for.

"I can explain," she says.

"And Tobias?"

"At first, he seemed really cool," she says, looking at the floor. "I could tell him anything. He's the only one who really understood."

*What about me?*

That's what I want to say.

"We used to play these games online," she mumbles. "It sounds kind of stupid now."

"You had a secret world."

"Yeah," she says. "Guess it's not so secret anymore."

"And he used you."

She lifts her head. "How did you find out?"

"I talked to him."

"When?" she asks, surprised.

I can tell she wasn't expecting that.

"A couple days ago. Me and Faron tracked him down at the cannery."

"You went all the way out there?"

"I figured if you're looking for trouble, it's not hard to find."

"What did he tell you?"

"He didn't know you were Amish at first."

She smiles. "That's why I loved going online. Nobody judged me there. I could finally be myself, you know?"

I do know.

When I hear Alice talking like that, I can't help thinking of Crystal. She told me the same thing, the day she called me a princess.

"It wasn't easy," says Alice. "Sneaking into the library, once my chores were done. I had to walk real far, just to get there. It was the safest place I could find."

If Alice wanted to do something, no soul on earth could stop her. That much I knew. And when she called the library her safe place, I understood that, too. Just like the doves inside a sand dollar, we kept our secrets.

"I saw these girls playing a game online. And it looked like fun," Alice explains. "Back home, we weren't even allowed to play baseball. Especially if you're a girl," she adds.

I nod, remembering what Faron told me. When you hear *no* all the time, you're aching to hear a *yes*.

"They showed me how to play *Warcraft*," she says. "It's this game where you can change into different people."

"Yeah, I know."

"That's how I met Tobias. We started talking online. At first, it was just about the game. Then he gave me his phone number. I couldn't call him from my house. So I needed my own cell. And he bought one for me." She shakes her head. "It was so amazing. I never had something like that before. But then I had to explain. I mean, about being *different*," she says. And I know exactly what she means.

"When did you finally meet in real life?" I ask.

She hesitates for a moment. "It was hard, trying to find a place to meet without Mom getting in the way. We had it all planned out. I'd go to the Amish Market, like I always did on the weekend. I'd make some excuse about staying behind to clean up."

"But you were with Tobias."

"That's right," she says, blushing. "He'd wait out in the field behind the parking lot until I came out."

The way she's talking, it sounds so exciting. Almost too good to be true. And that's when I can't sit still anymore. Can't listen to her talk about this boy as if he's the end of the ocean. After all, there's no such thing.

"Tobias said you ditched him at the party."

"Well, he's half right," she says. "We were supposed to go to the bus station in the morning. But we got in a major fight. He took my cell phone away. And he stole my money."

"Sounds like that's all he cared about."

"Well, he didn't get all of it," says Alice. "You want it? For real. You should have it."

"I can't take your money."

I want to ask another question. An important one.

"Did Tobias hit you?"

She doesn't answer.

I get up from the chair and put my arms around her. "It's not your fault, okay? You didn't do anything wrong. I just want you to know . . . I'm here."

Alice looks at me.

"Yeah, he did," she says, her voice shaking. "I kept telling myself, 'Oh, it won't happen again. It was an accident. He didn't mean to do it.' Most of the time, he was really nice to me. He'd buy all this stuff. It made me feel special, you know?"

"And he did it again."

She nods. "It was like he was wearing a mask. When we were at the party, it got really bad. So I grabbed my stuff and walked back to Pinecraft."

"You walked?"

"What was I supposed to do? Tobias just left me there. I was so drunk, I actually thought I could make it home. But I didn't get very far."

"You walked all that way?"

"Most of it," she says. "At least, I was walking until I passed out."

"What?" I can't believe this.

"I told you, Lucy. It's the most embarrassing thing ever. I woke up in the grass somewhere near Bahia Vista. Then I walked home."

"Your mom came to my house the next day."

"She did?" Alice says.

"I didn't tell her about your boyfriend or whatever."

"For real?" Alice hugs me again. "You're the best, Lucy. I'm so sorry that I dragged you into this. You deserve so much better."

"It's okay."

"Did you ever make it to Lido Key that night?" she asks.

"Yeah, I was on the beach."

"All by yourself?" She smirks.

"Faron drove me."

"So you guys are together now?"

"Maybe."

"I have a good feeling about him," she says. "You're really lucky. You know that, right?"

I don't believe in luck. But Alice has got me thinking. Maybe if I did, that's exactly what I'd be.

"Dad told me you were here with a boy," she says, smiling.

"That's funny. I didn't know ghosts could talk."

Alice blushes. "There's a lot of stuff I need to explain."

"I'm listening."

"My dad left the Old Order when I was really little. I didn't really understand what was going on."

"Why didn't you tell me?"

"It was a big secret. My mom told everybody he was dead."

"But you knew he wasn't."

"Yeah, I knew." Alice gets this far-off look on her face. "I used to see him sometimes. I'd be walking to church. But I had to act like he wasn't there. I wasn't allowed to talk to my dad. He was like a ghost."

"That must've been really hard."

"Mom always talked bad about him. I didn't know what to believe. But she doesn't control my life anymore."

"What made your dad change his mind about being Amish?"

She doesn't answer.

"Did something bad happen to him?" I ask gently. "Something that made him lose his faith?"

"It was a long time ago," Alice says, glancing at the wall.

I follow her eyes, and that's when I notice the Amish calendar above the desk. The black-and-white picture of a lake in winter. A pair of little girls in dark bonnets, marching through the woods.

"We were skipping stones on the lake," she says, her voice breaking. "He couldn't reach both of us in time. Me and my little sister. It happened so fast." Alice is crying now. All the world's tears pouring out of her. Everything she's held inside.

I try to imagine it. Alice dropping through the ice in one quick motion. Her dad pulling her to safety. The other little girl slipping away, her mouth open in a silent scream.

*. . . only one made it . . .*

"After the accident, he lost faith in himself," says Alice, looking at the floor. "That's when he left the church."

"So your dad wasn't shunned? It was his choice to walk away?"

"You always have a choice."

Yeah, that's what I've heard all my life. But it doesn't feel that way. Not when your choices have to be perfect.

I put my arm around her. "It's not your dad's fault. No matter what your mom says."

Alice finally stops shaking. She rubs her face on her sleeve. "Every time we came to Pinecraft, I had to act like he was dead. My mom was so embarrassed about him leaving the church. We got real good at pretending," she says, making me think of the games online.

The longer you tell a lie, the more it sounds like the truth.

"And my dad . . . he gave me a choice," she says.

"What do you mean?"

"He asked if I wanted to go with him."

"Before he left the Old Order?"

"Yeah," she says. "Of course I stayed with Mom. I was really small. I didn't know what I was supposed to do."

Alice was just a little kid. How could she make such a big decision? Maybe even harder than *Rumspringa*.

"How did you find him again?" I ask.

"I did a search online. It wasn't that hard. This was back at the library in Pinecraft. I found the place where he works. When I found out it wasn't too far away, I was really sad. I mean, he was right here, but I couldn't talk to him."

They were living in two separate worlds. It's not like Alice could do anything about it. Still, I know why she was sad.

"The day after the party, Mom was looking all over Pinecraft for me. You should've seen her face when I finally walked home. She grabbed all my stuff and we got on the bus. As soon as we got back to Maine, I ran next door and called my dad."

"Why didn't you tell me about this?"

"I didn't think you'd understand."

"Not even your best friend?"

"Things are different in Florida. The real world's a lot harder."

"That doesn't mean it's okay to hide from it."

"You're right, Lucy. I'm so sorry. I really messed up." She starts to cry again, big, wet sobs that make her whole body shake. "I tried to call your dad's cell a couple days ago. He said you were gone."

I almost start crying too. At the same time, I feel a complete sense of calm. It sweeps over me like water in a tide pool.

"It's okay," I tell her.

And it is.

"Come on," she says. "There's this amazing place I want to show you."

We head outside and start walking. In the woods behind Mr. Yoder's auto shop there's a slab of rock jutting above a stream. It reminds me of storm clouds on the beach, the way they brush against the horizon.

"You have to see it up close," says Alice, splashing across the shallow water.

I follow her through the stream. We make our way toward the slab of rock. I almost slip a couple times, but never fall.

"Now look," she says, grabbing my hand. She guides my fingers across the rugged surface. I feel like the rock's talking to me, whispering secrets from the past. I press my hand against it and trace something familiar.

"A seashell?"

Alice laughs. "A really big seashell."

I've read about fossils buried in the earth. This is the real thing, a glimpse of a world flooded with water, a billion years ago. I trace the bones in the rock and think of Lido Key, the seashells washed up at dawn, the secrets they keep, like the doves hidden inside a sand dollar.

• • •

When we get back to Mr. Yoder's shop, the garage door is flung wide open. Faron's sitting behind the wheel of that old car with the fins. Alice's dad is next to him, and the radio's cranked up real loud. They're having so much fun, I almost feel like I'm in the way.

Mr. Yoder climbs out and Alice runs over to him. She gives her dad a hug and whispers something in his ear.

"This is Lucy. We've been friends forever," she tells him.

"So I've heard," he says, as if we're meeting all over again. "Well, Miss Lucy. If you ever need a favor, let me know."

"How about a ride to the bus station?"

He laughs. "Which one?"

"The bus that goes to Florida."

"I think we can manage that," he says.

I glance at Faron.

This time, he's not coming with me.

Mr. Yoder seems to know what I'm thinking. "How come your boyfriend knows so much about cars?"

"He taught himself."

"Same here," Mr. Yoder says. "Guess it's not so bad, learning something if you love it." He takes out a pen and jots a string of numbers on a slip of paper. "Tell him to give my friend a call. Maybe they can help you out. We're all family, right?"

Maybe it's selfish, but I can't help wishing things were different. But Faron has his own dreams, just like I've got mine. I won't get in his way, no matter how much I want us to be together.

Mr. Yoder turns to Alice. "I'll get the truck started. Heat's frigged up again. The core's leaking something fierce."

"Just another reason I want my own car," she says.

I think for a second.

"You know there's a bunch of old cars at the lake, right?"

"What about it?"

"I heard there's a truck that sunk to the bottom," I tell her. "It's just sitting there, waiting for someone to make it new again."

"So who owns this mysterious underwater truck?" she asks.

"Whoever can fish it out."

Mr. Yoder gives me a sly smile. "I like the way you think, Miss Lucy."

Alice laughs. "How can you fix a truck that's drowned? By now, it's probably dead."

"Not always," her dad says. "If the water ain't salty, you can replace the engine. But that truck's going to need a lot of cleaning on the inside, starting with the brakes, the alternator—"

"So there's hope?"

He slings his arm around her. "Darlin', there's always hope."

The two of them leave the garage.

Now I've got one thing left to do.

I slide my finger inside my coat, where the paper's rolled tight.

Then I knock on the driver's side window.

When Faron sees me, he smiles so big, I get that electric jolt, letting me know I'm still alive. He pops open the door and I scoot next to him.

"How did it go?" he asks.

I tell him that Alice made a lot of mistakes. Lots of them. She's starting over with her dad's help. All that matters is that she's got choices now.

"Mr. Yoder told me to give you this." I dig the slip of paper out of my pocket and give it to him.

"What's this?" He squints.

"A place for you to work," I say, turning toward the window. I gaze at the interstate, the cars whooshing back and forth.

"The area code looks kind of familiar," he says. "It's up in St. Pete. That's like, an hour from Sarasota."

I've driven up to St. Pete lots of times with Dad, making his delivery rounds. Faron's right. It's not too far. The Gulf stretches between both cities, the same warm waters that circle the entire state.

"You take the Sunshine Skyway," he says. "You know. That big metal bridge?"

"I know where it is. I live there, remember?"

"Me too," he says. "The girls are much cuter down in Florida. Especially this one sweet girl I know. She even laughs at all my stupid jokes."

"Not all of them."

"Most," he says. "You ready to get out of here? Or we could stay in the car for a while."

"It's too cold," I say, snuggling against his chest.

"There's a way to fix that. Want me to show you?"

"Maybe later."

"You're right," he says, smirking. "It's cold."

"I thought you never got cold."

"Not if I'm with you, *fehlerfrei*," he says, kissing my nose.

## chapter thirty-one
# snowbirds

We buy a one-way ticket at the bus station. The ride down to Florida costs over a hundred dollars, which is all we've got left. It's Alice's money from the craft fair. Not much. But when you add it all together, it's more than you'd expect.

Everybody on the bus is dressed plain. I can tell who's Old Order or Mennonite just by the color of their dresses. We're all one big family, heading south. Now it's their turn to stare at us, a boy and girl in sneakers and blue jeans.

We sleep for most of the trip, taking turns, leaning against the window. I watch the miles of farmland. Empty pastures. Pylon towers. Hay bales rolled like cereal nuggets. After a while, I miss my purple iPod.

"Want me to sing to you?" Faron says.

He's not kidding.

Softly, he begins to sing.

It's a gospel song I know by heart.

I sing along, and, for once, I don't care if I'm in tune. The gray-haired woman next to me starts singing too. A man joins in. And another. Soon the entire bus is singing together, lifting their voices as one.

It's the most beautiful sound I've ever heard.

• • •

The bus rolls into Pinecraft a couple days later. We park in the exact same spot, as always, down the block from Big Olaf's ice cream stand. Neighbors are already lined up on Bahia Vista. They sit on lawn chairs or three-wheeled bikes. A little girl whizzes around on Rollerblades while a boy slumps in his truck, taking deep gulps from a paper bag.

I step off the bus and squint into the blazing sunlight. Faron squeezes my hand and together we walk across the road.

"There's my dad," I tell him.

When Dad sees me, he starts running so fast, his straw hat flies off. At first, I'm scared he's still angry. Then he sweeps me into a hug.

"So now you're an Amish snowbird?" he says, wiping his eyes.

There's so much I want to tell him, but I know there's time for that later. Time for everything. The lake filled with the bones of old cars. Alice's farm in Maine. The Amish Market, where I was shunned, and the Old Order girl slipping into the woods, quiet as a shadow.

Dad finally lets go and then he looks at Faron. I don't know what to expect. One thing's for sure: I never expected Dad to shake his hand.

"I hear you've been watching over my Smidge," Dad says, sizing him up and down. I'm a little embarrassed. Still, I can't help smiling.

"Lucy's pretty good at watching over herself," says Faron.

"Can't argue with you," says Dad, winking at me. "That's why I won't be so worried when she's away at college."

Did I hear that right?

"A letter came for you," he says.

I hug him again. "Thanks, Dad," I whisper. He's given me so much. Now this is the best gift of all. A chance to be free.

"You won't go too far, I hope?" he says.

"I'll be back to help at the shop," I tell him, "as much as possible."

"Good," he says. "And it's time we planted another orange tree. Doesn't look right with a space missing."

We start walking home in the late afternoon sun. In the distance, the wild parrots cackle as they swoop across the orange grove. I see me and Dad planting a new tree. Then I get another picture in my head. It's more like something I feel. That's why I know it's true.

On Lido Key, a pair of Amish girls kneel in the sand with their buckets and flashlights. The tide is low in the early hours before dawn. Nobody sees them except a passing jogger. He turns his head and wonders.

In Pinecraft, the *Rumspringa* boys slam a basketball against the pavement. Their feet skitter around the court. It's just them and the street lamp. An empty canal. A radio blasting songs about love lost and found again.

Not far from here, a parade of cars fills the parking lot. Their headlights spill across the picnic tables, the oak trees, the rusty baskets, for a game that nobody plays. A boy lights a cigarette for a girl he just met. They take a walk under the water tower, steal sips from a Dixie cup. Later, they steal a lot more.

I know because I feel it.

That's the way it's always been.

Is now.

And will be.

There's a boy driving across the bridge. He's speeding over the Gulf, in a hurry to meet someone. His fingernails are caked with grease. When he gets where he's going, he will dip his mangled hands in shallow canals, in warm ponds, in swimming pools where koi fish dart in the tangled seagrass. He will be whole.

There's a girl he's waiting to see. She's tired after a long day at school. A real school where she learns about the tides, the secret language that water speaks. Things come and go. This is something she understands.

The currents that slide along Lido Key flow up the coast to Maine. Seagulls dangle on the horizon. They hover above a red truck, following the shoreline. A girl in a denim jacket sits behind the wheel. Her dad rides shotgun. A gospel tune plays on the radio. It's a song they know by heart.

The truck disappears around the corner. For a moment, the song hangs in the air. It fills in the missing spaces, swallows them up like the sky, which brightens and fades. There's a strange kind of quiet. Then gently, it begins to snow.